I0717014

The Settle Down Society: Book Two

The Settle Down Summer

a romance

Natalie Keller Reinert

The Settle Down Summer
Copyright © 2023 Natalie Keller Reinert
All rights reserved.
ISBN: 978-1-956575-34-7

Cover Art: Dan Cunningham

Also by Natalie Keller Reinert

Sorry I Kissed You

The Settle Down Society
The Weekend We Met
The Settle Down Summer
The Business of Fairy Tales (2024)
The Tropical Update (2024)

Catoctin Creek
Sunset at Catoctin Creek
Snowfall at Catoctin Creek
Springtime at Catoctin Creek
Christmas at Catoctin Creek

Ocala Horse Girls
The Project Horse
The Sweetheart Horse
The Regift Horse
The Hollywood Horse

The Florida Equestrian Collection
The Eventing Series
Briar Hill Farm
Grabbing Mane: A Duet
Show Barn Blues: A Duet
Alex & Alexander: A Horse Racing Saga
Sea Horse Ranch: A Beach Read Series
The Hidden Horses of New York: A Novel

Theme Park Adventures
You Must Be This Tall
Confessions of a Theme Park Princess

Chapter One

THIS BAR IS not my scene.

But then again, what *is* my scene these days? I don't go out anymore. I hate being in crowds. Prone to panic attacks in packed subway cars. When the world shut down a few years ago, it took my sense of safety in this crazy city with it—and I've never gotten it back.

Even though everyone else seems to have moved on.

I look around the bar one more time—well, what I can see of it from under these dim, never-ending Edison bulbs—and take in rough wooden floors, sea shanties written in chalk on the dark blue walls, high tables surrounded by young men and women wearing clothes much cooler than mine. I can't even describe the fashion, that's how much cooler it is than my clothes. I'm just wearing black. The color that never goes out of style, right?

It feels out of style, believe me.

There was a time when I would have gone nuts for a bar like this, dim and loud and crowded and undefinably edgy. A place like this is the most essential thing about New York City to a certain group of people, the ones who like to consider themselves young and artistic and rebellious: these barely-lit clubs with their carefully curated playlists. When I came to the city ten years ago, a new art school grad, I wasn't cool but I could find a bar like this and I could pretend to be cool, and that was good enough.

Now, I just feel claustrophobic and dowdy. A winning combination, right?

Pull yourself together, Tracey. A little pep talk from me to me, we'll call it.

I'm trying, here.

After all, tonight I'm meeting someone.

And he thinks I'm cool.

His opinion should be good enough.

I practice my smile, beaming at myself in the mirror behind the rows of artisanal whiskey. And when the hipster bartender slinging beers at twenty-two-year-olds thinks I'm smiling at him, I shrug and order a shot of something brown that was distilled just over the bridge. No, not in Brooklyn. The other borough over the bridge. In *Queens*. For goodness sake! Queens! Brooklyn is just where people raise their kids now.

The bartender's sliding my drink over the stained wood of the bar when a rough touch jostles my elbow and I jolt forward, *way* more dramatically than necessary. (Thank you, raging claustrophobia.)

My hand knocks the glass of whiskey and it tips in slow motion, rolling in a semicircle. Twenty-two dollars in Queens County's finest slides over the bar, collecting loose pennies and a stray peanut.

"Oh, damn." I say, and look helplessly at the bartender. He is giving me what can only be described as the stink-eye. Something tells me there will be no free sympathy refills. I'm pulling out my credit card—I'll just start a tab, and cry over the bill in a month—when someone reaches past me and tosses a card on the bar.

"Put it on my tab," a deep voice growls, cutting through the music, and damn if my heart doesn't flutter a little bit.

My eyes follow the arm up to its owner. There's a man standing next to me—no, not standing. *Looming.* There is a giant of a man looming next to me, his face impossible to read in the eternal twilight of this bar. He's wearing jeans, a dark blue blazer over a blue-checked shirt, and judging by the width of his shoulders, he's the one who jostled my whiskey into oblivion. But since he's paying for it, all is forgiven.

"Hi," I say, and immediately run out of any other words.

The giant turns his attention from the bartender to me, and my breath catches a little. High forehead, short dark hair, a ghost of a five o'clock shadow—this guy has dramatic hero written all over him. And honestly, he's probably not abnormally tall. Maybe six-foot-four? It's important to note that I'm a shrimp. The view is different from down here.

I see crows-feet crinkle around his eyes as he takes me in. No spring chicken. Well, I see no problems here.

Listen, I'm here to meet someone, but I'm more than happy to take back-up candidates if the first date doesn't work out.

And then he says, "I didn't see you down there."

Of course he does.

Of *course* he does.

Why must people always say that?

"Well, maybe *you* should pay more attention," I snap. Yes, I'm sensitive about my height. You don't see me going around saying, "Wow, how's the air up there?" to tall people. Teasing someone about their size is about as fair as tormenting a dog because they can't open a door. Nature didn't give them thumbs! What do you want from them? Well, the same goes for me being so short that I can still duck under a subway turnstile. Not that I would do that. I'm too cautious to break laws.

This is the first time I've thrown caution to the wind, and so far, it's not going great. I just yelled at a giant.

Although he's looking down at me like he actually feels bad.

"I should pay more attention," the giant says. Maybe he's not as sheepish as I would like, but it's an apology. Of sorts. "Let me make it up to you. I'll buy you another drink."

"No," I say, and give the room a very dramatic scan. Maybe I flip my curls a little. What about it? "I'm waiting for someone. I'll let *him* buy it for me."

His looming presence seems to retreat a little at the mention of another someone. "I'll leave you alone, then," he says courteously.

And before I know it, he's taking his own whiskey from the bartender and melting away into the crush of people. I find myself watching him, his broad shoulders and height making him an easy target at first. Then he's swallowed up into a crowd near the front of the bar, where the front windows have been pulled wide open, letting the joviality spread onto the street outside.

I turn back to the bartender, who is watching me warily. Probably wants me to get a drink and give up this real estate. But the guy I'm meeting said to sit at the dead center of the bar. And I don't want to make things hard for him. Everything up until this point has gone so smoothly, so beautifully. Online dating was hard, and then suddenly, it wasn't anymore.

And that's how I know he's the one.

So I'm just going to wait right here, where he said to wait, and the scowling bartender can deal with it however he likes until his next therapy session.

"Can I get you something else?" the bartender asks.

"I'll take a whiskey sour," I say, because it will take a few extra seconds to mix, and I've got whiskey on my mind now. The bartender pointedly takes down another expensive bottle, and I guess I should have specified something cheaper, but that's on me. Another Manhattan ritual I've forgotten about.

It feels like I've forgotten *everything* about going out: how to dress, how to put on makeup, how to arrive late so I'm not sitting here being accosted by tall men with handsome faces, how to deal with sharing my space with more people than that occupancy sign can possibly allow.

But that's okay, because I'm about to meet Chase. And Chase is the one. The guy who will take me out of this city, sweep me onto a suburban lane with a white picket fence, and settle down.

Yes.

I'm ready to settle down at last.

Chapter Two

To hear us talking, you'd think we've all just been released from prison—not just three women sitting around drinking wine with our feet drawn up on the sofa cushions.

"We're finally free!"

"I'm *so* ready for hot girl summer!"

"This time, I'm putting it *all* out there!"

"I'm going to put my mouth up against the next hot guy I see on the street."

"Margot!"

We all throw popcorn at Margot, who, as usual, is the one who takes things too far.

She laughs and bats it away. In the six years since we moved to New York City together, Margot has only grown more outrageous, more uninhibited, than she'd been back in Iowa. And she'd been considered a *lot* of woman in Iowa, believe me.

A lot more than me. In our years rooming together at Prairie Arts, the prestigious but tiny art school in the Midwest where we'd done our degrees, Margot had been a girl you could rely on to start a party anytime, anyplace. I was a girl you could rely on to start a study group.

Everyone said we were perfect together.

But that was fourteen years ago and frankly, both of us were starting to wonder when the next phase of our lives would begin.

Summer always seems to shine new light on that question. Maybe it's because in school, we emerged into summer vacation with a sense of real growth. We'd finished something, and we were heading into the future.

Now we just get together for the same brunch date we'd had last weekend, only the calendar says it's June instead of May.

And, quite likely, the influx of young tourists and new grads which rushes into the city this time of year—kids on their real summer breaks, grads out on their own for the first time, running wild in this city of unlimited potential for excitement and trouble—makes us remember that feeling.

That huge, gorgeous, *what's next* feeling.

Whatever causes it, in summer, and more emphatically *this* summer, it feels like a decent chunk of the city is just going for broke. In the love and relationships department, that's for damn sure. It's not just Margot, Caitlyn, and me feeling the pull of fresh beginnings and sweet summer loving. The entire city is rocking with hormones and desire, love and relationships, sex and candy.

I see it everywhere I go: people are snogging on the subway, they're going at it in The Ramble, they're hooking up and bumping bits in every stairwell and alley and station from Battery Park City to the Bronx. They're young and they're beautiful and they're free and they're not even looking at me, but I still feel like they're judging me for being thirty-plus and single.

I'm trying not to be crotchety about it, but damn. A woman gets tired of constant sex hanging in the air when she, herself, is not getting any. Can't a woman commute from her Upper West Side apartment to her Chelsea art gallery without stalking through a fog of pre-, post-, and possibly current coitus?

"You sound like a grandma," Caitlyn laughs when I air this grievance aloud.

She's sitting in my favorite armchair—okay, my only armchair, because there is only space for a loveseat and a single chair along the back wall of my living room—with her feet tucked beneath her, long waves of red hair falling over her shoulders. Caitlyn has the smooth skin and confident features of a woman who still believes she will never grow old, only more beautiful. But she's just about my age, and single as well, and I know deep down she's feeling as crotchety as I am.

Her perfect teeth gleam—a shine bought and paid for, as Caitlyn has worked at a succession of television stations which have all required her to stay beautiful at all times—as she asks me, "So, are you just signing out of sex?"

"Please, I signed out of sex years ago," I retort. "Now I'm just mad at everyone else who is still having it."

I feel Margot on the loveseat next to me react, her shoulders twitching as she chokes on laughter, but it's no joke. It's *true*. All of us have seen our love lives dry up—even witchy little Margot, with her white-blonde pixie cut and her startling ice-blue eyes. During the pandemic, things got grim for singles with formerly exciting sexual escapades. Some folks we knew ended up hooking up with one another. Some of them got married. A few of them actually moved to the suburbs.

They're the ones I'm starting to envy. As the years go by and the city forgets its trauma, I feel like I'm the last one who can't get over lockdowns and mass panic. My therapist nods when I tell her this, but so far she hasn't gotten me past it. Supposedly, I am the only one who can fix myself. I consider searching for a new therapist.

"You could still have a sex life, Tracey," Margot informs me. "You are H-O-T *hot,* my beloved girlfriend."

"There's more to it than that," I say.

Margot snorts.

"No, I get you." Caitlyn sips her wine, gazing at a crazy painting of an elephant currently gracing the far wall, next to my living room door.

Well, we *think* it's an elephant. The artist was not forthcoming when I asked. She said it was whatever the viewer wanted it to be. As an art dealer, I know asking the buyer to pretend they have some kind of artistic vision is rarely a useful strategy, so I just tell everyone it's an elephant.

"I *totally* get you," Caitlyn goes on. "I know hook-ups are the hot trend this summer but I'm so over it. I want to go straight to the end, you know? Just me and my husband, dancing at our wedding reception."

"I guess we can wait the summer sex-fest out?" I swirl the wine in my glass. "Maybe the men will be worn out by the end of August and after Labor Day we can interest them in a few nice dinners and a short engagement."

Margot considers the proposition. "It's an idea. I mean, they can't sustain this energy for too long. It's crazy out there. It's like every subway car is someone else's personal strip club, and no one's bringing me a comped drink."

She's not wrong there. The subways are worst of all: the sweaty rush hours packed with laughing, grinning, groping people hanging from the poles, breathing in each other's faces, getting up close and personal with strangers. I usually have a front-row ticket to the show, because I like to sit in a corner seat, even though it can be hard to get out of when the train car gets full and your stop is coming up. I pretend to look at my phone, but all the while I'm feeling like I accidentally wandered into the wrong movie theater.

And the worst part is, I should love the summer shenanigans! The laughing, the grinning, the groping. I try to be jealous. I try to wish I was part of things. But it just isn't my scene. Not anymore. The world shut down, and when I finally ventured outside again, I was older, sadder, and less in the mood for a public ass-grabbing than ever.

Caitlyn leans over my coffee table, bottle in hand. "Was that sigh a hint, madam?"

I hold up my glass. "I mean, if you're serving."

As Caitlyn tops me off, I turn to check on Margot, who has been suspiciously quiet. She's thumbing the stem of her wineglass thoughtfully as she gazes out the window. My living room window can have that effect on people. I have the smallest apartment in my circle of friends, *but* I have a view of the Hudson River, and I arranged my small sofa and armchair so that everyone in the room can see out. Having a great view is better than TV in this town.

We'd had one of those rich, cerulean-blue summer dusks tonight, and now lights twinkle alluringly in the distance. Even if they're just the New Jersey skyline, those glowing lights have a way of reminding a person they're in magical, mythical Manhattan. A way of making a person feel good. We are in New York City and we are *making it*—how many people can say that?

That's how those lights *used* to make me feel, anyway—every day and every night. Now they sometimes make me feel lonesome, like I am on a lonely island in a sea of humanity. The part of me which loves this town withered to a few barren branches over the past few years, and now every day is a struggle.

But I'm trying to flourish here again. I really am. I don't *really* want to move to the suburbs.

I don't think.

Caitlyn waves the chardonnay bottle in Margot's direction, trying to get her attention. Margot would be wise to ignore Caitlyn. By tomorrow morning, we'll all regret drinking this stuff—it's cheap, awful, girl's-night-out wine, sweet and cloying as peach nectar. But I had three bottles left over from a low-key gallery opening I hosted last night, and none of us are doing *so* great that we can say no to free wine.

Margot doesn't look up. It's like she's lost in her thoughts, and not even the prospect of a refill is enough to get her back.

Caitlyn gives me a head-shake that says, *Here we go again.*

I shrug and toy with my short cap of chocolate-colored curls, absently looping them around my fingers the way I've been doing since I was a toddler. What can we do but wait Margot out? If she's dreaming up one of her new schemes, all we can do is watch the show and applaud when it's over.

I decide to keep our conversation going, let Margot do whatever brainstorming she needs over there. "So yeah, today was the craziest day yet. There was practically an orgy on the D train. I got off at Thirty-fourth Street and walked down to the gallery."

Caitlyn lifts her eyebrows appreciatively. "I *thought* your calves were looking hot. I was guessing Stairmaster."

"Twenty blocks in heels, actually." I look down at my feet, flexing them. "I still don't have it in me to go near a gym."

"I hear that." Caitlyn tucks in her stomach, patting what she assumes is excess. If anything, she has gone from a size four to an eight in the past two years. Hardly unhealthy for a woman of her height, but I can understand that is its own trauma. And she's been going through it, career-wise, which probably doesn't help with her self-image. Caitlyn's work in TV news reporting and production has been slowly drying up, and she's been devoting herself to her hobby, which is the weather. She developed a website for armchair meteorologists like herself, but she was the first to admit sitting at a desk coding was nothing like running around hot sets all day. "I was hoping shut-in weight would be sexy," she says morosely.

"That's another thing. All those beautiful young things out there—how do they all stay so skinny?"

"Easy," Caitlyn sighs. "They *don't* stay home like we do. Also: youthful metabolisms."

The wine is sticky on my tongue. I drink more anyway, because there's nothing else to do and I'm certainly not going to stick this bottle back in the fridge, save it for later. "I was looking forward to getting back out there this year," I confess. "But now I just feel like I'm just a bystander to everyone else's smoking-hot summer."

"Well, you're old," Caitlyn informs me with a wry grin. "We all are. It's okay to admit it. You wanna go up on the roof and yell at clouds? Should be some gorgeous high cirrus out there tonight."

"I can't." I stretch out my toes. "My feet hurt too much from walking twenty blocks in heels."

There was a time when that walk wouldn't have left me sore from my hips to my arches. But my commute went from daily to biweekly back when the city was shut down, and now my gallery is almost solely run out of my tiny living room. I only go downtown for special showings.

Here in the apartment, I change out artwork piece by piece on my best-lit wall, take quality photos, and put those on my gallery website. When buyers want to see something in person, I wrap the work up, take a car service downtown, and set up the gallery for their visit. I've been thinking of reinstating regular hours, allowing walk-ins, but my customer base has shifted online and it seems like too much trouble.

Also, I'm so short that I have to wear heels when I'm at the gallery, and once you *stop* wearing heels, it seems very hard to get back into them.

And yes, I really do have to totter around in high heels. It's no joke when you're trying to sell a big statement piece to a man almost two feet taller than you are. Well, it's a joke to him. "That painting's bigger than you are!" he says.

All of them say it.

Ugh, maybe it doesn't matter anymore. Do my feet matter more than my feelings about being short?

"I'm going to quit wearing heels," I say, testing the idea aloud to see if it has legs.

Caitlyn flexes her own beautiful toes at me. "You can't give up heels yet. That's the first step towards just plain giving up."

"Well, maybe it's time. I mean, look outside, Caitlyn. The city came back to life and it's ten years younger than we are. Everyone out there is an infant. We're the old ones now."

"Define old!"

"Do *you* want to hook up with a random guy you ran into on the D train?"

She wrinkles her perfect nose at me. "Eww, no."

"But you have before, right?"

"Yes, *but,* in my defense, that was the *L* train, and it was also six years ago—"

"Precisely my point. Six years ago."

We look at each for a moment. Comprehension is dawning on Caitlyn's face. "We can't keep up," she says slowly. "And I don't even *want* to keep up. Tracey, when did we get old?"

There's a moment of stunned silence while we take in the fatal shot of that word. *Old.* It means different things in different societies. In New York City, it generally means anyone over twenty-seven. Even that number might be a high estimate. It takes stamina to live and work and love in this city. You need a lot of energy. You need a lot of energy *drinks*—which make me sick, unfortunately. But the point is, everything takes everything in this town. Careers. Errands. Socializing. *Dating.* We've seen friends give it all up, shake their heads, say the city is a young person's game.

Are we next?

What are we even waiting for?

Chapter Three

(Still) Two Months Earlier

Margot puts down her wine glass with a startling *clink* on my tiny coffee table. She turns to us with a bright smile on her pixie face. We wait for her proclamation with interest. Margot is our dreamer. Margot is our woman of ideas. Whatever she says will be interesting and inspiring and probably knock us right out of this funk we've just found ourselves in.

She claps her hands, the same move she used on her little students back when she first moved to the city and taught art at a fancy FiDi school. "It's time to settle down, girls!"

That's...not what I expected. Not from Margot, anyway.

Looking across the sofa, I see Caitlyn is equally confused. She runs a hand over her face, as if trying to clear her mind for this.

For whatever Margot really means. "Settle down, like, how? Like, is it time we finally start that commune?"

About five years ago, we talked about buying a Victorian house in Ditmas Park, Brooklyn and starting our own commune. It was a bad break-up thing led by Margot and championed by Caitlyn. Abel wanted the attic for some ungodly reason. I was in because, hey, these were my best friends, and having a big house while still living in the city sounded pretty cool.

Ultimately, we couldn't get financing, and then Caitlyn met a new guy and Margot met a fun girl, and I decided to launch my own gallery, and the idea got left on the wayside. Like most commune ideas, probably. We're all better off in our own space, anyway.

But there have definitely been a few moments over the past few years when I really wished we were weathering the storms together in a big old house with stained glass accents, rather than separately, in three small one-bedroom apartments scattered around Manhattan.

"*Not* a commune," Margot says. "The opposite of that, actually." Her smile is a serene bow, cherry-red and twice as sweet. "We're going to get married and move out of the city."

I can feel my eyebrows lifting my scalp. "I don't think all three of us can get married. We have to pick one couple, and then the last person will have to be our very special friend."

"I'm not the extra in this scenario," Caitlyn warns. "Don't even try it. I'm a legal wife or nothing."

"You guys." Margot shakes her head, her white-blonde hair falling over her eyes. She looks like a mischievous fairy. Our friend Maeve says that Margot is a woodland spirit in disguise, and Maeve should know—she's a landscape architect and spends all her time in the forests and gardens of New York City parks, making them glow and bloom. "Seriously," Margot says, "we won't marry each other, although that's charming and I love that your minds went there first. But that's not what we want. Or what we need. I'm talking a regular, ho-hum, everyday marriage."

Caitlyn and I exchange a look.

"Is that what we *need*?" I ask, skeptical. "A ho-hum marriage?"

"It's exactly what we need," Margot assures me. "Peace. Stability. And *space*. This is the summer that we settle down, get married, and move to the suburbs. Or at least a glorious three-bedroom in Queens. Don't you want that? Don't you want to *stretch*?"

She stands up, reaching her hands out from side to side. I know the point she's going to make before she even does it, before she tilts her body to the left, leaning sideways at the waist with the litheness of many years of yoga, until her left hand hits the wall. Then she straightens, and does the same thing to the wall on her right.

Yes, my living room is small. But that's part of the New York story, right? Touching both walls of your living room without having to move your feet—that's part of living the dream, of being a New Yorker.

And so is being stir-crazy, wishing you had a three-bedroom in the Hudson Valley like your old gallery employee Liv, staying up late scrolling Zillow with "Must Have Pool" checked. It's all part of the lifestyle. Wouldn't trade it for the world. Don't look at my search history; it lies.

I shake my head. "Margot, you have a lot of ideas, but this one is without a doubt your craziest. You're just having a moment of Iowan nostalgia. It happens to all the farm girls eventually."

"I am not a farm girl," Margot says, still leaning against the wall with her right hand. "I am not a city girl. I am just a girl, standing in a tiny apartment, looking for some room to breathe."

"We don't want to move out of the city," Caitlyn says. "Come on." But she sounds uncertain. She looks around my living room, her brow scrunching up, as if she's suddenly remeasuring the tiny dimensions and wondering if she should have more.

We all want more, that's why we work so hard, but it's the first time I've thought maybe what I really need is more *room.*

All the anxiety, all the claustrophobia, all the drama—could that just be solved by getting out and moving on with my life?

'Goodbye to all that' essays are a constant joke amongst the city's stalwart, but suddenly, I wonder if it's time to pen my own.

Margot has seen the vulnerability on Caitlyn's face and she goes after it with the precision of a falcon loosed after a sparrow. "Don't we, Caitlyn? Do we really want to stay here and play the city mouse game? Or do we want to grow up, get married, and get out?"

Caitlyn tilts back her glass. She drains the tragic white wine, as if buying time to think. After the last gulp is gone, she looks over at me and shrugs. "You know, I think she's right. Maybe we've played this game long enough, like she says."

Margot cackles.

I can't stop myself from blinking a few times at the both of them. Somehow, leaving has never been on the table, through all the trauma and drama of the past few years. And if Margot suggests something wild, it's usually easy to laugh her off. After all, Margot is the dreamer of our group, the one who blames everything on Mercury in retrograde, the one who wore cowboy boots with a ballgown to a black-tie gala, the one who once spent a weekend starting a vineyard on a roof in Red Hook.

But now Caitlyn agrees with her? Caitlyn is the realist among us. And she is not afraid to own that title. She went on record telling Margot that teeny-tiny planet next to the sun was not causing her bathroom sink to drip all night; she warned Margot that going off-script at the gala would get her in trouble with her boss; she suggested that Margot not sink every last dime of her savings into a bunch of vines on top of a six-story building.

Margot laughed her off every time, but she also didn't get a decent night's sleep for two weeks before she finally got her sink fixed; she landed in the doghouse at her job for wearing those boots and missed a promotion over it; she lost her investment three months into the vineyard when a hurricane blew through the city, taking out her precious vines in what the insurance company callously named an "Act of God" which they couldn't be responsible for.

We don't like to say Caitlyn is always right, but we all know Caitlyn is always right. She knows how to put her finger on the truth of the matter, without bothering to get all sentimental. A useful, if not always comfortable, trait to have amongst a circle of friends.

Oh, and what trait do I bring to the table, you ask? They call me the mom of the group. This is not a compliment to me, but they think it is. I see myself as a helper to my talented friends. I am kind of artistic—hence the gallery I run. But I am also kind of ordinary—hence it's not *my* art gracing the gallery walls.

I'm very average. It took me a while to learn that, but now I consider this kind of self-knowledge one of my strengths.

Margot finally straightens up; she walks over to the living room window and flings it open dramatically. The sounds of the city flood in: sirens, car horns, a jet on approach to LaGuardia, an Amtrak train rumbling north in its tunnel along the Hudson, a woman laughing from another building's tiny courtyard. For years, this has been a symphony to my ears. There were times when just hearing the city out there meant we were all alive, we would all make it. It was a comfort.

The noise feels intrusive now, like I got used to the silence and I want it back. I remember days when I could leave that window open and just hear the odd barking dog, the occasional siren. Days when the rattle of leaves from the spindly courtyard trees seemed to be a song all their own. These are the sounds of the suburbs, and I know it, and I want them back with an intensity that makes me wonder who I even am anymore.

Margot closes the window, shutting out the din. She spreads her arms dramatically, saying, "I'm *done* with it! I'm ready to write my *Goodbye to All That*. Aren't you? Don't you want to just wash your hands of this city, of this madness? I always meant to have four kids. Where will I ever put *four kids* in this town?"

"You'd have to be a millionaire," I say.

"Try a *billionaire*," Margot insists.

"You're saying we should jump ship," Caitlyn says, tilting her head as she regards Margot with interest. "Leave the city to the strong. For we are weak. Is that it?"

"Leave the city to the *young*," Margot corrects her.

"I guess being old is better than being weak," I say.

Caitlyn snorts.

Margot isn't done. "Let's get out. Let's allow the kids to grind on the subway in peace. Let's be good to our feet and stop commuting in heels. Let's buy houses and have yards and raise kids and maybe get some of those backyard chickens everyone loves so much. No roosters, though."

"But we're not going to marry each other," I say. "Just to confirm, that's not the idea?"

"Oh, we'll get married," Margot says. "All three of us. Not to each other, though. If we put all our effort into it, and look in the right places, we'll find husbands in no time. I guarantee it."

"Why does this sound like a pyramid scheme?" Caitlyn asks. "How many boxes do you have in your apartment right now? What happens to you if you don't get enough members to sign up?"

"This is not a pyramid scheme. This is just a plain old scheme." Margot's glacier-blue eyes are glittering with excitement, and I feel myself leaning forward, absorbing her craziness into my own body. "A house! A yard! Kids! A dog! A cat! Chickens!"

"A Lexus!" Caitlyn adds. She's always had a secret yen for luxury. "A home office that isn't also my bedroom!"

"A husband," Margot announces gleefully. "Out mowing the yard, getting all sweaty, jumping in the pool, calling you to hop in with him—"

The fantasy is getting more vivid by the moment.

Let's do it, I think feverishly. *What could be worse than what we've already got?*

"Let's get married!" I leap to my feet, spilling what's left of my wine across the floor. The dry old floorboards thirstily drink it up. Let them drink and be drunk; this apartment isn't where my bones will rest forever. I do a spin and shout, "Let's *settle down!*"

Margot takes my hands and we do a quick, thrilling dance around the room which ends when she bumps into my TV table, nearly sending the flatscreen crashing to the floor.

"Let's buy houses where there's enough room to dance," she teases, straightening the TV.

Chapter Four

And so here I am, in this bar, waiting to meet the person I'm pretty sure I'm settling down with.

So far, the settle-down pact seems to be going really well. Margot got us onto Lifer, a new app she'd heard about. She swore it would be the answer to finding true love that wanted an end. "This isn't about dating," she said solemnly. "This is about *marriage.*"

We all took really nice pics of each other, and we helped one another write awesome-but-not-too-awesome bios for our profiles, and then we waited for magic to happen.

My first day on Lifer, I got sixteen messages. Eight of them wanted pictures of my toes, but the other eight seemed like they were actually on the app to find a life partner. Fifty-fifty was not bad, I figured, and I responded to the second half. The ones who wanted marriage to a person with any old kind of toes.

Two of the eight ghosted me; I guess they didn't like the way I texted. One of the eight lived in Bahrain; I had to let him down gently because I didn't want a long-distance relationship and also moving that far from my parents in Iowa wasn't on the agenda. Another guy wanted to take me bowling, which was fine, but he wanted to take me bowling in New Hampshire, which was too much too far, too soon and anyway, this specificity made me think maybe he was too into bowling for this to work out. The fifth guy was lovely, actually, but he was married already and if I wasn't going to have Margot or Caitlyn as sister-wives, I wasn't willing to try plural marriage at all. The sixth and seventh guys—what can I say, we just didn't click? They were fine, but we weren't going to spend our lives together.

The eighth and last, though, was Chase.

And that's who I'm waiting for tonight.

Oh, Chase! I get shivers just thinking about him. He's everything I could want in a guy. For one thing, he's a normal size—yes, I'm talking at *you,* giant man somewhere in the bar— and for another, he's an artist. A sweet, brown-eyed, chestnut-haired artist with a dimple in his right cheek, a funny way of furrowing his brow when he's considering something I've said, and all the right opinions for a lifetime of marital bliss. I can't argue politics over cornflakes every morning, I really can't, so aligning opinions matters.

We've been talking nonstop for a month. Via text, I mean, and some DMs and a couple of video chats but honestly, we're so sick of video chats in general, it felt like we should just dispense with that stage of the relationship and move right into a real-life, face-to-face, you're-real-and-so-am-I, meet-up.

Margot is cheering me on; she thinks getting together ASAP is the only way to overcome any lingering doubts about meeting our future husbands on the Lifer app. Margot went to see her top match, a real estate investor named Damian, after three days and three chats. Caitlyn is more cautious, but she's also video-chatting with a really nice guy now, and it seems like she's getting on board.

Two months into our settle-down summer, things are looking pretty good for the three future brides of the Upper West Side.

Although to my mind, Chase is the kind of guy who should be snapped up already, so I'm a little nervous about tonight. The questions pile up as the minutes tick by: what if he doesn't show up? What if he does show up, but he only has six months to live and he wants me as a nursemaid through the final hours?

These are normal nerves, though, right? Typical things to worry about?

I sip my whiskey sour, which tastes exactly like Caitlyn made it for me from her home bar, using Jack Daniels, which means this bartender has fleeced me with his top-shelf liquor, but it's fine, it's *fine*—because there he is. My heart stops, and my drink nearly slips through my numb fingers.

He's here.

Pushing through the crowd is my average-sized online boyfriend, wearing loose jeans and a slouchy striped shirt and a blue knit hat that just covers his mop of brown hair—um, okay, it's like seventy-two degrees outside and this bar is warm, so maybe the hat is a weird choice—but that's fine, too. If he is the kind of person who makes weird hat choices, he's hardly alone in New York City in that. We can work it out. We can make the hats work.

Over-the-top eager to see him, to hug him, to *feel* him and know he's real, I hop down from my barstool...and lose sight of him immediately. Taller people have closed in, including, oh god, the giant, and somehow his face comes between Chase and me.

My gaze, which must be all sunshine and rainbows right now, lands on his face, which is not. Or, it wasn't. Because for just a moment, the giant looks back at me, and his dour expression bursts into something bright and beautiful, like a butterfly has emerged from its chrysalis. Not that his face was like a gross little caterpillar before, nothing like that, but it's just that startling a shift when he goes from dour to delighted.

The giant turns out to be *so* handsome, *so* lit from within like a lightning bug on a summer evening, that I have to take a moment to catch my breath.

While that happens, we're just staring at each other, and in a split-second the mood goes from wow to weird.

The giant tilts his head at me, like I'm a puzzle he can't figure out.

And then our moment is over.

Because now Chase has emerged, pushing past the giant. And since he's a foot shorter, my gaze physically drops to his. Our eyes meet for the first time in person.

This is real.

A white-hot surge of excitement takes hold of me; I'm shaking all over; he's coming towards me; this is all so real—I reach out my hands for him—

Crash. Broken glass tinkles, causing a momentary pause in the bar's conversational buzz. Someone coughs.

"Oh." My cheeks are burning red-hot. "I completely forgot I was holding that glass."

Chase has already stooped to start picking up the pieces of glass; he's heaping them carefully in his palm. I look around, hoping to god no one has seen me drop my drink, and over Chase's bent back I see him—the giant, shoulders shaking, as he laughs at me.

Chase finds us a table in the bar's backyard, and with the crush and noise inside dispensed with, I can finally relax. I've got another drink now, but it's just a glass of white wine. Non-staining, cheap. The bartender gave me a very meaningful look as he handed Chase the glass. A look which said, "Drop another glass, and you'll be drinking out of a sippy cup for the rest of the night."

I let Chase carry the drink to our table, which earns me an approving nod. Well, at least I am now on better terms with the bartender.

And now we're actually sitting across from each other. It's really happening, and in all the right ways: the full moon finding us from between two apartment towers, the cool evening breeze playing on my bare shoulders, tugging at tendrils of my loose curls, hopefully giving me a winsome look and not a mussed one. Also helpful: the white lights strung in the trees, the scent of the honeysuckle climbing up the brick walls, which also serve to muffle the sounds of the local buses plowing their way through the East Village. I wondered why Chase would want to meet me all the way down here, when we'd talked about feeling like fish out of water in the new, reborn New York, but this little garden is all the explanation I need.

He's a romantic!

"I'm just so glad we're really doing this," he's saying, his voice husky and earnest. I'm obsessed with his voice. I want him to read me poetry. Specifically, Yeats. I wonder how to introduce this into the relationship. "My friends said it was so soon, but I just felt like—" he scoffs at himself, shaking his head, and I melt. "I just felt like we had a real connection."

I slip my hand across the table, thankful for the manicure Caitlyn insisted upon, and place it over his. He has soft, peach-colored skin. An artist, I think. Chase does not toil in the dirt nor dirty himself with money. He paints, he told me. Watercolors, some oils. Cityscapes, and, he admitted with some cajoling, ships at sea.

"Of course we have a real connection," I say. "That's why I came all the way down to the East Village for you. I haven't lived down here in years, let alone drink here."

He laughs, long eyelashes falling over his cheeks. Swoon. "Are you not a fan of this neighborhood? I thought there were some galleries we could walk past, later on. If you want."

The galleries on this side of Second Avenue are usually a little avant-garde for my taste, but I agree readily. We'll figure out how our tastes mesh later. "For sure, that sounds really fun. You'll probably think I'm old and stodgy when you see what I like, though."

"I could never think you're old and stodgy."

I pluck at my sleeveless tunic's collar. It's silk and plum-colored and probably the most boring piece of clothing between this table and the East River. I have a cardigan in my purse, too. And I'm not afraid to wear it. Who wants cold shoulders? Twenty-three-year-old Tracey, that's who. She never would have pulled a sweater over a revealing top. But here we are. Getting older.

"I really feel like over the past couple years, I did get stodgy," I admit. "I started prioritizing comfort over everything else, because I was just too stressed to think about things like fashion or, you know, *waistbands*." He grins. "I sort of fell out of the whole New York stay one step ahead of the trends kinda thing. If I was ever really in it."

"That's not my thing," Chase says. He turns his hand over and squeezes my fingers. "It all feels kind of tiresome, you know? I'm like you. I learned to stay home and relax. And now, honestly? That's all I want to do."

This is what I want. A man who will stay home with me and eat cheese on the sofa, wearing only his boxer shorts. I'm sure of it. "I do, too. I almost wish I hadn't reopened the gallery at all."

"That's right! Your own gallery. Tell me more about it. Is it near here?"

"Oh, no. It's west of Union Square, near Fifth Avenue. Just a small space, really. A lot of my sales go to regular brokers, so I don't have a lot of frills. They just want to come in, get a feel for the piece, and then they go make the case to their bosses or clients or whoever they're shopping for. I do occasional opening nights, with cheap wine and the works." I smile deprecatingly, and Chase does, too. I suppose he knows all about gallery openings.

"But you worked from home for a while, right?" he asks, his fingers tracing a pattern on my palm.

"Oh, yes. I still mostly work from home. I keep a lot of gallery work on my walls." I smile, thinking of the so-called elephant on the living room wall. Still there, two months after it watched Caitlyn, Margot, and me decide to settle down. And now here I sit. With *him.* I try to focus on the conversation. "Everything I sell now is based on photos I take in my apartment. It goes to the gallery for showings on request."

"That's so funny. So your apartment is part gallery?"

"I guess you could say that. I've liked working out of the apartment, although obviously it can get very lonely. Confining. *You* know." I watch his face, looking for confirmation. I need to know I wasn't alone in my feelings. That he has been sharing my journey out of the woods, somehow, even though we hadn't yet met when I was deep in the forest.

He nods understandingly. "Of course, it was. You've got to get out and interact with other humans. That's in our makeup. But tell me more about your artists."

I spend a little time describing the artists whose work comes through my gallery. I'm proud of my artists, and I have clever scouts scattered around the country, old art school friends who know what my clients are looking for. "It's the kind of work I would have done, if I were an artist," I finish.

Chase lifts his head at that. "Why aren't you, then?"

I snort, then immediately regret it—what kind of dream woman snorts? "Ah, I'm just not very talented. It took art school to teach me that."

"But you loved art enough to go to school for it?"

"It's not uncommon to go to school and realize you're not good enough," I say, taking my hand back.

He notices and grabs at it, grinning. "I apologize. Don't be mad at me. And honestly, I love that you have a gallery. I've always wanted to be involved in the art world somehow. More than just painting for myself, which is what it feels like most of the time."

"Well, that counts," I tell him. "And you could sell your work, I'm sure."

"Even more than that, I want to know more about how great art is created, and what makes a piece go from cafe gallery to Soho gallery. You know? Like if I walk into some random cafe in the Village, am I going to see a watercolor which belongs on the block at Sotheby's?"

"Probably not," I laugh. "But that's the kind of idea that keeps a lot of artists creating long after they should consider going back to college."

"How long did you keep creating for?"

I shrug. "Not very long."

"Do you think about it?"

"Being an artist? Not really. I'm surrounded by artists, my best friends are in the art world, and that's good enough." There's no need to mention the three boxes of sketchpads shoved under my bed, or the occasional longing I have to turn a doodle on a post-it note into a full-fledged study. Or the way I make myself crumple up the paper and throw it away. We're not going to focus on what we don't have, I remind myself. We're going to focus on what we *could* have. I let him rub his thumb across my palm and smile at him to show him: no tragic backstory here. "But if you want to know more about galleries and the art market, I can definitely show you that."

There's movement behind him, a party coming through the door into the garden. They're laughing, and somehow I recognize the giant's voice, even though I've never heard him laugh before. I flick my eyes back to Chase. He's watching me, his face warm and open, and I decide it's time to leave. I don't want anything to mar this evening we're having.

"Do you want to go get some food?" I ask.

"Sure. You have a place in mind?"

"The perfect place. Trust me?"

He smiles. "I trust you, Tracey."

"You shouldn't," I tell him. "Because it's seven blocks away, and we're walking."

Chase is looking around warily when I finally stop our march across town. We've walked clear over to Union Square, but I didn't stop at any of the obvious places here, instead taking him past the bustle of the park and the flagship stores, and now we've paused on a fairly quiet street.

It's lined with practical Manhattanite stores at street-level, fine and upstanding trades like Persian rug dealers and vintage picture frame galleries. Above the storefronts, brick apartment houses loom, their cornices decorated with ornate shields and scrolls. I can tell Chase is wondering where all the restaurants and cafes are. But this isn't that kind of street.

"It's right ahead," I say. "Almost there. You're not winded, are you?"

"You didn't say it was seven *long* blocks," he points out. "That's an important distinction. Especially on a hot summer night."

"Sorry," I laugh. "I guess I didn't think about that. But I promise the crosstown walk will be worth it." I point at the shop ahead, the only bright spot on the street, although its welcoming fluorescent glow is hindered somewhat by the semi-permanent construction scaffolding overhead. "This place has the *best* falafel."

If Chase thinks it's crazy that we just walked across lower Manhattan to get falafel when we were already in the East Village and probably drinking within spitting distance of three falafel shops, he doesn't say anything. And that's how I know we're going to make a great couple. No complaints, just a chipper, "Great, I can't wait to try it."

I really need someone to have that kind of confidence in me. It doesn't have to be blind devotion, but a little trust goes a long way for me.

Of course, Chase pauses again when he realizes it's literally just a walk-up counter, and we're taking our food to go. But he follows me without a word as I take our paper bag and lead the way back to Union Square, and when I find a bench under the trees for us to sit at, he dutifully doles out the foil-wrapped pitas and enough napkins for a daycare having popsicles for snack-time.

We eat in silence for a few minutes, and I savor this moment: the breeze playing in the thick trees, which almost block out the tall buildings around us; the rumble of trains beneath us; the hushed conversations of couples passing us on the wide walkway. On the far side of the square, some kind of social justice rally has given way to a drum circle. It's surprisingly melodic, a low undercurrent of rhythm that rumbles through the soles of my sensible flats. No, Caitlyn could not make me wear heels tonight, and thank goodness, because that really *had* been a long walk.

"So," Chase says eventually, "now that we're all the way over here, I guess my gallery itinerary is kind of out the window."

I'd forgotten all about his idea to look at East Village galleries. "Oh, I'm sorry! It was a good idea, too."

"Another time, maybe. If I'd known you were *this* into falafel, I'd have taken you to my favorite place in the Village."

"I just—" I hesitate. But he's looking at me expectantly, and I figure I've told him everything else. Might as well admit this. "I wanted to eat outside, that's the thing. So, I dragged you over here to make sure we had to."

"Um, why? You could have just said so."

"I sometimes have panic attacks in restaurants," I say, with an effort.

Chase's eyebrows lift. "All restaurants, or just the really dirty ones? Because, seriously, we won't go inside if it has anything besides an 'A' on the health department card, I promise. I sometimes risk a 'C' for myself, but your comfort is worth more to me."

"Oh, a 'C' rating is fine, it's just crowded restaurants I hate," I say, and laugh afterward because of course, that's every restaurant in Manhattan. "I know. It's…it's just leftover from the whole thing, you know…" We say *thing* a lot, my friends and I, when we mean pandemic. The Late Unpleasantness is another way we like to put it, although Abel can't do it without putting on a Foghorn Leghorn drawl that makes us all shriek with laughter—effectively raising the mood. Smart guy, our friend Abel.

I study Chase's face. He looks like he gets it. Like he doesn't think I'm a total freak.

"Sorry," I say anyway.

And I'm not only apologizing to Chase, but to myself. For not being able to bounce back, for not being able to return to my old life. But I mean, that's what this is about, right? Finding a nice guy and getting the hell out of the city? Because I can't hack it here anymore, remember?

"It's no problem," Chase says gently. "I'd rather be out here with you, in the park, than in a crowded, noisy falafel joint where I can't even hear what you're saying. You should have told me before; I wouldn't have suggested meeting in that bar."

"The bar was a little outside my comfort zone," I admit. "But I wanted to try it. And the backyard was really nice."

"It *was* nice," he replies, and now he's leaning towards me, brushing a wild curl from my forehead. His eyes catch the glow of a nearby streetlight, and my breath catches in my throat. "It was nice, and so is this, out here in the dark with you. It's like we're not in the city at all." His voice has dropped to a whisper. "It's just you—and me—"

His lips touch mine, and I can't help a little gasp of surprise at their warmth, their softness, that mysterious silken pressure that makes me instinctively lean into him. My lips part, and as our kiss deepens, the crowded city and all its discontents simply melts away.

Chapter Five

MY HEART IS still flooded with endorphins when I call an emergency meeting of the Settle Down Society the next afternoon.

Maybe emergency is the wrong word. The truth is, I've been daydreaming through my day, a sultry August Sunday filled with mundane errands like picking up dry-cleaning and buying three different kinds of bread at the French bakery near my apartment and scooping up some new wine at the bottle shop on the corner. I still buy most of my necessities online; I got used to having my toothpaste and my socks come in the same box, and I see no reason to brave the cramped stores where I used to shove my way through crowded racks and narrow aisles.

But there are a few shops in my neighborhood which still remind me of why I love New York, and I'm not giving up fresh croissants and brioche, no matter how long the line or what the cost to my mental health might be.

So when the girls come over, I've got red wine uncorked on the kitchen counter, and a plate of sliced baguette alongside some interesting cheeses and a salted Amish butter I recently discovered at an Amsterdam Avenue hole-in-the-wall shop. Margot and Caitlyn are both very enthusiastic over the offerings. Caitlyn was an on-again, off-again vegan back when she first moved to New York City, but good cheese is hard to ignore and she's been back on the dairy train for years now.

"Should have called Maeve over," she says when she sees the cheese. "Maeve loves a good brie."

"She and Dane are upstate this weekend," I say. "They were taking the dogs to Lake Placid."

"Oh, I forgot. They're always at that country house," Caitlyn says. "Lucky them."

"*This* is going to be the hardest thing about leaving New York," Margot announces through a bite of bread heavily layered with the creamy brie. "They don't have cheese like this in New Jersey. I checked."

"Well, we still have time to enjoy what we've got," Caitlyn says. "And maybe someday you can live near a cheesemonger. Play your cards right and see what happens."

"Here's hoping," Margot says. "Because we're looking at neighborhoods next week."

My wine glass collection narrowly misses annihilation.

"You're doing *what?*" Caitlyn demands, slamming her glass onto the table. "Who is *we?*"

"Me and Damian," Margot says, wide-eyed and innocent. "I *told* you we hit it off." Damian is the guy she started seeing less than a week after we named our agreement The Settle Down Society, as if she had him waiting in the wings for just this moment.

"It has been less than two months! We haven't even met him yet, and you're buying a house together?" I slouch onto the loveseat next to her. "I was just going to tell you about my *first date*. How did you get so far, so fast?"

"I chose wisely," Margot says, shrugging. "He said he wants to move to Montclair and live in a house with an elm tree in the front yard. And anyway, the sex is amazing."

"A house, an elm tree, a good lay, what else could you want?" Caitlyn's voice is dry. She has been non-committal with the matches she's made on Lifer so far. A few dates, but nothing she's wanted to pursue.

Margot isn't bothered by Caitlyn's tone. "No rules saying you can't hit the jackpot on the first try."

"That's how the casino hooks the newbies," Caitlyn says darkly.

"Well, what about *you?*" Margot rounds on her, nearly losing the chunk of cheese perched atop her baguette slice. "Are you dating anyone?"

"No." Caitlyn folds her arms and looks away with a stubborn expression I know too well. "I haven't met anyone worth my time yet."

"Well, you have to go on some dates!" Margot insists. "This isn't going to work if you don't at least meet some people."

"I've gone out with some people. They just aren't right for me. Most of them, I'm not interested in meeting in person at all."

"But you have to go out and meet them in person! It's a completely different ballgame in real life. The app is just to give you a starting point. You use the app to find people you want to *meet.*"

"Again," Caitlyn says, "I feel like you're in deep with a pyramid scheme when you start talking up this app."

"You're just stalling." Margot rolls her eyes. "I'm not talking to you about it anymore. Tracey, how are you doing?"

I take a breath. This is the moment when I tell them that last night, I saw stars. "Pretty good," I say.

Pretty good? I wonder where that phrase came from. Wasn't it more than that? I had a great time!

"Oh, that's good." Margot is looking at her phone. I'm already boring her. "You went out with that guy, right? What's his name? Chess?"

"Chase," I correct her. "I went out with Chase."

"He's the artist, right?" Caitlyn asks encouragingly.

"Yeah, he paints," I say vaguely, realizing that I don't fully know what else he does with his life. He paints on the side... what does he do for a job?

"We can always use more artists," Margot says cheerfully. "Oh, I need more of that brie."

I watch her scrape cheese across a hunk of baguette, trying to figure out why I didn't tell them I had an *amazing* night. Our twinkle-light tryst in the garden, our walk across town to my favorite falafel place, our dinner on the park bench, the drums beating as we shared our first (and second, third, and fourth) kiss. His face in the window as he closed the cab's door behind me. I'd decided I couldn't face the spotty service of late-night weekend trains, and he'd called a car service for me. It had been a perfect first date, especially within the confines of my tightly-drawn comfort zone.

"Well, what was he like?" Caitlyn is peering at me suspiciously. Not a lot gets by Caitlyn.

"He was really nice," I say. "He was—sweet. Understanding. Accommodating."

"Well, if you're looking for a new doorman, he sounds like the man for the job."

"No, it's not like that. I'm explaining it wrong."

Margot rounds on me and demands, "Were there fireworks?" She waves her bread around her head to illustrate pyrotechnics.

I close my eyes, remembering our night.

It was good.

Where did amazing go?

I decide not to worry about it.

"Yeah," I say. "Something like that."

Summer weekends are slow, but when Abel calls me up in the late afternoon and asks for a quick meeting at the gallery, I agree to head back down to Chelsea. Caitlyn and Margot have both headed out on their own adventures, and I'm feeling strangely discontented with the way our wine-and-cheese afternoon went. The goal had been to talk about Chase and figure out my next step with this guy, but we'd ended up talking about Margot's impending house-hunting trip to New Jersey while I puzzled, in the back of my mind, why I'd ended up saying next to nothing about our date.

Well, maybe Abel will be able to prise the truth out of me. He's pretty good at getting honest answers. Abel's one of my oldest friends; he and Margot were my best friends in art school and nothing changed when we got to New York City. We met in an anatomical drawing class in art school, where we bonded over our lack of skill. When the professor tactfully suggested we consider abstract visions for our body studies, we drowned our sorrows in dollar cans of PBR at a campus watering hole and planned out our future, art-free lives. Abel decided he would be a Pilates instructor—"That'll show Professor Ryman how to sculpt a body," he snorted, only slightly marring the punchline with his verb—and I would go into interior design, which required a good eye, but not actual artistic ability.

In the end, neither of us followed those the paths. Abel has done his share of bouncing around, but we found that his work as a broker and my work as a gallery owner meshed well.

I've had months when Abel's patronage was the only thing keeping my rent paid, and Abel has had months in which the only pieces he could move were from an artist I had an exclusive on.

So by now, we have a sort of symbiotic relationship.

"Tracey! My bestie! My dearest! My sister from another mister!" Abel is standing in front of my locked and gated gallery, looking dapper as ever. He's opted for a full-on eccentric millionaire get-up this evening, his rounding frame draped in a three-piece suit with a gorgeous check pattern. His receding hairline is covered with a fedora.

It is eighty-two degrees and humid, a hint of thunder in the air. He has to be dying in all that fabric.

"What on earth are you wearing?" I present my cheek for his kiss. "Let's get you into some AC before you melt into a puddle."

"Isn't it gorgeous?" Abel fingers his lapel as I unlock the gallery's heavy front gate and push it up with one monumental heave. It's an action I have perfected over years. When I first rented this space, I couldn't open the gate alone. I had to ask the nice owner of the deli on the corner to help me. Now I get coffee from Ahmed at least two times a week to say my continued thanks, even though it's terrible coffee.

Abel watches my athleticism with an absent gaze. "Nice job. But seriously, this suit? I'm so in love. It just arrived from my tailor and I couldn't wait to put it on. And I thought, Tracey appreciates nice things. She will appreciate this suit."

"I do appreciate it." We step into the gallery, which is cold and dry. I have to keep climate control running all the time in here, an expense that gets more monumental every summer. "And now that I've appreciated it, why don't you take off that jacket and air yourself out."

"Not necessary," Abel declares, but he does remove his hat, dropping it artfully onto the coat-rack just inside the door. "So, show me this elephant."

I stare at him in dismay. "Why didn't you say that's what you wanted? The elephant is in my living room."

"Fiddlesticks!"

"Sorry, Scarlett O'Hara. I had some interest in him online a couple months ago, so I brought him home for pictures and never brought him back. He's huge. A real pain even in a town car. But," I flip on the lights with a flourish. "The same artist also did *these*."

"Oh my god!" Abel stares at the canvases in front of us. There is a long pause. Then he ventures, "What...what are they?"

"Well, I think that one might be a lemur." I point to the one on the left. The canvas is four feet tall and three feet wide. This artist loves working with big space. The better to confuse people with.

He squints. "I can see a lemur, I think. Those squiggles would be the...paws? Lemur paws?"

"And the black orbs would be their giant eyeballs," I suggest. I've had these paintings for several months; that's a lot of time to stare at them. "Why the interest in the elephant all of a sudden?"

"The artist is doing someone dramatic in Rio."

"Something, you mean?"

"Oh, no. Someone." He laughs.

"Well, this is the work. The elephant at home, this lemur, and that's maybe...a dolphin? If you turn your head slightly."

"Charming." Abel glances at me, and for just a moment, I see a hint of hurt feelings. "And they said *we* didn't have enough talent to be artists."

"Well, we said that, too, to be fair." I push through a hidden door and into the galley kitchen. The fridge is always stocked with San Pellegrino and white wine. Abel accepts a mineral water with a grateful expression, and finally sheds the coat. I take one for myself, saying, "I think the difference between an art dealer and an artist might be more in ego than in talent."

"And you're utterly lacking in ego." Abel gives me an adoring older-brother smile. "Now, while we study these specimens, tell me about your love life. Still planning on getting married and moving away from me as soon as possible?"

"That's the goal." I pause, still not sure how to express myself over last night's date with Chase. "I met up with a guy," I say finally. "We had a really nice evening. I like him a lot."

"Oh! Is he the one?"

"He could be. I think." I thought so last night. Where did that certainty go? I'll have to see him again soon; I need that connection back.

"You should know," Abel says. "Right away. Like lightning! That's how it was with Dev and me. Like a bolt from the blue. He walked into the room, kissed another man passionately, and I said to myself, *that is my future husband.*"

I laugh weakly. Now is not the time to bring up Margot's lightning-fast courtship with Damian, but it does seem a little unfair that two of my best friends seem to be blessed in the relationship department. "I don't think it's like that for everyone. You two are a special case. But we get along really well, and he's really sweet. I think there's something there."

Again, I mourn the loss of "amazing" from my personal description of my first date with Chase. Where did the magic go, in just one night?

"Do you, now?" Abel is peering at me now, missing only a lorgnette to give me the full ducal inspection.

Something occurs to me at that moment. The name we'd given ourselves and our little brainchild. *The Settle Down Society.* The goal was to find the right guy to marry and move to the country with, but had we overlooked the key word in the title? *Settle?*

Were "nice" and "sweet" and "we get along really well" all codes for settling?

And what if they are? A scolding voice intrudes, a voice I recognize all too well. It's the one that told me to stop playing with pastels and find a job selling other people's art, it's the one that intrudes every time I think about going to a concert or a reading or a play like I might have before my anxiety got so serious. I've always assumed this voice was my common sense, and listened to it. And so far, has it really led me astray?

It's time to make your move, the voice says. *Nice and sweet and getting along are all more than you've got right now, alone in your apartment for years on end.*

I lift my chin and meet Abel's gaze head-on. "Yes, I do think there's something there," I tell him. "Chase is great. He might be the one. I'm excited about him."

Abel watches me for a moment longer. Then he cuffs me gently under the chin. "Fine, you've convinced me. But this painting? Tracey? It's not a lemur. I think it's a raccoon. How are we supposed to sell a painting of a maybe-raccoon to a guy who had his heart set on an elephant?"

Chapter Six

ABEL'S GONE MORE quickly than I expected, announcing he has to meet friends for dinner at nine in Queens—"Queens," he repeats, blinking elaborately at me. "When did everyone move to Queens?"—and I find myself alone in my gallery as the streetlights begin to replace daylight.

This is a quiet street on a Sunday night, mostly residential, with grand old brick buildings housing the affluent, older New Yorkers who have probably lived just off Fifth Avenue for their entire adult lives, and can't imagine life any other way. Shadows pass the gallery's plate-glass windows, couples walking matching sets of small dogs, the occasional cab or town car, a group of loud twenty-somethings, the girls wearing almost nothing in the summer heat, laughing and grabbing at each other as they stumble past.

When I see them, it's like my heart seizes up. It's that reaction I keep having, every time I try to imagine my old life in the city, back before everything changed. After all that time spent alone in my apartment, after moving the gallery online, people make me nervous. Panicky, even. Everyone's too close together, everyone's breathing each other's air.

It isn't supposed to matter anymore, but I can't convince my brain to let go of these primitive fears.

In any crowd, I quickly get sick, and nervous, and my palms start to sweat, and I know, beyond a shadow of a doubt: *I can't stay here.*

And there's not much going on in New York City that doesn't involve a crowd.

I flip out the bright display lights and let the gallery sink into a half-lit stillness. I can't see the sky outside, because the buildings here are too tall for that, but I know it's dusk. A summer dusk, the sweetest time of the year. I should be happier. I should be embracing the city. At the very least, I shouldn't be alone.

I want to talk to someone, and for a moment I'm lost. Who to call? Who to text? Who do I want?

Then I remember. I can call Chase.

Chase comes over in a flash. I'm actually startled at how quickly he appears outside the gallery, knocking on the glass door. He's peering inside, his hands cupped against the glass, when I unlock the door.

"You weren't kidding when you said you were nearby!" I laugh, letting him in.

He flows into the dark gallery, bringing a burst of welcome energy with him. "I was lurking nearby, hoping you'd call me." He holds up a bouquet of flowers. "Also, I caught the very last vendor in Union Square."

"Oh my gosh, beautiful!" I take the flowers and theatrically breathe them in, hoping I won't catch a nose-full of pollen. As I look for a bowl to set them in, I wonder if I've ever mentioned where my gallery is. I suppose last night I said it was close to Union Square and Fifth. That must have been enough for him to go on. "What have you been up to all day?"

"Just wandering the city," Chase says. I hear his footsteps as he walks the gallery, pausing in front of each painting. "You know, some days it's just nice to walk and take it all in."

"I used to love doing that. I haven't so much, lately."

"Why not?"

I glance back over my shoulder. He's looking at the painting that might be a lemur, might be a raccoon, depending on the viewer's frame of mind. With his thumb to his chin, studying the painting's strokes, I wonder which one he sees on the canvas.

"I guess it just makes me a little anxious, all the crowds on the sidewalks these days." I shake out the flowers in the big bowl, a ceramic dish I usually use for pretzels at openings. It's a pretty arrangement, unconventional but pleasing. I carry it out to the gallery floor like I'm presenting a grand prize. "What do you think? Fun, right?"

His glance is absent. "Mmhmm. I like that. So, this painting. It's a Pocchiano, right?"

I nearly drop the bowl. "You know Alphonse Pocchiano?"

The artist who is doing someone dramatic in Rio. How does Chase know about him?

"I know a thing or two." Chase steps a little closer, his nose just inches from the canvas. I have to restrain myself from asking him to back away. "He's had a few hits at auction. The sloth abstract? Almost a million dollars?"

Three years ago. "A lucky night," I say. "Two dealers who just broke up with each other were bidding on it." Abel had told me all the juicy details.

"Ah, love," Chase says, chuckling.

"Well, I wouldn't count on this lemur getting anywhere near a million. Or the dolphin, or the elephant. Or—whatever that is." We hadn't been able to reach a satisfactory conclusion on my third Pocchiano, with Abel going all-in on panda while I am pretty sure it's a box of tissues.

"I like the dolphin. You have to turn your head just a little… But, where's the elephant?" Chase ignores the third canvas, too.

"That's the one on my living room wall," I say. "I brought him home for pictures and never brought him back, remember?"

"Right." He gives me a slow smile, and in the low light filtering in from the street, it's almost seductive. I feel a shiver of pleasure and put the bowl of flowers down on a nearby table. Just in case something interesting is about to happen. He says, "I'll have to see this elephant of yours one day."

I like where things are going, so when I lightly reply, "I didn't realize you were a fan of elephants," I'm already closing the space between us. A little tremor races through me as his hands grip my arms and pull me to him, a survival instinct clicking in to shriek, *Too close! Too close!* But I manage to shake it off, turning my face up to his. My lips part of their own accord, and I feel my knees weaken as his lips find mine, gentle pressure that sends a shock of heat through my core.

"Mmm," Chase murmurs between kisses. "This is nice. Tracey, I think—" He stops and rests his chin on my shoulder.

I can't stand the waiting. "What? You think what?"

"Nothing, nothing." His lips are warm against my throat. "Speaking out of turn. Ignore me."

I turn my head, willing him to say it. Willing him to move us to the next step. I don't care if it's too soon. Months too soon. Years too soon, even. There's no time to waste; my life stopped for too long.

"Tell me," I whisper. "You can say it."

"I think I'm falling for you." His words end in a groan as I take his lips with mine, forcing the feelings coursing through my nerves to be as real as his are.

Be the one, I think desperately, giving myself into his kiss. *You have to be the one.*

There's not a soft spot or protected corner in my entire gallery; I pulled out the sofas when I reopened the space to visitors, reasoning that I didn't want to encourage people to stay too long, breathing my air. The plush couches were listed online and sold within hours, lifted away by enterprising New Yorkers, the first of the rush of new residents pouncing on momentarily low rents.

We have to settle for a chair in the pantry, with the door pushed mostly closed, letting in just enough light from the street that we can see what we're fumbling with, zippers and buttons and waistbands. It's not the romantic setting I'd wish for, not for our first time together, but it does the trick.

And anyway, now we have a fun story that proves how passionate we are, how perfect we are for each other. We couldn't even wait to get home, to a nice comfortable bed, and at our age! It will go over great with certain factions at the wedding reception. A fun, raunchy story for the bridal shower, when our mothers are out of the room.

There's nowhere to go afterwards, though. No snuggling when your calves are threatening to cramp from propping yourself up on your toes. I'm tucked into a corner of the tiny kitchen, sitting on a puffy winter coat I left here when the seasons changed irrevocably into summer, as Chase straightens his clothes and gets up.

He glances around the kitchen like he's measuring the space for new wallpaper. It's a small space—just a counter with a sink and cabinets above, a refrigerator with a too-robust hum, and the chair in one corner. Nothing on the walls, even, except for the control panel for the gallery's electrical systems.

"What's this?" he asks, touching the panel with one finger. The LED screen lights up for him. "Ah! Temperature control."

"Among other things, yeah. I have the climate control, lighting, and alarms wired through there. It's a smart system, they say."

"Smart, huh?" Chase keys through the menus. "Look at this, you have motion sensors in every gallery. How high-tech of you."

"I like the sensors, but I *should* have cameras. Priced it out, and the installation was going to cost a fortune. And the back room sensors don't even work." I shake my head. "This place was a mess when they put all that in. Ripped it to shreds. Even had to put in new drop ceilings afterwards. You'd think for that kind of trouble, I'd at least get fully working system. But not in New York. I used someone's guy...I should've known there'd be a catch."

"Everyone's got a guy in New York," Chase snorts. "Some guys are better than others."

"And every guy has a guy. And *that* guy knows how to get around inspections. They tell the gullible lady, hey, saved ya some money! Anyway, the security system does the job for now. Careful or you'll set it off and we'll have the cops here in about a minute."

Chase removes his finger from the panel and puts his hands behind his back.

I laugh at his naughty-boy expression. "Afraid of the police?"

"Not so much afraid as...eager to allow them to do their jobs unimpeded by me?"

"A good answer. The guys at the local precinct know me a little bit, but I've never actually needed them. This alarm is probably mostly for show. And it helps me sleep at night when I've got big works of art down here. Of course," I add, grinning, "the real prize is the elephant. That's why I keep him in my living room."

"No alarms on your door there? I'm surprised."

"Who'd bother little old me? A fifth-floor apartment is an awful lot of trouble to burgle. Especially as slow as my elevator is. I live in one of those big pre-wars near Riverside Drive, you know the type." My beautiful limestone building has one of those tiny, groaning elevators from around the dawn of lift technology. Pre-wars: we love them, except when we're bringing home groceries. Which I rarely do anymore, thanks to online shopping. I hang my winter coat back on its peg and dust myself off. "What's your building like?"

"Shabby," Chase admits. "I could do better. But I don't want to deal with apartment-shopping in the city again, so I just deal with it. And rents are going wild."

"Boy, I know it." I remember Margot's announcement from earlier that day. Leaving the city. Incredible. "I have a friend looking at houses in Montclair," I say, watching his expression. Could he be up for it?

"That sounds interesting," Chase says. "To be honest, I've always seen myself in a colonial with an elm tree in the front yard."

"Maybe someday?"

He smiles and pulls me close. "Maybe someday *soon*."

* * *

By the time our stomachs start rumbling, the neighborhood has retreated indoors. Golden rectangles of light shine in the upstairs windows all along the street as we step outside. I lock the door and then put down my purse, preparing myself for the leap to catch the gate strap. It would be tough to reach even if I were a more normal height. At sub-five feet, it's all about launch strategies.

Chase is staring at me as I do some quick stretches. "What are you doing, getting ready for your floor exercise?"

"I have to grab that strap." I point at the nylon strap hanging almost two feet above my head.

"And then what, dangle from it?"

"I have a system." Years ago, I found that if I hang on with both hands and draw myself up into a ball, the gate will give way and slowly rumble down. I just ride it until my feet can touch the ground, then I jump out of the way. It saves me having to drag a ladder in and out of the gallery. And it's kind of fun, besides. "Trust me, I've been opening and closing this gallery by myself for a long time."

"Oh, let me do it." Chase is able to give one little hop to grasp the strap, and the gate follows him down obediently, squeaking its way to the ground. "There. Isn't that easier? Where's the key? I'll latch it."

I hand over the key, feeling a little miffed. The gate isn't a hardship for me. It's an accomplishment. Every time I manage to tug that gate down by myself, I'm reminded of how much I can do without help.

Of course, in a relationship, I don't *have* to do everything by myself.

That's supposed to be one of the upsides.

So I show Chase how to wiggle the key just right, and how to listen for the right number of clicks to know the finicky old tumblers have fallen into place. By the time we're done, Chase could easily open and close the gallery by himself. He hands me the key with a grin. "See, I'm already learning more about how the art world operates."

"I didn't realize you were being so literal."

Chase laughs and kisses me. It's our first off-hand, casual kiss, the first one that isn't layered with long looks and deeper intention. That in itself is enough to make it feel powerful and real. I pull him towards me, ready to kick things up a notch, and he trips. Except it's almost like he was shoved, and I fall to the sidewalk. Chase tugs me up, looking around. "Did you see anyone?"

But I didn't—the street is so dark, beneath the thick summer foliage of the plane trees. "Did you get pushed?"

"I thought someone was just in a hurry," he says, still looking around.

And then I notice my purse is missing.

Chapter Seven

THE OFFICER WHO takes down my report isn't surprised by my story. "Just your everyday mugging," she says, tapping keys. "Most of them aren't violent. They're just a surprise, someone noticing your guard is down and taking advantage."

"Is there any chance you'll catch the person?"

"I'd get a new purse," she says.

Chase is waiting for me in the precinct lobby. It's one of those old-fashioned ones, with the grainy wood and the globe lighting, but the floor is covered with mint-green vinyl of a seventies vintage. He's kicking at a dark splotch of gum stuck just in front of his chair.

"Think about the hardwood under this stick-on vinyl," he says.

"Chase, that's so gross. Stop putting your shoe all over that gum. It was in someone's *mouth*." My fear of germs will probably never leave me. I'm going to be a paranoid mother.

Chase just grins. He gives the gum another kick for good measure. "I'm sure all the bacteria has dispersed across the rest of the floor by now."

"Don't make me throw up. Come on, I need a drink." I'm trying to think of a quiet bar in the neighborhood. Maybe the White Horse...? There's a tap on my shoulder and I spin around in surprise.

And I find myself face to face with a broad chest beneath a crisp white shirt.

I take a step back without meaning to—he's too close to me. Everyone is too close to me. And I'm probably two feet away before I look up and see his face. Even under the ghostly fluorescent lights, it's impossible not to recognize him as the same tall man who bumped into me at the bar before I met Chase.

It's the giant, and he's every bit as handsome in a blue button-down shirt and green tie in this rundown police precinct as he was in casual clothes at that crowded bar.

He's looking down at me with an expression just like the one he wore at our last meeting, as if I've inconvenienced him with my mere presence. His pursed lips and slightly narrowed eyes seem to make more sense in this setting, as if he's suddenly put into context by the ringing phones and ticking keyboards behind him. I'm about to ask him what his problem is when I realize there's an NYPD shield clipped to his belt.

Of course, I think. *He's a cop.*

Doesn't that explain everything? Rude, pushy, incapable of apologizing? A cop. Sure, he paid for the drink he made me spill. But he didn't buy me another one. (I may have told him not to, but I don't remember. So we'll leave that detail out.) And he certainly never said he was sorry for knocking into me in the first place. *And* he made fun of me for being short. So yeah, he's a jerk. I don't owe him anything.

But he's still a cop, with all the authority that implies. And we're in his office, not mine. So I temper my sharp tone when I say, "Did I forget something back there?"

Not that I have anything to forget. My phone is in my back pocket, thank goodness. Everything else is gone.

He lifts his eyebrows. "You're asking me? I don't even know why you're here. I was just leaving for the night. Then I came around the corner, and you were standing here, looking lost."

"I don't think I was looking *lost,*" I argue. "That's kind of rude."

"Oh," he says, surprisingly taken aback. "Well, sorry about that. In that case, are you—uh—going out, or—"

"Do you know this officer?" Chase is suddenly at my side. I'm so grateful for his presence, I could just melt. "Officer, can you help her get her purse back?"

He looks from me to Chase, and his brow furrows. "Who's this guy?" he demands, his tone hardening again.

"This is the guy I was waiting for last night."

"Oh," he says again. He regards Chase for a moment, like he doesn't like what he's seeing. "You were late. That neighborhood can get rowdy at night. Don't let her wander around down there alone anymore, okay?"

"I don't need a *babysitter*," I snap, just as Chase tries to stutter out an apology. It's like the cop is his dad or something. Or my dad. This feels kind of like we're standing in front of some parental figure, like I got home late from prom. I wonder if Chase has an issue with authority figures. When I asked if he wanted to come down the hall with me to file the report, he was quick to say he'd be better off waiting in the lobby. "I have an awful head for details," he'd told me, and I'd accepted that. But maybe he's actually afraid of cops.

"No one's saying you do," the cop says to me, ignoring Chase's babbling. "I'm just saying, he should be a better boyfriend."

"Detective Reilly?" The officer who took my report has appeared in the lobby.

The cop holds up a finger at me. "One minute."

I look at Chase incredulously as the officer walks back to the reception desk and leans on the high counter, his head close to the speaker holes in the bulletproof glass. "What on earth is this? Did he just tell me to *wait* for him?"

"I don't know what's going on," Chase says. He gives me a suspicious look. "How do you know him?"

"Believe it or not, he was at the bar last night. He spilled my first drink, before you got there."

"So you don't even know him, and he's giving us both instructions like he's someone's dad?"

"That's what I was thinking!" I giggle. "Shush, he's coming back."

"No, I'm not hanging around for this." Chase heads for the door. "Come on, Tracey."

I start to follow, but Detective Reilly's voice pulls me back.

"Miss, be careful out there, okay?" He looks genuinely concerned, his eyebrows still drawn together. I like the protective expression it gives him, like a wise and worried hound-dog. But in a nice way. "I don't like to share scary statistics, but there's been an uptick in crime lately. Summer nights bring out the worst in people. Make him walk you to your door, that kind of thing."

"Oh, I don't live down here," I assure him. "I have a gallery down the block. I live up on West Eighty-Second towards Riverside. You know, kind of near the museum? Of Natural History?"

His mouth twitches. "I know which museum's on Eighty-Second, yes."

"Good. Um. Right. So you know, it's a really safe neighborhood, and..." I seem to have forgotten how to end conversations with strange men. "So I guess I'll just—"

"Be careful," he says, that protective look still on his face. "Goodnight to you."

"Thanks," I reply, because he seems to really mean it. "Goodnight."

Despite the police officer's request, I don't ask Chase to walk me to my door. For one thing, I've already had about all the close human contact I can handle today—a girl has to work her way up to these kind of things, and in one day I've met up with my friends, had a long chat with Abel, and had sex on the floor of my gallery. Plus, I remind myself, settling into a cab, there was whatever *that* was with the police officer.

Detective Reilly, the other officer called him. Not sure why I remember that.

It was just weird, seeing him twice in two days. And both times, hardly a hint of a smile and yet his interest in my wellbeing was palpable. Anyone who heard the basic outline of the story would think it was a classic New York City love story unfolding, meeting the handsome stranger in a bar, then running into him again the very next night. But this isn't a Nora Ephron movie, and this isn't the New York City it used to be, either. This is someone else's city, and, I suppose, that's someone else's love story.

With my purse just a fond memory now, I have to stop at Caitlyn's apartment to pick up her copy of my keys. She's in a mood, something about a celebrity interview she'd picked up freelance getting canceled at the last minute, and only about two minutes pass before I've got the spare set of keys tucked deep into my pocket and am walking up Amsterdam.

Sunday night doesn't slow down the sidewalk cafes and crowds spilling from bars along the wide avenue; here, people go to bed late, and walk home slowly, hand in hand, to the apartments or brownstones where they've raised their families. I moved to the Upper West Side four years ago. I'd always thought it was for old, boring people. I figured I was just getting old and boring.

But it's nice now to have other people around, not too close, to hear their voices and know I am not alone as I walk beneath the plane trees.

Just in case Detective Reilly's warning about summer crime was correct.

Chapter Eight

BY THE MIDDLE of August, the Settle Down Society has its first engagement. Margot, fresh off another house-hunting trip to New Jersey, is flaunting a diamond ring the size of a June bug on her slim finger. "I'm getting married, getting married, getting *married!*" she sings, dancing around her living room. Caitlyn is looking at her skeptically, and I have to wonder if Caitlyn has bought into this thing at all. Maybe it's just Margot and me.

The idea is worrisome. Margot is not the person you want to follow in an emergency situation.

But I also know I'm in too deep to try and get out now. Things have proceeded very quickly with Chase. We've been seeing each other for about two weeks, and already he's sleeping in my apartment every other night. He has mentioned two specific starter homes in Rockland County.

"Unless you'd prefer to move south," he suggested just last night over takeout, as we slurped up ramen noodles. "Maybe you're ready for a change from the ice and snow, I don't know."

"Where in the south would we move?" I was picturing palm trees and blue water, a white clapboard cottage and a rowboat pulled ashore a sandy beach. The scene was washed out and pastel, like a watercolor hanging in a Holiday Inn.

"Atlanta? Charlotte?" Chase laughed as I wrinkled my nose. "Okay, okay, not those!"

"I don't know where I'd want to go," I admitted. "Not back to the Midwest. I've lived here most of my life, or at least, it feels that way."

"But you definitely want to leave the city," Chase persisted.

"Definitely."

That's not up for discussion; leaving New York City has become my obsession. I need room, I need my own air. That is one of the major points of the Settle Down Society, right? Finding someone to whisk us out of here? But Chase seems less willing to whisk me away on his own. He wants my input, and it's a conversation I'd rather not have with myself. I need a hero to do the work for me. I pretend I'm a damsel in distress, who can't take care of herself, even though nothing could be further from the truth. I have taken care of myself, with varying degrees of support from my friends, for over a decade.

At three a.m., lying awake and staring at the crack in my ceiling, I know the truth of why.

I'm afraid I might talk myself out of leaving.

And I can't let myself do that.

"That ring is so flashy," Caitlyn says, bringing me back to the present.

Margot has run out of breath from her dancing and throws herself onto the sofa. I hold up my champagne flute to avoid spilling it all over both of us. "I can't believe it," she gasps. "I'm getting *married*."

"And moving to the suburbs," Caitlyn adds, in an unenthused voice. She drains her glass. "You know what, ladies? I'm not sure I'm up for this."

I shake my head like I haven't been having my own late-night doubts. "Come on, Caitlyn. Don't back out now."

"I haven't met a single guy on Lifer who could be my life partner. Or even a girl, and I checked a couple out, so don't ask. It could be that not everyone can find their life-match on an app."

"That can't be it." Margot shakes her head. "I have all the faith in the world in Lifer."

"Maybe too much faith is a bad thing, Margot." Caitlyn looks around Margot's living room as if searching for something. "By the way, I apologize for insisting it was an MLM scheme. I don't see a single box of miracle drugs or weight-loss shakes anywhere in this apartment. You're clean."

"I told you! This is about moving on to the next stage in our lives." Margot turns to me. "What about Chase? Any closer to popping the question inappropriately quickly? That's part of the app's user guide, you know. Marriage ASAP!"

"I feel like he might!" I try to infuse some of Margot's excitement into my own voice. "If he doesn't propose, I think he'll definitely ask me to move in with him."

"Where does he live?"

"Oh, I mean the two of us moving out of town. But he lives in Clinton Hill right now." The Brooklyn neighborhood is clean and renovated, with expensive restaurants. Less crowded than the Upper West Side, too, but I'm sure that won't last. The towers get taller every day.

Caitlyn makes an impressed sort-of face that says *not bad.* "I would have expected Staten Island, to be honest."

"Caitlyn! Oh my god. Be nice. He's not Staten Island at all. He's from northern Virginia originally. Not from up here." Even now, as the boundaries of where's cool to live in the city expand outwards, there's still very little chance someone would live in Staten Island without having been born there and simply neglecting to move away. And once that changes, I'll know the city has grown unrecognizable.

But Caitlyn isn't convinced. She has met Chase a few times and they haven't clicked. She says, "He's just a little...I don't know, it's like he's trying too hard? But don't listen to me. I haven't hung out with the two of you very much. You still somehow manage to have a dating life *and* be a shut-in, which is impressive."

"You know I don't like to go out in crowds."

"It's August. No snow on the ground. There are *parks.* When's the last time you went for a walk in the park?"

"In summer? Too many tourists." The last time I went to Riverside Park, I felt like I was going to be swallowed up by the number of people on the pathways, taking selfies, biking, walking dogs, pushing strollers. "I go to the community garden a couple blocks over now and then. That has to be enough fresh air for now."

Caitlyn is giving me a look I don't like, a look which says, *you are lying to yourself and to us, and it needs to stop.* She's very good at this look. Caitlyn is going to be an amazing mom.

If she will just settle down with someone and get busy having kids.

Margot, on the other hand, has gone back to leaping around the room. It's hard to see how she is the one in the room who is closest to a husband and a family. Margot is artistic, wild, free-spirited. That's not to say all those talents won't make her a superb partner and mother—any kid would be lucky to have her for a mom. But I find myself wondering how on earth she'll ever make it as a stay-at-home wife in Montclair.

Chase is in my living room when I get home, typing away on his laptop. He closes it as I shut the door behind me, sliding it into his leather messenger bag. His smile is everything I love about him: open and cheery. "Hello, my love," he says, standing up to greet me.

Yes, things have progressed a lot in two weeks. But again, that was the point of all of this. Move fast, get married—before I can change my mind.

"Hey, sweetheart." I busy myself taking off my shoes and hanging up my keys—a replacement set, to go with the replacement purse I had to buy myself, since my old one was never found. I like to keep him waiting, teasing him, because I know exactly where we're going to end up. The sex is good, it is constant, it is rich and unfolding...just like my life, right?

But Chase doesn't take me by the hand and lead me into the bedroom. Instead, he takes out his phone and fiddles with the screen for a moment, then holds it out to me. I take it, confused.

There's a photo of a house on the screen. Well, a cottage, really. One of those sweet little mock-Tudors with the swooping eave over the front door, the shingles nearly level with the ground. It's surrounded by thick trees, their leaves lustrous with summer rain. "What's this?" I look up at him, befuddled. "Is this a friend's new house?"

"It could be *our* house," he says.

I stare at him, then look back at the phone. I start flicking through photos—it's a real estate listing, and there are dozens of pictures, inside, outside, front yard, back yard. The details make themselves clear: a small house in a small town up the Hudson River, a recognizable enough place where I could get down to the Manhattan gallery if I had to, but mostly where I could start anew with summer tourists and online sales.

A place where we could start a family and breathe clean air and never step foot on a crowded subway train again.

The enormity of leaving New York City makes my hands shake.

This is what you want.

"Chase, I don't know what to say…"

"Say you'll marry me, and run away with me to the tiny town of…" He furrows his brow. "Oh god, I forgot the name again. I rehearsed this, too!"

I choke back something that is half a laugh and half a sob. This is it! This is the proposal. "The town of Hallenbeck," I say.

"Not the poetry I was going for, let me tell you. I tried and tried to find the right place in a more melodious-sounding town, but—"

I cut him off with a kiss.

"Let's do it," I say afterwards.

"Okay." Chase gives me a cartoon leer.

"No, I mean, let's get married and move to Hallenbeck." I'm laughing now, because he's already dragging me into the bedroom, unbuttoning his shirt with his free hand. What kind of proposal is this? It's different, it's carefree, it's completely unconventional.

It's Chase.

The girls insist on taking me out to dinner. And because they're my best friends, they know that dinner needs to be outside for me to feel totally comfortable. So, it becomes a picnic. A picnic in Central Park, with booze packed into water bottles because it's illegal to drink alcohol in New York City parks, but no celebration in our group is complete without drinks.

Margot suggests a little pocket of grass she knows about in the North Woods where the park police are unlikely to find us imbibing, and so on a golden, breezy Sunday evening I climb the slanting paths through the forest that covers the northwest corner of the park. The views can be surreal up here, looking through thickets of old-growth trees to see the symmetrical lines of pre-war apartment houses lining Central Park West.

But it's still wild and green, and I savor the nature all around me. Soon, my whole life will be surrounded by forests like this. We've driven up to Hallenbeck already, a tiny sliver of land along the Hudson, just north of Saugerties. The house is small and welcoming and smells of lemon polish, and we've made our offer. I could be leaving New York City in a matter of months. I've already started thinking about subletting my apartment.

It's all happening.

When I spot the girls, some howls of welcome go up, scattering squirrels.

For a moment, I wonder how I'll live the rest of my life without them.

"Pour me a glass, girls," I demand, throwing myself on the picnic blanket.

We're three water bottles deep and the sun starting to sink when Margot and Caitlyn start packing up our things, waving me away when I try to help. There's some chatter of taking the party back to my place—Margot's apartment is a sea of packing tape and cardboard, and Caitlyn has a cousin in town she can't stand—and I'm considering what a success my life has become, tipped over in the grass, when my phone rings.

I glance at it. A *212* number. Huh, I think. Don't see a lot of those from spam calls. Curious, I roll over and answer.

"Ms Tracey Adams?"

"Mmhmm, yes?" I'm blinking now, trying to get my wits about me. But it's hard when you've been drinking champagne from water bottles for the past two hours.

"Are you the owner of Adams Galleries at 314 West Sixteenth Street?"

I sit up. "Yes. Is there a problem?"

"Ms Adams, we're going to need you or a representative to come down to the location and speak with the police. There's been a burglary."

"I—yes. Okay." I'm stammering now, as the woman on the phone says a few more official things, then ends the call.

Caitlyn and Margot are staring at me. "Is everything okay?" Margot asks.

"My gallery—a break-in? I think? I'm confused."

Caitlyn has maintained her composure; Caitlyn was probably drinking water half the time Margot and I were throwing back wine. "Let's get you some coffee and protein," she says. "Something a little heavier than brie and water crackers before you try to get into a cab."

"My gallery?" I say wonderingly, the words seeming to wobble on my tongue. "It's *daylight*. Who would break in on a Sunday evening?"

Caitlyn gives me a steady look. "Do you want me to even say what I think?"

Chapter Nine

THANKS TO THE isolated spot where we picnicked, plus the need to change clothes, sober up, and contain my shaking hands enough to call a car, it takes me two hours to get to the gallery. The streets are packed and the drive seems to take forever.

By the time my car reaches Chelsea, the sun has set and a cool afterglow has settled over the city, but the streets in the lower third of Manhattan Island are still warm and sticky, as if the breeze we were enjoying all afternoon never made it down here. I'm full of ham sandwich and black coffee from a bodega on Columbus Avenue—uncomfortably full, actually, but no longer drunk, and that's what counts.

But no, maybe I'd rather be drunk. I step out of the cab and looking at the little cluster of police officers standing near my gallery door. It all looks like too much to handle without a fortifying shot of whiskey.

Plus, that's Detective Reilly standing there, arms folded over a blue button-down shirt, looking like he's tired of waiting for me.

You're my bad luck penny, Detective Reilly, I think, squaring my shoulders to walk over and face the investigators and officers.

He stands to one side and lets the officers take control. Their questions are brief, but probing. I stand outside my violated gallery and answer the officers until the combination of humid August heat and an encroaching champagne headache makes me feel faint. Then I insist everyone comes inside so that I can have some air conditioning and sparkling water.

I try not to look at the empty walls as I walk to the kitchen. It's all gone—even the lemur. Maybe especially the lemur. That bizarre tangle of loops was the last Pocchiano canvas I had in the gallery; just a few days ago, a few collectors began to snap up the artist's work just as I'd always expected, and the panda/box of tissues sold for a stunning sum. I still have the elephant back at my apartment, hanging on my living room wall like a trust fund waiting for me to cash in.

"Is the Pocchiano canvas what triggered a robbery?" I ask, sipping carefully at my water. I'm sitting on the lone chair, with the detective and a few officers standing around me. I can't get it out of my head—this is the chair where Chase and I had heart-pounding sex. We haven't done it here again—it's really not very comfortable—but to me, it gives the chair a sweat-soaked aura, and I'm afraid these starch-shirt men are going to notice it.

Reilly shrugs as the officers exchange confused looks; art crime is beyond their beats. "Triggered isn't really the right word here," he says. "In this case, we're dealing with someone knowing how to get in, *and* knowing you wouldn't be here. This is about timing, more than anything. You've told us no one knows the alarm code but you, which makes sense since it went off when they went out the back. But they came in through the front door, with a key. Who had a key?"

"My purse was stolen," I remind him. "You were there, remember? When I filed the report? I had business cards in my purse, along with the keys. It would be easy for anyone to figure out what the keys are for. It could have been *anyone* in this city."

I have to say it, because I know what Reilly's thinking. And the two officers standing next to him exchange glances; they're thinking it, too.

But it wasn't him.

It can't have been him.

Reilly regards me for a moment, his expression easy to read. *This chick's in denial.* He's about to say something else when a new officer elbows her way into the kitchen. She glances down at me and gives me a sort of apologetic grimace before saying, "I got a description from the guy who runs the deli on the corner."

"You talked to Ahmed?" I ask, my blood suddenly chilling in my veins. Ahmed loves standing in the front door and watching the street life around him. If anyone knows who has emptied my gallery, it's him. And if it was—anyone I know—Ahmed will have recognized them.

The officer nods, looking at her notebook. "Yeah, that's him. Ahmed Zayat. He said he's seen the guy who let himself in a couple times here, with you, ma'am."

My heart sinks. No, it has stopped beating.

"But the details on his description are pretty average. Brown hair, white skin, about five-foot-six, favors t-shirts and jeans, plain sneakers." The officer shrugs and hands her notebook to Reilly. "And he said this guy has never gone into the deli."

"Average white guy." Reilly looks at me over the notebook. His eyes are giving me a message I don't want to receive.

"No," I say, my mouth so dry the words are a croak. "Can't be."

"Call him," Reilly says. "Find out where he is right now."

"No." I feel it coming. I feel the crash. I feel the end all around me. I'm not going to just invite it in.

"Call him," Reilly says, pitiless. "Or I'll find him myself."

Chase doesn't answer the phone. Not the first try, not the second, not the sixth, not the seventh. I finally put my phone down, shaking my head.

Reilly has already dispatched an officer to Chase's address. "Just to ask questions. As a friend of yours and a known visitor to the gallery, it's completely normal to ask him a few questions."

As a friend of mine who was spotted entering the gallery by my eagle-eyed corner deli coffee buddy. Ahmed is just doing what I've always loved about him—keeping an eye on the neighborhood. But I'm still furious with him, however unreasonably, for breaking my heart.

Maybe it wasn't him.

There's a part of me that still thinks it's possible and I cling to it, with everything I've got.

"Chase didn't do it," I tell Reilly.

"Then he won't mind answering a few questions," the detective says, shrugging. His phone buzzes and he scoops it up, puts it to his ear. His eyes lock on mine, gray and cold. "Not there, huh? Wait a while. Uh-huh. Thanks."

He puts his phone back in its clip. "You can guess."

I shake my head. I'm too disappointed to speak.

When we finally adjourn and spill onto the warm street, a guy from a 24-hour locksmith company has arrived and is fitting a new lock to the door. For a moment I think the police are locking me out, and I look accusingly at Reilly. But the guy holds out a set of keys, nodding for me to take them.

"Insurance company sent me," he says. "Already did the gate. Said you were a rush job."

"Thank you," I murmur. The keys are bright and shiny, unused. I suppose the new lock won't require a sophisticated series of wiggles at just the right time. "Where's the old gate lock?" I ask suddenly.

He gestures to a little heap of metal by his workbag.

I stoop and pick up the lock. It's heavy and battered, and it smells of the grease I occasionally have to pour in just to keep it operating. I should have replaced this lock a long time ago, but it worked. And I didn't think anyone else could figure it out.

No one else should have been able to open it. Even with the key...they would have had to see me do it to understand what trick popped this lock.

I sniffle a little, because there's no denying the truth anymore.

I hold the lock out to Reilly. One last test.

"Try and unlock this," I say, giving him my key-ring.

He doesn't have to ask why. And a few minutes later, after he's found no amount of cursing and jiggling will release those tumblers, he's giving me a disappointed look. "You showed him how to do it?"

"Last month," I admit. "He offered to help me, because the gate's so high—I mean, you can see it's hard work for me to get it closed."

Reilly is looking at me like I've somehow shamed him, personally. "How long did you say you knew this guy? Two months? And the *first* thing you did was show him how to get into your gallery?"

"It wasn't like that—we had been talking for a while, we connected, we—"

"This was a set-up from start to finish." Reilly's face is stony. "You know that, right?"

I don't need a lecture from a cop right now. Especially a cop who has *still* not apologized for spilling my drink the first night we ever laid eyes on each other.

"There's been a mistake," I tell him, my voice tight, hanging on to the most stupid lie I've ever told myself. "Once we get hold of him, you'll see. Chase would never rob me. We're getting married, for god's sake." I'm hanging onto that truth with everything I've got, even as it wriggles wildly, snaking through my fingers. The last good thing in my life.

Reilly rocks back on his heels, regarding me. His nose is a little too long, I think spitefully. If he thinks that it gives him an important, handsome profile, he's absolutely wrong.

"Ms Adams," he says, "I hate to break it to you, but you're not marrying this guy."

"That's incredibly rude—"

"Ma'am, this guy isn't even in the city anymore. I would put money on that. Hell, he might not be in the country anymore."

And then my last wall of resistance tumbles down. He's gone. He duped me, he robbed me, he left me.

I am that woman. I am *that woman.*

I let myself tip against the rough bricks of the gallery wall. Reilly is close to my side, his hands out in case I wobble. He's ready to catch me. At least someone wants to keep me upright. My brain certainly isn't interested. My head is spinning, equilibrium lost.

"Ma'am, do you have anyone who can come pick you up?"

I do. I have friends. They love me. But I can't face them now. So I shake my head, and say I don't want to bother anyone. "I'll call a car," I murmur.

Then, I remember that my gallery is empty, and I have no income. Car services might be the first thing I have to cut. At least I have one more painting: the Pocchiano hanging on my living room wall. Thank goodness for that elephant. He's got to go. And if I sell him for enough, I can cover my bills for a few months. Long enough to figure out what's coming next, deal with whatever insurance headaches are coming my way, and find a way to resuscitate my business.

"After I get a coffee," I amend, putting my phone back into my bag. Once I've gotten around the corner, I'll head to the subway.

But Reilly is already shaking his head, like he knows my plan. "Come on," he says, pointing to an unmarked black sedan. "I'll drive you home. You shouldn't be going anywhere alone for the next couple of days. Not until we know where this guy is."

I realize he's saying Chase could be a danger to me, and my head starts to spin all over again.

Chapter Ten

WE DRIVE IN silence for a few blocks, the lights of Fifth Avenue flashing by. I assume he'll take West Drive, the wide thruway along the river that turns into the West Side Highway, so I'm surprised when he settles down for the long haul up the center of Manhattan, turning a few times until we've settled into the heavy traffic on Eighth Avenue. The radio is mumbling softly, two co-hosts talking to one another about the mysteries of bees. I realize it's Radiolab and give Reilly an appraising look from lowered lashes. Could this detective really drive around the city looking for clues while listening to public radio all day?

He notices my surreptitious glance and gives me a half-smile. "Rough day today, huh, kid," he says, his voice a gentle rumble from his chest. "I'm sorry you had to find out about him like this."

"Aren't you supposed to consider him innocent until proven guilty?" I challenge, still somehow clinging to Chase against all odds.

"You watch a lot of cop shows?" he asks, amused. "That's for the courts. When a case is this easy, all I have to do is collar the guy and haul him in. It's too bad he had the key, because that bought him enough time to get away. But he'll show his hand sometime. When he tries to sell one of those pieces, if nothing else."

"They're not high-profile," I admit. "Just the Pocchiano, and even then, it won't make the news. It's not like he stole a Monet or something. I don't know how anyone would ever find out if those pieces go through a private sale."

"You'd be surprised where we have people," Reilly says. He slows down as Midtown traffic crawls beneath the skyscrapers.

"Why are we driving this way? We could have gone up the West Side Highway and saved a ton of time."

"You in a hurry?" He glances at me again. "I didn't realize."

"No, it's not that. I just wondered. Usually drivers are in a rush."

"I like to drive through the city. I like to take it all in, remind myself of where I am." He points as we pass a cross-street, and for a moment we have a perfect view of the Chrysler Building's Art Deco spire. The lights beading its curves are exquisite, like seed pearls on a wedding gown. "The highway is just for people who wish they weren't here anymore."

I tip my head back against the headrest and watch the city whirl around us. It's Sunday night, and presumably most people work tomorrow morning. But you'd never know it to watch the crowds heaving on the sidewalks, rushing through the intersections every time the lights change. Pedicabs slip around cars, daringly using every spare inch to their advantage, while tourists hang on in the back, squealing and snapping selfies. On a corner lit by a glowing marquee, a woman reaches up to pat the neck of a police horse. Everyone here wants to be here.

Everyone except me.

"I'm moving out of the city," I tell Reilly, seized with some perverse desire to hang onto my fantasy. "I'm moving upstate. We have a house picked out. It has a cherry tree in the backyard and three bedrooms and—" My throat closes, and that's the end of my fairy tale.

He's looking ahead now, watching the brake lights flash scarlet as another traffic light turns red. "What makes you want to leave the city?" His voice is quizzical, as if I'm presenting him with a puzzle he can't figure out. "How long have you been here, anyway?"

"About ten years," I say. "I moved here right after college. I'm from the midwest, originally."

"A farm girl," he says amiably. "Charming."

"Corn-fed," I admit. "Chores before school. Slopping hogs. Plumes of fertilizer polluting the water. The whole experience."

"And you want that back?"

"No, of course not. But I want space. I want to be able to walk down the street and not feel like everyone is on top of me. I want to be able to breathe my own air."

I feel his gaze settle on me. "I've heard that from a few people over the past few years."

"Well, then you know what I'm talking about."

Traffic is moving now; we've crossed Columbus Circle and we're gliding up Central Park West at a stately twenty miles an hour. The stone wall lining Central Park slides along beside me, blocking my view of the trees and paths. We'll be at my building in just a few minutes, and suddenly it feels too soon to consider being alone in my apartment. I long for the park, the pools of light surrounding each cast-iron light-post illuminating my walk. "I just want to get out," I say. "Can you pull over?"

The natural history museum appears ahead, its vast stairs rearing up the sidewalk. "You said you live behind the museum, didn't you?" Mason asks.

I stare at the back of his head, speechless. He remembers that?

Reilly moves the car into the left lane. In the mirror, I see that half-smile on his face again. "West Eighty-Second, right?"

"How do you remember where I live?"

We stop at the light. Reilly's grin is impish. "Something about you is hard to forget, Ms. Adams."

"Oh, really? Like what?"

"Well, you're extremely short—"

"Hey!"

"But feisty. You're not afraid to get into a fight with someone bigger than you. You're loyal—you wouldn't let me buy you a drink because you were waiting for this other guy, even though I was the one who made you spill the drink you had. You believe in people even when they don't deserve it, which, honestly, is kind of refreshing for a guy like me. I don't see that very often. And, not to bring it back to the physical, but your hair is incredibly curly. Do you have to pay for that kind of hair?"

I can feel myself touching my curls, which have wound themselves into tight coils in the summer humidity. I force my hands back to my lap. "The curls are natural," I say flatly.

"Amazing. It feels like most women have such straight hair."

I guess he doesn't know about flat-irons. "They'd certainly like for you to think so," I tell him, and he tips his head at me but doesn't ask for clarification. Maybe he knows about women and their hair; maybe he has a sister who is high maintenance.

We cross Columbus and now he's looking at me for directions. I tell him the building number and start playing with my purse, tucking the handles and the straps into place as if I'm going to simply leap out the door of the moving car and need to be prepared. But when he pulls up in front of my building, I let him put the car into park, turn on the hazards, and walk around the car to open my door.

He's a cop, I remind myself. *It's normal for him to call the shots on when a person gets out of the car.*

Sure, it's just his job. But it's also incredibly gratifying to let a tall man with graceful movement swing open the car door and gesture, with a flourish, that I may now exit the vehicle.

In the narrow space between his car and the ones parked along the curb, we stand chest to chest one more time. I find myself lingering. He feels so large and safe, two feelings I can't relate to in my own skin. "Are you the one who is going to be working my case?" I ask, stalling.

"Probably, but with the high-dollar items it might be moved up the flagpole. You'll get taken care of, though, don't worry about that. When we collar that kid, we'll find out just where everything went and get it back. It's not like that purse of yours."

I can't believe he remembers the purse. That was weeks ago. "How do you mean?"

"A purse gets emptied and thrown out. The phone gets jailbroke and sold on a corner. There's nothing to recover. Artwork isn't like that. There's no value if it's destroyed. So the paintings will come back to you...eventually."

The paintings will come back, but my fiancé is gone. And with him, so are my plans. My hopes. I turn and look at my building. Suddenly, I'm yearning to be inside that solid masonry, safe within those stout brick walls. That apartment has felt like my prison, but it's also been my safe haven. I should try to remember that, when I'm despairing about how I'll ever leave the city behind. "I better go," I say. "Thank you, Detective Reilly."

"Mason," he says.

I hesitate, somehow unable to walk away.

His lips are turned up, his smile warm under the white glow of the streetlights. I remember, fleetingly, the old amber lights, the way the streets wore a yellow sheen beneath the shadows. They replaced those lights with piercing LEDs, so bright that residents of street-front apartments had to buy blackout curtains just to get some sleep. Some of the mystery went out of

New York City when those new lights came in, with their heedless clarity. Some of the charm was lost, when moments like this, facing a person you don't quite understand, trying to piece out the meanings behind their words and their expressions, could take on a new hue in that shifting amber light.

"My name is Mason," he repeats. "I'm off-duty now. I'm only Reilly when I'm on the clock."

And then, even without the magic of the old streetlights, I know.

We could have been something.

But I'm engaged.

To an art thief.

But maybe he isn't.

Crazy faith claws for my allegiance, even if I know I'm being ridiculous, ignoring all the evidence. Such cold, such hard, such clear evidence.

What can I say? I guess I've always loved rooting for an underdog.

"Goodnight, Mason," I say.

His eyes glitter down at me, and I hope he's satisfied I used his name, the way he asked.

I hope someone is satisfied tonight.

And I turn, to go upstairs, to lock myself in my apartment.

Chapter Eleven

IT TAKES ME an embarrassingly long time to recognize that Chase isn't coming back. And, sadly, it takes a few more days after that for me to accept that he robbed me.

Twice.

I am grateful for the passing of summer, because it means that our settle down summer is over. What a waste of a season that turned out to be! Margot is unmarried, Caitlyn is unbothered, and I am unhinged.

The case is passed on to another detective. No one ever bothers telling me why Reilly is no longer my contact. I take the new number and email address with the same numbness I'm feeling as I handle everything else in my life right now. Nothing has flavor, nothing has zest, and nothing feels worth reacting to. All I feel is disappointment, loss, and, overwhelmingly, *shame.*

I simply can't believe I let this happen to me.

My new contact, Detective Deepa Patel, is kind and business-like, collecting information and updating me with admirable efficiency. When she tells me they're tracking Chase through Europe and have recovered two of the paintings—one in Belgium, one in France—all I can ask is if one of the pieces is a painting of a lemur. She blinks at me with dark brown eyes and says she really can't share which pieces have been recovered and which remain missing. "But," she admits, "I saw the source material from your website and I have to tell you, I didn't think *any* of them looked like a lemur."

"It was just a guess," I say wearily. "We didn't actually know if it was a lemur."

"I never really understood modern art," Detective Patel confides.

"I used to." I glance at the detective's calendar, a splash of color on the institutional beige wall. A watercolor of a cardinal with a berry in its mouth. Everything is warm and welcoming, and *realistic*: red tones, green leaves, ruffled feathers. It might as well be a photograph, and for that reason alone, I should scoff at its simplicity. But I find myself drawn to it. I haven't been to a gallery in months; haven't checked the auction catalogs, haven't even looked at the elephant on my living room wall. My last Pocchiano. I took the elephant off my website, hoping to avoid notoriety as the word got out that other Pocchianos were on the loose somewhere in Europe.

"It doesn't really speak to me anymore, though," I say.

"You've had a shock," the detective says, turning back to her files. "Give it some time."

Tell that to my landlord, I think. *Understanding art is how I'm supposed to pay my rent.*

On the way out of the precinct, I always take a good look around, pausing at the end of corridors, glancing surreptitiously through open doors. But he's never there. It's for the best, obviously; Detective Reilly isn't even my type. If we seemed to have a connection, it was probably just a response to all the emotion in the air that night. I'd just found out my fiancé had robbed me blind and skipped town, for crying out loud. I was in massive denial and going into shock. It was a wonder I hadn't invited Reilly upstairs and dragged him into my bedroom. Anything for a little comfort.

Luckily, it's easier than ever to find comfort at home, away from the unseasonable heat of an endless September. An Indian summer marches into the city and sets up camp, smothering the streets with a blanket of hot, muggy air that fills with smog and makes everyone cough like another plague has arrived. With my shades down, my air conditioning running at full blast, and my groceries delivered to my doorstep, I hunker down. I've gotten good at that. It's just me and my bad news, my letter from the bank telling me the application for a loan on a house in Hasselbeck can no longer be considered; emails from dealers asking why I'm not running any shows; calls from my mother asking if there's any news on my missing fiancé.

I tell myself it's hot out there, and I'm happier at home, and I'll start putting my life together in a few weeks, when some autumn air filters in. I'll have more energy in October. Who could find the strength to rebuild their life in this heat? There's no way. And when my friends ask, when Caitlyn and Margot try to reconvene a session of the Settle Down Society, or Abel asks me when I'm going to sell the elephant, I simply tell them not now.

Later.

They worry and fret that I don't leave my apartment. What they don't know is that I go out and walk at night.

I don't tell anyone about my walks, long midnight rambles through the city that won't let me leave. I walk down Amsterdam Avenue as the sidewalks empty, through Times Square as the crowds melt. Sometimes I walk as far as Chelsea, to look at my shuttered gallery. At Ahmed's bodega, closed for the night. At the trash cans rattling with rats, the graffiti on the security gates, the blue lights of the watching cameras. My block is a different, creepy place at night. It's where criminals walk, I tell myself. This is where Chase would be, if he were still in the city. On a dark, spooky block filled with robot watchers and rodent scavengers.

I always turn and leave the way I came; I never walk past the precinct house. There's no reason to avoid it; they lock their front doors at night, anyway, and it's not like he'd be there, working all night as he tries to capture my fiancé. It's not his case, and that's not how things work. This isn't a crime drama. There's no sixty-second commercial break right before the case is finally cracked.

I get home late from my wanderings, sometimes just before dawn, and that's perfect because it means I can sleep all day, waking in the hot afternoon to order in some lunch and listen to the delivery person tap tentatively at the door before going back down the stairs.

Margot and Caitlyn are understanding at first, but as the sultry September finally fades and the first crisp days of October arrive, their impatience begins to rise. The phone calls and texts finally turn to an in-person visit. I let them in warily, pretty sure it's an intervention. They've brought Maeve along, tanned and freckled Maeve who spends every day overseeing gardening projects in the parks.

"You can't stay in on a day like this," Maeve insists, flopping across from me in the arm chair. She's wearing leggings and a long-sleeve shirt. Maeve can handle hot weather like no one else I know. "It's gorgeous out there, and the weather isn't going to last. Let's go for a walk in Central Park before it gets nasty and hot again."

"I'll buy you a hot dog," Margot says cajolingly. "Or an empanada? Whatever you want."

"You don't have to lure me outside with treats. I'm perfectly capable of buying my own lunch."

"Are we talking lunch?" Caitlyn glances at her phone. "Because I'm thinking we could grab sandwiches from the cafe by the Sheep Meadow."

"Oooh, they have this chicken salad I love." Margot claps her hands. "Let's do it!"

Caitlyn swings her head to look at me again. "Well? You coming?"

I could say no, but then they wouldn't leave. They'd just hassle and harass me. I know my friends. "Let me get dressed," I sigh.

Central Park is pretty as a picture. That's the thing about living in New York City for a long time—you get used to things other people only see on magazine covers or in movies, and then one day, the sky is the perfect shade of blue, the sunlight is the perfect balance of bright and warm, and whatever you're looking at, be it city streets or lush meadows, just pops back into your consciousness. You think, *Wow, this place is amazing!* And you remember, with a little feeling of smug satisfaction, that you live here. That this is all yours, every day.

Then, you'll forget what this feels like for a while, and New York will play its usual tricks: the subway will arrive precisely three minutes early every day for a week, making you miss it and end up late for wherever you were headed; clouds will settle over the skyscrapers and block out light for an entire weekend; you'll get stuck behind a garbage truck on a narrow street because you decided you couldn't miss another train and chose to take a car service. Things like that.

And then another beautiful day will pop out and surprise you. Make you think you can never leave. Remind you that you live in a totally amazing, unique place—even when you're determined to get out.

It still happens, even now, with nothing but escape on my mind. So that when I walk through the Seventy-Second Street entrance and look down the slope towards the lake, past park drives filled with happy families walking dogs and tourists buying hot dogs and a pair of police horses clopping along the Bridle Path, I am filled, once again, with a rush of gratitude.

Oh, city, aren't you beautiful? I think.

It's a little bit of a walk towards the Sheep Meadow and its adjacent cafe, so I settle into stride behind Maeve, Margot, and Caitlyn, trying to hold on to this feeling. What for, I don't know. It's just been such a tough summer, on top of a tough year, on top of *another* tough year before that. It feels like any bit of happiness is worth clinging to, even if it's fleeting.

With sandwiches and lemonades acquired, we find a patch of grass in the crowded Sheep Meadow we can call our own and spread out a blanket. It's good to sit here, shoes off and toes curling into the cool grass to remember what the earth feels like. Even if after a few minutes, my ass feels like it's falling asleep. The others are talking about Margot's wedding, coming up in five weeks. Just another month, I think, closing my eyes against the sunlight. A month, and then Margot will be married and off to Montclair, the first and only success of the Settle Down Society.

Margot is droning about her catering when Caitlyn suddenly interrupts her. "Should we be talking about this when we're here to cheer up Tracey?"

I open my eyes. Both of them are now looking at me with deep concern, as if I've been over here trying to nap off a terminal diagnosis or something.

"I'm fine," I say. "Please, I need to know what's happening with the puff pastry. Will it be filled with mushrooms or not?"

Margot cracks a smile. "Not. Damian's mother hates mushrooms."

"But *you* love them," Caitlyn argues. "Shouldn't you have mushrooms at your own wedding?"

"I planted a mushroom plot in the Shakespeare Garden a few years ago," Maeve says dreamily, gazing at a clover blossom.

"Did anyone eat from it?" Margot asks, momentarily distracted. "Did you kill anyone?"

"They were all edible, just in case."

Caitlyn grumbles something about mushrooms getting a bad rap and mushroom-haters pushing mushroom-lovers around. I suspect it's a passion left over from her vegan days.

Margot rolls her eyes. "It's about compromise, Caitlyn. Surely you've heard that saying before."

"I have," she says crossly. "And that's why you haven't seen me finding someone to settle down with, after all. I'm just not *there*, mentally. I would have an all-mushroom buffet if someone told me I couldn't have mushrooms in one silly appetizer."

"It's just not important enough to, I don't know, blow up my entire future over?"

"You have a future without Damian. You're just choosing not to see it."

Margot gasps, her fingers coming to her mouth in a hurt gesture. "What's *that* supposed to mean?"

I lean forward and put my hand on Caitlyn's thigh. "Have you considered, I don't know, *not* trying to make Margot feel bad about getting married? Especially when a few months ago you were all in? What happened, anyway? You never told us anything besides hating the guys on the app."

"That's the whole story," Caitlyn says, waving me away. But she's not meeting my eyes, and I know there's more to it than that. "No one out there for me, apparently."

"It's not the app's fault," Margot mutters. "I could have figured it out if she'd let me."

I give Margot a little hug. "Forget the app. Forget the society. You got the guy, the proposal, the wedding, the house—everything! Caitlyn and I will be fine. We'll figure it out in our own way."

"You've got this," Maeve says fondly. "Look for someone with a dog."

"*Are* you seeing anyone?" Margot demands of me. "You have to tell us if you are."

"Only if Abel counts." I've let him put on a couple shows at the gallery, and so far, so good. "His boyfriend probably would say no, though. That's okay. He'll make a good business partner when I finally leave the city."

"Decide where you're going yet?" Caitlyn asks, sounding skeptical.

"I've narrowed it down to somewhere in the United States." I try to put a laughing face on the problem. "I just don't know where that would be. Where does a person go after New York? And don't say Los Angeles. Because I don't think that's right for me, either. The traffic, for one thing. I can barely drive as it is."

"I never really saw myself in Montclair before this year," Margot admits. "But this house is perfect, and it's where

Damian wants to go. It works out. You never know where the right place will be."

"I was considering Florida," Caitlyn says. "But when I say it out loud, I know how foolish that sounds. Would I last a day in Florida? The weather's exciting, though." Caitlyn's probably thinking of her side-hustle as a junior weather girl. I hope she makes it someday.

Margot pats her hand. "I think you could go anywhere and make a go of it."

"Oh, I don't know. I'm working some here, and there's no guarantee I could find TV work anywhere else." Working in broadcasting has always been an uncertain career for Caitlyn. "Maybe I could commute from Rhinebeck or something."

"Oh, yes, do that! Then we can all stay close together." Margot glances at me. "Assuming you stay around here, too."

"Rhinebeck's on my short list," I assure them. Along with Santa Fe, the greater Portland area, some artsy-type tourist town in the Rockies I haven't identified yet, and the entire amorphous region known as Maine. I haven't been able to nail down where I could live and work outside of New York City, and while I like to blame it on practical reasons—things I'd need for work, like access to an airport, or reliable high-speed internet—I know it's also because if I leave here alone, I have to start an entire new life all by myself, and I'm not ready for that.

I'm not ready for *anything*.

It's like I've been cast in stone by Chase's disappearance. He came into my life and seemed like he brought everything I had ever wanted, all at once: a chance at escape, a chance at true love, a chance at a life spent with someone else who was really a kindred spirit. And for it to suddenly be exposed as a lie...how am I supposed to bounce back from that?

If I could just talk to him—if he'd just reach out to me (and yes, I know how ridiculous this sounds) and I could ask him to tell me the truth, maybe that would do something for me. I'd like to just say, "Hey asshole, give it to me straight—did you love me? At all? Were you actually a disappointed artist? Did you really love that piece you told me changed your life? Or was it all a lie, from top to bottom, soup to nuts?"

Maybe the answer wouldn't be what I wanted to hear. But wouldn't it just be nice to clear it up, once and for all?

And so while Caitlyn and Margot start discussing the ins and outs of the artsy towns along the Hudson where so many displaced New Yorkers have taken their talents, I let myself fall back onto the grass and closed my eyes again, imagining that impossible conversation over and over again.

If I could come up with a plausible conclusion for it, maybe it would stop haunting me. Maybe I could get my life going again.

Chapter Twelve

I WAKE UP a half-hour later to find the conversation has stalled and the party is down by one. "Where's Margot?" I ask, sitting up and blinking. The sun seems to have shifted quite a lot during my nap; it's hanging closer to the apartment houses along Central Park West than I expected. But the Sheep Meadow is still crowded with families and groups of friends. No one is willing to give up their claimed patch of grass, not on the first day New York City has been bearable in months.

"She went to get a bottle of wine," Caitlyn says, not looking up from her phone. She's laying on her stomach, bare feet up in the air. A royal purple manicure shines from each toe. "And I told her to bring back some crackers and cheese for later. No point in leaving while this weather's so perfect, right?"

"I guess not." I wonder if Margot will adhere to the water bottle rule, or if she'll just show up with a tote bag filled with clinking bottles. Looking around, it seems like most people have decided there is strength in numbers when it comes to flaunting the no-alcohol rule. There are beer cans, wine bottles, and champagne flutes everywhere I turn. Maeve doesn't seem concerned, though, and I think the park police know they'd be outnumbered if they tried to ticket this crowd. Wine it is. "Just one problem, though."

"What's that?"

"I have to pee, and the toilets are all the way up at the cafe."

"See ya in twenty, I guess."

Twenty minutes is a pretty solid guess, I think later, waiting in line to wash my hands. The park restrooms are so packed, I have a hard time making myself go inside. But this isn't the North Woods; there aren't any quiet patches of forest where a girl can cop a quick squat behind a tree. I've got no choice but to queue up, wait my turn, and try not to hold my breath the entire time I'm inside.

It's not necessary, I remind myself. We can breathe the same air in a crowded restroom.

But I still feel dirty and a little panicky when I finally make it back outside. I take a deep breath once I'm a few steps away from the restrooms. *Ah,* I think. *Everything is fine.*

Then I see the officers.

They're making their way into the Sheep Meadow, a little cluster of uniformed men and women. I pause, my hand on the rough bark of an elm tree, while I watch them divide into pairs and start walking across the grounds. At first, I think they're looking for someone, and I can't help but feel a start of horror—

what if it's Chase? But I know that's ridiculous; Chase is hardly the only fugitive the NYPD are looking for today, and the last I heard, they were still tracking his movements somewhere in the Czech Republic.

No, I realize, watching each pair stop by picnicking New Yorkers. It's a lot less sinister than that.

They're really ticketing people with alcohol, merrymaker by merrymaker. A few raised voices are quickly silenced, probably by threats of jail-time.

Ugh, cops, I think. Imagine that I actually thought I had some kind of connection with one of those guys.

I send Margot, Maeve, and Caitlyn texts, letting them know that the party is about to get broken up. I see Maeve pop up and head for the hills; she's not going to risk getting caught anywhere near an illegal open container. Margot texts and says she's heading back to her apartment to drop off the bottles she picked up—unless we'd like to come over and drink them on her roof?

This gets an affirmative from Caitlyn. *I'll grab our stuff, you wait there,* she instructs Margot. And me, too, I decide. I'll wait for her over here where it's less contentious.

I'm watching a group of barely-clad young women arguing with the police over their bottle of Prosecco when I hear a chuckle. The sound is too close for comfort; I whip my head around, ready to move away from whatever weirdo is getting into my space out here in a park, with plenty of room for everyone.

And then I stand very still, because it's Mason Reilly.

He doesn't see me; in fact, the chuckle wasn't even meant for me or, more than likely, about the police activity in the Sheep Meadow, it was meant for his phone and whoever he's texting. He taps back a reply to whatever he found so funny, then slips his phone back into his pocket. He's either on the job or he's been working, because he's wearing tan trousers and a pair of comfortable-looking oxfords. But despite his somewhat professional attire in a city park, his face is relaxed, and when he looks back over the Sheep Meadow, I can tell he's not part of the alcohol operation taking place out there.

I wonder if he's just walking home from work. If he was on the east side for some investigation, this would be a convenient way to stretch his legs on the way back to Lincoln Center.

My phone pings with a message from Caitlyn—she's at the gate, and where the heck am I? I begin to text back—*under the trees by the cafe*—but I don't want to call attention to myself, so I start forward, hoping if he only sees my back, he won't recognize me.

"Ms Adams?"

Well, that didn't take long. I turn slowly, smiling apologetically, and pretend I'm seeing him for the first time. "Oh, Detective Reilly! What a surprise!"

"I'm not on duty," he says, shrugging. "Please call me Mason."

He's not going to quit until I actually call him by his first name.

"Oh. Well. Call me Tracey, then."

"Thanks...Tracey." He smiles. "What brings you to Central Park?"

"I was just hanging out with friends in the Sheep Meadow. Actually, my friend is waiting, I should go—"

"Hope you guys didn't have any booze." He winks. "Park enforcement waits for holidays and nice afternoons to remind folks of the rules."

"Nope, we just drank lemonade, like the law-abiding citizens we are." I squeeze out a smile. "I better leave. Nice seeing you, though."

"Yeah, my niece and nephew are just around the corner." He picks up a bag I hadn't noticed before. "Better change into something lighter before they start running me ragged."

I glance at the bag, curious despite myself, and see the bulge of sporting equipment. Not what I expected, though—"Are those roller blades?" I can't help but sound incredulous. I wouldn't have pegged Mason Reilly for a roller-blading enthusiast.

He gives me a sheepish smile. "Briar and Sebastian love ice-skating, so I told them we'd start blading to get ready for the winter season. Do you ice skate? Or, um, roller-blade?"

"Neither, actually." It's a regret of mine, that I've never learned to ice skate. Everyone has that dream of a big romantic date at the Rockefeller Center skating rink, but it can't come true if you can't skate. Roller-blading just looks like an opportunity to skin my knees on asphalt. I lie politely when I say, "It looks fun, though. You go over to that spot past the meadow where all the roller skaters hang out?"

"Just for inspiration. I wouldn't dream of trying to join them. Those guys are geniuses on four wheels.

I can't believe it. Big, scary Detective Reilly actually looks a little intimidated. By the Central Park roller skaters! Sometimes people really surprise you. In good ways, I mean. They nearly always seem to surprise me in bad ways.

He's looking past me now, and I sense some of the constant shouting of children is actually directed at him. When he waves, I know it's really time to go. "Have a good time," I say, turning.

There are two kids hurtling towards us, with a frazzled-looking woman being hauled by a plunging Golden Retriever a few dozen feet behind them.

"Uncle Mason!" shouts the shorter of the two, a girl with a head of blonde curls. She grabs him around the legs and he staggers, laughing. I watch his hands go to her shoulders, steadying her so she won't fall while he pretends to stumble around the uneven ground beneath the trees. The boy, slightly taller and with short, golden hair tumbling above a mischievous face, wraps his arms around both of them.

I stand there longer than I should, watching Mason Reilly as he's accosted by his family. I can't help it; I want to be like that —okay, maybe not like he is right now, surrounded by grasping, shrieking children, but like their mom is. Standing off to one side, hand on the leash of a beautiful dog, watching her family play with a favorite uncle.

Whoops, she's also watching me, wondering why I'm staring at her children as they assault their uncle.

Before I even know what's happening, my cheeks are wet, and I turn away quickly. I wipe my face clean with my shirt as I head for Caitlyn, who is waiting for me, arms folded, by the gate to the Sheep Meadow.

"Who was that?" she asks immediately.

We fall into step on the path. "That's the detective who was on my case at first."

"I thought Detective Patel was on your case. The woman?"

"Yeah, but the first day, it was Detective Reilly." *Mason,* I think. *Call me Mason.* "And I met him once before, at the precinct when my purse was stolen that time."

"Whatever happened with that?" Caitlyn has lost interest in Reilly. "That purse getting stolen. Did they catch anyone?"

I shake my head. "It was obviously organized by Chase. It's how he got my keys."

"Oh, right. I knew that."

I give her a sidelong glance as we wait for a gap in the racing bicycles on the West Drive. "You did know that. Why did you ask?"

"I wanted to see how you'd answer," Caitlyn says, shrugging and stepping into the street. "If you'd just up and say it was Chase, or if you'd still say the police *thought* it was Chase. I don't know if you knew this, but that's the first time you admitted it was him."

I linger a little too long at the street's edge, watching Caitlyn cross and wondering if she's right. Another phalanx of bicycles, men in spandex suits, goes flying past, blurring my view of her. When they're gone, she's across the street, smiling at me. And I know that Caitlyn has made her point, and won't bring it up again—possibly ever. Chase did that; I've admitted it; and as far as she is concerned, now we can all move on.

I hope she's right.

Chapter Thirteen

WHEN ABEL SUGGESTS that I escort his cousin Monty around the city on a sunny weekend towards the end of September, I say no so quickly, it shouldn't be possible for him to talk me around it.

Naturally, though, he tries. Abel is a tenacious brat of a man. It's one of the things I (usually) love about him.

"But *Tracey,*" he moans, "I *need* you. Your city tours used to be legendary. And I am going to be dealing with clients and brokers at your gallery all weekend. *Your* gallery, remember? The one that you won't go near and I'm keeping open for you?"

"That's not only a low blow, it's not true."

Abel does not look repentant. He pouts, pushing out his lower lip like a large toddler.

"You can stop that," I tell him, pouring him a fizzing glass of prosecco. Abel currently only drinks sparkling wine, an affectation his current partner swears will go away in a few months. Before that, it was martinis mixed in a pitcher a la Dorothy Parker. I shudder to think what's next. If he decides that gentlemen only drink rare Kentucky bourbon, I'm going to hand him a can of Miller Lite and tell him it's me or the trendy booze.

He sniffs at his glass and takes a healthy gulp. "The least you could do is buy a better brand for the man working his fingers to the bone to keep your gallery going," he says sulkily.

"Do a better job keeping it going and I'll be able to afford something nicer than soccer-mommy juice," I retort.

"Well, we don't have to talk about money like we're farmers," Abel grouses. "Anyway, come on, you have to help me out with my cousin. I don't know the city like you do. I mean, I know the parts that *matter,* but you know all the history and old-time places. And Monty *loves* that stuff. He went to a battlefield on summer vacation last year. A battlefield! In Pennsylvania! You see why I can't be responsible for him."

Abel waggles his fingers in desperation.

"So he went to Gettysburg?" I'm interested despite myself; my brain is already ticking over battlefield sites around the city. I do happen to know a decent bit about NYC history. And it would be nice to talk to someone who doesn't think that's totally ridiculous. I love my friends but damn, they do not care about the Revolutionary War *or* the Civil War. Or any other wars fought in this town that don't involve the best burger or most ridiculous doughnut. "I guess I could take him to

Brooklyn and show him where old battlefields were, if he likes that kind of thing."

"Yes!" Abel hugs me elaborately, spilling his wine all over my cardigan in the process. "Please! Take my cousin Monty to Brooklyn!"

"Fine. Have him meet me here on Saturday morning, and we'll have a field trip." I think about the state of trains over the Manhattan Bridge on Saturday mornings. This could take a while. "And if he wants to bring coffee, that would be fine, too."

"You're an absolute angel," Abel says.

Monty, fresh-faced and curly-haired, brings the coffee, and croissants besides. "I heard about this French place just up the block and had to try it," he says. And *then* he slips off his shoes just inside my front door. I think I'm in love. Too bad he's ten years younger than me and in town to visit his girlfriend, who is doing some kind of zoology internship at the Bronx Zoo.

"She's obsessed with lizards," he explains. "It's weird, but when you're in love, you're in love."

"So I've heard," I reply, taking down plates so that we can eat our flaky croissants like civilized humans, and I am now so evolved that I do not even mention that I was in love with an international art thief and it's entirely possible that I'm still in love with him, despite the fraud, the lying, and the grand theft.

The zoology internship requires working weekends, which is how Monty ends up my responsibility on this sparkling Saturday. He's a nice guy, excited about the battlefield sites we're going to see and enthusiastic about seeing new parts of New

York. When we finally head out onto the street, I am almost happy about the day I've planned for us. Fall has finally made a late but dramatic entrance, and there are fluffy white clouds scattered around the sky, drifting on a breeze with a decided chill to it. It's going to be cold, but gorgeous, when we get to Green-Wood Cemetery. But that's our second stop.

First off, I tell him, is the spot where the Maryland 400 fought the Battle of Brooklyn against terrible odds.

"Excuse me?" Monty's eyes are bugging out of his head. "That is amazing!"

I'm quick to bring his expectations down to reality. "All that's left is the park and an old farmhouse. The Old Stone House is cute, but it's next to a soccer field and surrounded by the kind of bistros that foodies like to blog about."

"I like food," Monty says, shrugging. "Food and history can coexist."

"Well, then you'll love this place. And then we'll go to Green-Wood Cemetery and see some more of where the Revolutionary War battles were fought, and see the statue of Minerva gazing out at the Statue of Liberty."

"Holy crap." Monty stops dead in his tracks, where he is immediately jostled by no less than three New Yorkers who have not ceased to be in a hurry just because it's a Saturday. "That sounds incredible."

"That one actually is incredible," I agree. "It's going to knock your socks off. Well, down the stairs we go."

I find it easier than usual to stand on the subway platform and wait for a train, even with the spotty weekend service to contend with. Having a person to talk to is a welcome distraction from my nagging anxiety over crowds and close spaces; having a person as eager as Monty is to talk about the city's past is the ultimate in diversions.

He walks over to the map on the station wall, and I point out our route, finger following the yellow and orange lines of the BMT. "We change here for the D train, and take that over the river, and then we switch to the F here, and get that to Ninth Street in Park Slope—"

"Do you just know all of that by heart? Or do you have to look at a map to plan your trip?"

"I know this part by heart, but some places I don't. Like if we went to the Bronx, or most of Queens? I'd have to look at a map. There are even some parts of Lower Manhattan that throw me a curve ball from time to time," I add, laughing. "It's complicated down there. And I used to *live* down there!"

"This all looks complicated," Monty assures me. "Don't sell yourself short. This is amazing knowledge to have in your head."

Sure, I think. *It's amazing*. And it will be utterly useless once I leave.

I'm leaving, right?

The Little Stone House is a hit, as is the short walk through the Park Slope neighborhood surrounding it. Monty is impressed by the dominance of low buildings, many of them just three or four stories high—a big difference from the canyons of Manhattan. Even my historic neighborhood is more shadowy than this; the apartment houses and brownstones there tower five or six stories above the street. The high-rises are coming along, but for now some blocks of Brooklyn still feel open and airy, like we've gone to the countryside for the day. The stiff wind off the harbor only enhances that sensation.

It's a slog up a hill lined with shabby row houses clad in vinyl siding to get to Green-Wood, but as we approach the Gothic stone gates, I know it's worth the sweaty climb. A flock of green parrots are flocking around the entrance pillars, squawking and squabbling with their high-pitched voices. Monty is texting his girlfriend as quickly as his fingers can go, demanding to know if she was aware there were whole colonies of parrots living in Brooklyn.

"I'm sure she is," I tell him. "It's not exactly a secret."

"You have to share information like this the moment you receive it," Monty counters. "This is huge news."

It turns out Monty is a big bird fan. Not quite as big as his girlfriend is a lizard fan, but still. We stand around for a while watching the birds, who seem engaged in a never-ending battle for the best perch on the pillars. Monty takes about a dozen videos. I like the parrots okay, but after a while, my attention starts to waver. I look down the sloping drive, towards Fifth Avenue. There's an old store on the corner that sells cemetery memorials. I see some kids hopping around the assortment of statues, and a tall man trying to rein them in. He finally gets them to grasp his hand, and turns to cross Fifth. As they run across the street and start up the cemetery drive, I feel a strange flutter in my midsection.

I don't really know how I can tell from this distance, but that's definitely Mason.

Detective Reilly, my stern inner voice immediately instructs me. *Keep it professional.* But just like when I saw him a few weeks ago in Central Park, this guy is not on duty. He's out amusing his niece and nephew. Whose names I remember—Briar and Sebastian. I rarely remember anyone's name without meeting them two or three times. Why would I remember this guy's little relatives?

They're skipping up the driveway, a pace guaranteed to get them within hello-distance in just a few minutes, when Monty taps my shoulder. "You, uh, want to go check out that statue?"

"Oh, yes," I say, turning my back on Mason Reilly. "It's awesome. Can't wait."

It's another tiring climb to the hilltop where Minerva stands, draped in stone folds of fabric, with one hand raised to hail her stone sister in New York Harbor. The statue isn't tall, and stands between a few opulent monuments, but her grandiose surroundings do nothing to take away from her own grandeur... or popularity. We have to hold back a few minutes, waiting for a selfie session to finish, before it's our turn to inspect the Roman goddess of war.

" 'Her hand is on the Altar of Liberty,' " Monty quotes, having pulled up some article on the statue while we were waiting. "How's that for symbolism! She's literally looking right at the Statue of Liberty. I'm obsessed."

I don't mention one of the fun facts at my disposal, that Minerva was originally designed to face the Woolworth Building, which was nicknamed the Cathedral of Commerce as it rose to become the tallest building in New York. Millionaires might have built this city, but apparently cooler heads can occasionally prevail and choose actual poetry over unrelenting capitalism.

"Incredible, right?" I say instead, and stand in front of Monty to take his picture with the armored goddess.

As I snap a few shots, I realize he's not alone in the picture. Sebastian and Briar are cavorting through the grass between the mausoleums behind Minerva—and Mason is right behind them, laughing.

"Don't run up to Minerva," he calls. "Wait your turn!"

I am clearly being haunted by this man. He's a ghost and he is haunting me. There's absolutely no chance this is happening by —well, by chance. I have been placed under some sort of curse, probably the moment I kissed Chase for the first time. But it could go back further. This could go all the way back to my birth. I wonder if my mother ever offended a fairy.

Whatever's going on, it needs to stop now. I beckon to Monty. "Let's go over and look at this cool mausoleum," I say, as if it's the most urgent and awesome thing in the whole of the city. "It has the best—uh—carvings on it."

"Sure," Monty says, giving Minerva an affectionate farewell pat. "But did you take a minute to really look at the view? I mean, just give yourself a second. It's incredible."

So I turn and look, a Minerva-eye view opening up before me. The dramatic drop-off as Battle Hill slopes down and is swallowed up by the apartment houses and homes between us and New York Harbor. The dark blue water lapping at the hull of an orange Staten Island Ferry as it charges south towards its hilly destination. The distant shore of New Jersey, the low mountains along the horizon. And right in front of us, so close I swear I can see a twinkle in her great green eye, Lady Liberty.

It's *always* worth a look, no matter how many times you drag your tired bones up this hill to show it off to relatives or because you ran out of ideas and needed some exercise. Whatever the reason, this view holds the infinite capacity to raise goosebumps.

And as much as I have longed to leave New York, I know instinctively that I'll never feel quite the same way about any other view. Because something in this scene *speaks* to me, something in these acres of asphalt and blue water knows me. I look out, and the city looks back.

It's a shame I am too broken to stand by her. I'm no Minerva.

Kids are squealing behind me, and a familiar voice is booming, "Hey! Do not climb on the art!"

I tear my eyes from the harbor view and look back at Mason. Just a few dozen feet away, he comes to a stumbling halt and stares at me. Then a smile spreads over his face.

"Well," he says. "Tracey Adams. Fancy meeting you here."

"It's weird," I agree. "Very weird. Are you following me?"

"I promise I'm not. Although I recognize that as a detective, you have every reason to be suspicious of my ability to trace a person through the city."

It's almost a joke. I think. He's still smiling. "Well, I guess we have been together at two very popular places on nice days. It *could* be by chance."

"Briar and Sebastian have soccer up in Park Slope on Saturday mornings. Somehow, that's not enough to run them dry, so I bring them up here to tire them out before they go home. Gives their mom a break. She lives a couple blocks away, on Twenty-Third Street." He points at a line of trees separating the north boundary of the cemetery, and I can see tidy streets lined with row-houses beyond. "Right up there actually."

"Seems nice over there. Quiet."

"It's very quiet. I like to come over here and clear my head now and then. There's a cafe over there that makes an excellent cup of coffee..."

Suddenly, I feel he is eyeing me speculatively, as if an invitation is coming on.

We can't have that, my stern voice reminds me. I'm leaving New York. Why spend time with someone who is clearly still happy here? It will just make parting even tougher. And after my moment communing with the city view, I know it's going to hurt, wrenching myself away from the city I've loved.

Even fully aware the city doesn't love me back, not anymore.

"Well, I'd love to chat, but we have to get going." I point to Monty, who is dutifully inspecting the Roman columns of the nearby mausoleum. "Don't want to lose that guy."

Mason's smile shifts, from warm to fake in a second flat. "I'm sorry, I won't keep you. I hope you two enjoy the rest of the day."

I half-expect him to offer up the name of that cafe, and I linger for a moment, hoping he will—coffee would be great to warm up after we're finished here. But he looks towards the kids, who are abusing poor Minerva, and as he goes to pull them off the statue, I slink away to join Monty, feeling like I've done something wrong.

Chapter Fourteen

"I LOVE NEW York in fall."

I glance at the man gazing through my living room window, trying not to judge him too hard. It's not his fault he can only express himself in cliches.

At least, I don't think it is.

Then again, if it's not his fault, whose is it? Who is to blame for the endless parade of unoriginal expressions I get from this guy?

Be nice, I chide myself.

And honestly, it's not hard to be nice to Sam.

My date for Margot's wedding is an unexciting lawyer named Sam Peterson, a friend of Margot's fiancé who was assigned Tracey-duty when it became clear I was not going to find someone else to date after Chase vanished. Something about moving on immediately because I was dangerously close to rationalizing Chase's robbing me and disappearing into thin air. *Not true,* I argued weakly, and then I found myself reading Chase's old texts to me sometime around three o'clock in the morning and decided I'd better go out with my friends' choice for me, because I clearly couldn't be trusted to make my own choices.

So, Sam and I have gone out a few times. We get along. It's fine.

Everything's *fine.*

Sam's a bland, nice sort of guy, with a forgettable face and a plain navy suit, and I shouldn't be surprised he just said the most unoriginal line of all time, but I'm a little surprised he's looking at me now as if he expects an enthusiastic response, like he has hit on some kind of hidden truth.

I mean, in the words of President Joe Biden, come on, man.

Everyone loves New York in fall. It's incredible. The rich blue hue of the sky, the pumpkin-colored trees lining the brownstone blocks, the beautiful earth-toned rainbow of the parks, and the always-delightful return of fall fashion: scrumptious sweaters and cozy coats and scarves, scarves, scarves.

What's *not* to love about New York in fall? Even the rainy days have a special feeling to them, a nostalgic heart-tug for the New York City that only exists in Technicolor and the imagination. I used to seek out bars with fireplaces—there are a few of them out there, if you know where to look or who to ask —and cozy up to the hearth just as close as I could get, listening to that snap and smelling that smoke, pretending I was living in a romance novel.

"Sure," I say, because Sam is waiting for a reply to his ground-shaking revelation, and everything I just thought is too much for him to contemplate. "I love New York in fall, too."

Even now, as I angle for a way out of this city, I have to admit it remains true—I love New York in fall.

Killing time, I sift through the mail on my counter, because Sam is still enamored with the view, gazing out towards the river. We've gone on three dates to get to know each other so that we would have fun at the wedding. None of them were particularly exciting, but he's been nice enough, dealing with my phobias about eating in restaurants by bringing over sophisticated take-out and excellent wines. He is really partial to that view of the Hudson out my window, and I am starting to wonder if he's going to propose and then ask if we can stay in this apartment forever.

Absolutely not, I'll tell him, but he's welcome to sublet it from me the moment I land a place outside of town. I am off the marriage market, because once burgled, twice shy. But I'm still shopping for a life outside the crowds.

My fingers pause in shuffling the envelopes—here's a thin one from a mortgage company. I've been trying to get a pre-approval on a loan so I can make an offer on a Victorian house outside Red Hook—meaning the town just up the Hudson, not the neighborhood in Brooklyn with the same name. The house would make a great spot to start my life over. There's space for a gallery that I can run in the summer, when tourists are in town. I could give the Chelsea gallery to Abel to run full-time for me, or I could simply close it when the lease ends and forget all about Manhattan.

My eyes skim the typewritten letter. *Not enough credit*, blah blah blah. Long story short, they're not giving me the money.

Well, that's another dream out the window. I toss the envelope aside. I'll think about it later. Or never.

Yeah, I like never.

I glance at the clock, almost as tired of our silence as I would be of our conversation.

"You ready to go?" I ask Sam.

He leaves the window obediently, winding his Tiffany-blue scarf around his neck. I take in the sight of him for a moment, imagining what we'll look like as we greet friends and Margot's family at the wedding. I appreciate his diminutive height; that way he doesn't make me look ridiculously small standing next to him.

The way I would if I were going to the wedding with Mason Reilly, local giant.

I bite back a snort of laughter that's anything but humorous. Why am I still thinking about that detective? Bumping into him twice outside of work doesn't mean anything. And I haven't seen him in weeks, not since we ran into each other atop Battle Hill in Green-Wood Cemetery. That meeting wasn't a sign; I *wasn't* being haunted. I know that because I've looked everywhere for those broad shoulders and that jutting chin in the weeks past, and haven't seen them. A haunting doesn't just end. It goes on and on.

Well, there's nothing broad, tall, or jutting about Sam. His suit jacket clings just a little too snugly around his chest and upper arms; it's probably seeing its first outing in a while, and it's a little too tight.

My fingers fumble with my coat buttons and the top one flies off, landing somewhere under my fridge.

"Whoops!" Sam is on it like a dog after a bone, dropping to his knees to reach under the fridge.

"Sam, get up!" I'm afraid he'll get his pants dirty, and worse, I'm afraid of what else he might see under that fridge. I'm a clean person, but not pull-out-the-fridge clean. "It's not a big deal. The coat can be open at the collar. It's not *that* cold."

"If you're sure..." He climbs up and straightens my collar, looking down at me with his average brown eyes. They're kind, and I think if I look closely enough, I'll see flecks of gold in their depths.

But no sparks. There aren't any sparks with Sam.

Unbidden, my thoughts turn once again to Mason. Where is he today? Why haven't I seen him again? He seems to have dropped off the face of the earth. At least, *my* earth. The streets that I walk, the city that I frequent, the hours that I keep. Maybe I'd have a better chance of seeing him if I went out more during the day, but my wanderings remain strictly nocturnal; even more so as the sunsets grow earlier. I'm growing to love the dark, empty sidewalks. Maybe I could stay in New York City if I only went out at night.

I should try to take Mason's disappearance as a sign, just like I tried to take our unexpected meetings as some kind of haunting.

Not necessarily a sign that I don't need Mason in my life because I'm going to have a happily-ever-after with Sam—that seems pretty unlikely, unless he displays some hitherto hidden depths or saves me from an out-of-control bus or accidentally develops a personality overnight.

But maybe it could be a sign that I don't have to rely on the sporadic appearances of charismatic people in my life to keep moving forward. Chase arrived, broke me, and left. Mason in turn arrived, but I didn't let him get too close, and he didn't have a chance to ruin me. I'm getting better at this. I'm keeping men at arm's length, where they belong.

I'm not relying on a man to get me out of the city now. Of course, I am relying on a bank, and that's not going great, either.

But it's fine. I'll recalibrate. Maybe a house in a frilly Hudson Valley suburb with a gallery in the garage isn't what I'm meant for. And if it turns out I'm actually meant to be an artsy spinster in a shack in the forest, well, that's not the worst case scenario, right?

Sam brushes my neck as he finishes tidying up my collar, so I return the favor, straightening the knot in his scarf with a little smile, and when he's inspired to kiss me, I give in for a moment, softening my midsection and leaning in towards him. There's no heat in my core, there's no rush of lightheadedness, but there's kindness and comfort.

Sam's wearing a satisfied smile as we head out the door. It's not a bad look for him. I resolve to give him another slow, sultry kiss just outside the church doors. Enough to waken his tiny inner devil, and show everyone at that wedding that I'm over Chase.

Including myself.

Chapter Fifteen

THERE'S A CROWD outside the church Margot has chosen for her wedding—an imposing, stone edifice I've passed a million times since moving to the Upper West Side, but have never actually gone inside. I've often wondered who in this big, intellectual, diverse community still darkens church doors like this one on a Sunday morning, when the exciting allure of a too-brief weekend morning in the city is glittering just down the sidewalk.

I haven't been into a church for services since I was twelve. And most of the weddings I've gone to have been in odd, artsy places: a restored freight warehouse along the East River in Brooklyn, or atop an old factory (also in Brooklyn) or in a community garden, surrounded by odd sculptures welded by the local crank.

So now, I have an odd tightness leftover from childhood collection plates and a fear of going to hell gathering in my chest, as I scuff at the wet leaves on the church's green side-yard and know that I'll be going inside a house of worship in a few minutes, sitting in the colored light cast by the stained glass windows, probably looking at some fairly graphic religious imagery. The Episcopalians are big on the crucifix art, right?

This isn't Margot's church, of course. It's Damian's. He unveiled his religious side after the proposal, which I think is a tad sneaky, but Margot says it's part of that same old-fashioned charm which is leading them to their white colonial with a colonnaded front porch in New Jersey, so she's all in. She says she can hardly be expected to live the perfect suburban dream if she isn't dropping off her kids at Sunday school. But she also wants to take them to other services, she assures us at her bridal shower, as if to placate the rainbow of religious histories found in our extended circles.

Caitlyn asked why she doesn't just request Damian switch to a Unitarian church, but Margot has assured us it isn't that simple. "His family lives in the next town, you know," she confided. "And his father's a doctor, his brother's a lawyer, his uncle's an alderman...it's one of *those* situations. We all have to keep up appearances like crazy."

I have to hand it to Margot, as the only winner of the Settle Down Society's summer challenge, she has *really* hit the ball out of the park with this one. So many cliches in just one relationship! Sometimes I think she's marrying him for the Hallmark Movie-ness of it all.

But I have to admit to myself, with the right guy, I'd do the same thing.

Sam isn't that guy, but I still like it when he pauses outside the wrought-iron gate and asks if I'm going to be okay in there with all the other attendees crowding around us. "Just remember that you have nothing to worry about," he tells me, gripping my hands in his. His eyes are very serious, boring into mine. "Everyone here is healthy and safe. We've all had our shots—" he grins at this, it's a favorite expression of his, "—and we are going to be okay in the same room for an hour or so. Okay?"

My heart is fluttering, although sadly not because of his intense gaze. If only! He's so solicitous, so kind, so anxious to be there for me. Sam wants to rescue me. That's really refreshing. I need to be nicer to him, I decide. On the inside, where I tease him and make fun of him and say he isn't enough.

That has to stop.

Sam *could* be enough, if I let him be.

The idea is so startling that I let myself lean forward and tip my lips against his, and then he's wrapping his arms around me, pulling me close and deepening the kiss to something that's probably inappropriate for outside a church gate—but is utterly romantic minutes before a wedding. It's an altogether hotter kiss than the one I imagined giving him back in the apartment; even I feel a tingle.

There are a scatter of *oohs* and a few appreciative guffaws from the other early arrivals. "I guess we know who's next," a familiar voice shouts, and I can't help a laugh that erupts against Sam's lips. He lifts his head and smiles down at me, and I gaze up at his eyes, looking for the spark.

It's not there.

Keep trying, my stern inner voice commands. *This guy's great. Well, not great. But pretty good.*

I turn around to acknowledge the cluster of people at the gate. Margot and I go back to our first days in the city, so we have a lot of overlap in our circles. There's our old friend Maeve with her kind-eyed husband, Dane, and of course there's Abel and Caitlyn in her bridesmaid dress of deep blue, hurrying into the church, and there's Kitty Lewis, a painter friend from art school, and there's—Mason?

"Oh, you've got to be kidding me." I shrink back against Sam's chest.

He still has a possessive hand on my shoulder. "What's wrong? Are you having a panic attack? Deep breaths—I'll get you some water—"

"No, it's not a panic attack," I say brusquely. I actually feel surprisingly fine about the gathering. Probably because I know so many people here. It's a crowd, but it's a crowd of friends and acquaintances, not strangers. "I just didn't expect to see some of these people here," I add, lowering my voice. "A few surprises in the group."

"Ah, say no more." Sam starts to turn me towards the church gate. "We'll just go find our seats and it'll save you the trouble of talking to them."

I let him walk me up the steps and along the short walk into the church, stepping under a pretty bower of white wicker and green ivy being set up outside the door. "Careful, miss, there's wet leaves on the ground," one of the workers warns me.

I step around the slippery leaves on the sidewalk and nod my thanks to the men. The arch is going to make a lovely photo op for the newly married couple, I can imagine them posing here for photographs after the ceremony, like an English couple outside their charming parish church. And maybe they'll get some shots in before the wedding, too—I notice a photographer setting up already, and a few tense-faced men in suits and bowties standing around, boutonnières clipped to their lapels. They must be the groomsmen, chosen by Damian, of course, so no one from our crowd.

So strange, to think of Margot leaving us behind to live with an entirely different family. *We've* been her family for a decade now, and she's going to cast us off, find a new version of herself.

God, I hope she loves it. Because we're going to miss her so much.

"Why weren't you a bridesmaid?" Sam asks as we find our seats, near the front of the church.

I finger the blue ribbon bedecking the wooden pews. "Oh, Margot asked me. But you know how I get...I didn't want to risk having hysterics in front of the entire church if I realized I couldn't handle the crowd." I look around me; the church isn't as large as I expected. "But you know, I think this is going to be alright."

"I'm so glad," Sam murmurs, squeezing my hand.

I'm starting to think this entire wedding thing is making him feel romantic and dreamy, which is...interesting, considering we've only been on three dates and I wouldn't have considered any of them something I'd like to repeat over and over until death.

We glance across the aisle as Damian's immediate family arrives—imposing, red-faced men with close-clipped haircuts and a mother with a feathered hat straight out of a villainous queen's dressing room. They are deeply stereotypical. I catch Abel's eye a few pews away and he raises his eyebrows hilariously. I shake my head at him.

"Everything okay?" Sam asks. It occurs to me he's going to ask me that constantly, and it's going to get old.

"Fine. I just can't imagine Margot with that family."

"They do look pretty terrifying, don't they?" Sam's head is tipped close to mine; it's the only way we can whisper such awful gossip without being overheard. The church is still quiet, although I see chairs set up for a four-piece string quartet off to one side. "Honestly, I was surprised by this whole engagement. I thought Margot was your hippie, artsy type and Damian's really...not."

"She is. That's what makes this kind of weird. You know, when we all talked about getting married this year, I figured we'd still hold out for the right guys, but she just went for it with this one and—" I stop short, realizing what I've admitted aloud.

Sam is the only one of my dates I didn't meet on Lifer. He isn't in on the game.

But his expression is simply amused. "Seriously, you and your friends *planned* on getting married this year? I didn't know marriage worked like that. Thought it was more random."

"Oh. We were being silly." I wave my hand dismissively. "Using the summer to get back out there and everything. You know how it felt, after the past few years have been such disappointments. We were going for that whole seize-the-day thing...but it was just for fun, really."

"Margot took it pretty seriously," Sam says.

"Well, that's how she is. Margot isn't afraid to go all-in on something for the story, or for the photo, or whatever. She's the most adventurous person I know. That's why—" I cut myself off.

Sam tilts his head at me. "Why this doesn't make sense?" he guesses.

I bite my lip.

Sam doesn't know us, not really. We've been on *three* dates. But still, somehow, Sam gets it, just from looking around this church. Margot's wedding makes no sense.

Margot's Aunt Ellen and her two sisters, the only members of the family to shun the corn-fed bounty of the Midwest back in the lawless 1960s, have been seated in front of us. Ellen is wearing a flapper headdress with two peacock plumes set over her right ear and a beaded dress to match—and knowing Ellen, it's probably vintage, not a reproduction. Liza and Emilie are similarly gowned. They look like they stepped out of a cream-colored limousine and will be quaffing pink champagne after the vows are spoken.

They're also exchanging tense looks with the black-clad groom's family across the aisle.

These nonconformist women are so clearly Margot's inspiration in life, it's scary to think she's about to have a traditional white wedding in this stalwart stone church.

Eventually, Sam murmurs, "You know, Damian's my friend and all, but...I'm not sure this is the life Margot was going for."

I can't reply, because it's what I'm afraid of, too.

He doesn't even know her, but he sees it. Margot jumped into this with both feet, all the wild-eyed fun of a girl playing in a puddle. But marriage isn't a puddle in Central Park. It's more like the Reservoir. Jump in there, and it's a serious commitment —so serious that if a person isn't careful, they could find themselves in serious trouble.

Danger of drowning.

Okay, the metaphor is getting too serious. But still, what are we all doing here?

Why is Margot giving up on her bohemian city life? I know why I'm doing it, because my anxiety has reached such a fever pitch that I can barely function around other people...

Although, I'm here, not freaking out, so that's something.

Isn't it? Maybe I'm rushing things, too. Maybe Margot and I both rushed, and I was saved by Chase's inability to respect basic laws and Caitlyn was saved by her own good sense, and only Margot—

I have to focus on the wedding. On Margot's day. She chose this for herself.

And hell, if it goes wrong, there's always divorce. With that unromantic thought, I shake off my last internal protest. On with the show.

Everyone around us has settled into their seats, including the string quartet, who have begun to play a rather somber ode. I would have expected something more spritely for Margot's wedding, but I suppose they might be saving their energy for the preludes to the wedding march.

Then the groomsmen file in and take their places by the altar.

This is the wedding. It's happening.

I smile and accept another hand squeeze from Sam, who is still watching me closely in case I start to have some sort of manic episode. But for the moment, at least, I don't feel hemmed in here. It might be the first time I've managed a crowd without a racing heart since I went back into society this year.

Maybe I'm getting past it, I think, my head slipping back into that crazy train of thought. But maybe it's not crazy? Like, what if all of this dramatic life-changing nonsense of the past few months has actually changed my life, and not the way I expected? Maybe the way I've had to put myself out there—however slightly—in order to date and fall in love and be heartbroken and pick myself up again and get to know some new people has really all conspired to make my chosen life less caustic to my system again.

I mean, I loved this city once, not so long ago. What if I could love it here again?

What if we all could, and what if the Settle Down Society, our cute little joke name that turned into something so real that we're sitting in this church today, is really working its magic in the opposite way than what we had planned?

What if what I *really* want to settle down with is the city itself?

It's an interesting thought, and I'm just starting to unpack it when I hear a shriek from behind us. Well, we all hear it. And as everyone rises as one, whirling around to see what happened, I do feel a little woozy. All those people towering above me? Turns out there *are* a lot of them.

I slump down in the pew and put my head down, hoping to avoid a fainting episode. "What's wrong with Tracey?" Margot's Aunt Liza asks, noticing me for the first time, but whatever Sam says sounds like it's coming from deep underwater.

Chapter Sixteen

I OPEN MY eyes to a half-emptied church. The groomsmen are gone, and the quartet are playing determinedly, but there are strained looks on their faces. I blink at Sam, who is leaning over me. "What happened?"

"Everyone jumped up, and you fainted," he explains. "It must have felt like too much of a crowd. But you've only been out for a minute."

"And here I thought I was doing so well." So much for dating the city. I rub at my forehead and glance sideways. The pew in front of us is empty. The aunts have vanished. "Where did Margot's family go?"

"Someone at the doorway shouted for the bride's family and they took off. Then a lot of people rushed after them. I don't know what's going on now."

I slowly work my way to a sitting position. "Crap. Can you find out? This sounds serious."

Sam is clutching at my elbow. "Should I leave you?"

"I'm fine. I promise."

He gives me a doubtful look, but he gets up and heads up the aisle. I reach for my purse, thinking I'll send Caitlyn a text and ask what's up. Caitlyn *is* in the bridal party, so she should be out with Margot, wherever they were waiting to make their grand entrance. But my efforts to contact her are stymied by the stone church, which wasn't designed for cell phone signal.

"No service?" I groan, and there's a gentle chuckle from a few pews back.

A *familiar* chuckle, one that sends a shiver of recognition rippling across my skin.

I turn in the seat and look over the back. There's no one in the pew behind me, but the next one has a single person sitting in it: Mason Reilly.

He's wearing a tuxedo, and he looks amazing in it. His gray bowtie brings out the stormy elements in his blue eyes, but his hair is just a little too long, giving him a slightly bohemian look. He's leaning forward, his elbows resting on the pew in front of him. I feel a sudden, simple sense of longing, and all of a sudden everything makes sense.

I have a crush on Mason Reilly.

A massive, ridiculous crush.

I don't know why I didn't see it before; because it seems pretty obvious now! Just looking at him is giving me a tingly feeling that Sam has failed to evoke in all of our bland, kind outings.

Oh, my poor confused brain. This must have happened back when I was all confused about Chase, and Mason seemed like someone I could rely on. Even after he turned the case over to Detective Patel.

Yes, that has to be the reason. I mean, think about it: no one knows my heartbreak the way Mason does. He'd been there that night. He'd gotten the story from me as it came to me. He'd seen right away that Chase had betrayed me as badly as a person could, and I just wasn't ready to admit it yet.

There were only two options for me after displaying my insides like that: I could either hate him, or fall for him.

Clearly, I'd done the latter. Because I wanted to jump over the pew and plant a kiss on his smiling face. Hopefully a lengthy kiss, with some hand stuff.

Only, his face isn't smiling anymore. He's frowning at me.

Like a child getting a glare from a teacher, I try to think of what I've done wrong.

And then I remember Sam. The sizzling kiss we shared in front of the church gate. The quick, glancing eye contact I'd had with Mason right before I'd turned and tugged Sam's lips to mine.

Oof. I've messed this up, big-time. Why couldn't my stupid brain have realized I have the hots for Mason fifteen minutes ago, before I smooched Sam like we're hot and heavy?

Well, I can try to at least warm up the water between us. We're still staring at each other. His lips open, like he's going to speak, but then he thinks better of it.

All up to me, then.

"How do you know the bride?" I ask, since he's sitting on my side of the aisle. "I had no idea you were connected to Margot."

Mason shrugs, "I don't. My girlfriend is a bridesmaid. She does some PR work for Margot. The charity art projects Margot gets up to, the shows, that kind of thing."

Disappointment twists my gut. I know exactly who he's talking about.

"Girlfriend?" I repeat, and then swiftly name Margot's public relations assistant to cover up my dismay. "Um. I mean, is your girlfriend Roxy Weinberg?"

The word *girlfriend* is bitter on my tongue.

"You know her?" Mason asks, mild surprise in his tone. I suppose that's the heaviest emotion I'll get from him.

"Sure," I say. "I've met Roxy at some of the shows she's helped Margot with."

I know Roxy as a slim and fashionable woman of about our age, with a sixties-era smooth brunette bob that suits her pointed chin and big brown eyes perfectly. She's also taller than me, but who isn't? I say, with an attempt at hearty normalcy, "Roxy's great. You guys must be—great—together."

I would love to have another word in my vocabulary, but apparently *great* is all I've got.

"She is great," Mason agrees smoothly. And then he stands up, looking around. I realize at that moment that something truly odd has happened. This isn't just about Margot needing help with her dress or feeling faint.

The quartet has given up, the bridal party are scattered, and the people left in the church are buzzing with conversation. No one is whispering anymore; it's like the wedding has been called off and no one has told us. Even Damian's parents have gotten fed up and are stalking up the aisle.

"Well, I think we might have a jilting on our hands," Mason says.

I blink at the old-fashioned word. "A jilting? You can't mean —"

But I trail off as I realize he's right. The church is in disarray. This doesn't feel like a place that's about to see a wedding. This looks like a party that is breaking up unexpectedly. I see Sam coming back down the aisle, his face carefully composed. "Oh, my god," I say.

Mason pauses before leaving his pew. "Are you going to be alright?" he asks, his voice suddenly soft.

I remember the night of the break-in, when he drove me home. The concern in his tone then feels very much like it does right now.

But he has a girlfriend, and I have a boyfriend—of a sort. And anyway, if the wedding is off, then we have Margot's heartbreak to sort out, not mine. I have to go be supportive. There's time to work out whatever has gone wrong in my brain later.

"I'm alright," I tell him, and for a moment we are gazing into one another's eyes, as if to reassure ourselves—each other—that we are both just fine.

Then Sam is back, taking my elbow as he slides into the pew next to me. "Tracey, the wedding isn't happening," he says.

I look one more time towards Mason, but he's already walking up the aisle. All I see is his broad back.

Moving away from me.

I turn back to Sam, who is looking down at me with an expression of extreme care in his eyes. Those average brown eyes. *Oh, Sam,* I think sadly. And then I listen as he explains what happened to Margot.

Those slippery leaves.

For whatever reason, the workmen who were putting up the archway didn't bother to sweep them up. Probably they just shrugged and said it wasn't their job, but they sure hoped whoever's job it *was* got there before the wedding.

Or maybe I should give them the benefit of the doubt, maybe they went off to get a shovel to scoop them up or something. And by the time they came back, the damage had been done. Either story is just as likely. The outcome was the same.

Whatever the story behind those wet fallen leaves, they sat there under the triumphant arch of white wicker and green ivy. And when Margot arrived, resplendent in white satin and lace, a chic little veil pulled over her pert nose, and turned to smile for photos with her bridesmaids, she slipped, foolish little shoes sliding on the detritus of autumn in New York, and she fell into the mud.

Caitlyn always pauses here, for dramatic effect. She has told this story a dozen times since the wedding that wasn't. Margot has given her the go-ahead; it's all officially sanctioned. In fact, now she's laughing, leaning over Caitlyn's shoulder, urging her on. Our friend Fern, who was out of town and missed the debacle, is listening with wide eyes, utterly entranced.

I lean back in the easy chair, my eyes slipping to my view of the Hudson, which today is gray and somber with the icy promise of an oncoming November. I have heard this story too many times.

"And then she sat there," Caitlyn continues, in her broadcaster's clear voice, "just sitting in the mud, while the bridesmaids screamed, and I held out my hand because no one was doing anything, not even Margot! She was just sitting there like a pig in a sty."

"Oh, Margot," Fern sighs. She's sitting on a pillow against the far wall, beneath the elephant. Maeve is stretched out alongside her, shaking her head as she remembers Margot's big day.

Maeve and Fern came over today specifically to eat frozen wedding catering, work through a few bottles of wedding champagne, and hear this story once more from Caitlyn's lips. It has been a week since the abandoned wedding, and all of us have to host these parties or we will never get through the chicken marsalas and vegetarian samosas and assorted other dainties which were meant to fill up Margot's guests. She offered to go halves with Damian and his family, but they weren't speaking to her, so she told the caterer's to just divide it amongst the three of us.

"It's fine," Margot assures Fern. "I promise, I'm not broken-hearted over my botched wedding. Keep going, Caitlyn."

"So I pull her up, and she just starts laughing. And then she twirls, which of course slings mud and leaves all over *me,* and now I'm telling her off because I was going to wear that dress to my fifteen-year reunion, *Margot,*" Caitlyn pauses to give her friend an injured look, "but now of course the dry cleaner is having to try some miracle cure from China on it..."

"I'll pay for it," Margot says airily. "Or I'll buy you a new one."

"You can't afford a new one," Caitlyn informs her. "That dress was vintage. Irreplaceable. But anyway. I suppose it's a small price to pay for my friend's freedom, in the long run. Because next, Margot throws her bouquet to Hannah Kauffman and takes off running, her skirt pulled up to her knees, and she runs right through the guests still standing at the church-gate and was all the way to Broadway before any of us realized what happened."

"I felt like I could *fly.*" Margot grins, showing all of her teeth. They'd been whitened for the wedding. I will never admit it, but I'm jealous of those sparkling smiles she's throwing around. "I was free for the first time in months—in *years.* I felt like *myself* again. That's all it took—I just had to threaten to shackle myself down, and my spirit rebelled and I was set free."

"That's all it took," Caitlyn says. "She just had to invite a hundred people to a white wedding and con some poor man into buying her a colonial in Montclair, but now she knows herself again."

"I *am* sad about the house," Margot admits. "It would make a really nice commune. Remember our commune idea, girls? But

Damian's going to sell it. He wouldn't even think of letting me have it."

"Girl, no one is going to give you a million-dollar house as thanks for running out on him!"

"Well, maybe he should. I heard that Sabrina Barbarossi was more than happy to cheer him up that night."

Gasps all around.

As the gossip flies around the room, I refresh everyone's mimosas. We've all had so much champagne over the past week, it was getting tiresome without some juice to flavor the stuff. Who could have predicted we'd get tired of real French champagne?

But that's what this year has been, I think wearily. It's been a nonstop surprise. And I am getting very tired of the constant action.

I retreat to the kitchen and drop the empty into the recycling bin with the other empties. It's overflowing; I will have to take it down in the dead of night, in case a neighbor or, heaven forbid, my landlord, sees it and gets suspicious about how much I'm drinking. I can see my reflection, upside down and frowning, in the green glass. I try on a smile, but even in the upside down, I can tell it's fake.

No worries, I have time to pull it together. Time to stand here and think, and breathe, and remember that I'm in a good position.

That Sam is a nice guy, and I am lucky to have him.

After the wedding was officially called off and I knew Margot was safe, he called an Uber and took me to a diner on Broadway which had tall dividers between each booth. We had gravy fries and cheesecake and cup after cup of coffee. It wasn't until I'd been there for about an hour and was utterly full of fattening food that I realized I wasn't looking around at the other diners, wasn't feeling their presence as if they were breathing down my neck and pressing against my skin.

It was a glimmering of hope, the same one I'd felt in the church.

I looked at Sam, smiling across from me with a fat diner mug of coffee in one hand, and I thought maybe, just maybe, I could get better.

And hell—maybe Sam was the one to help me get there. Unexciting, kind Sam. No sparks, but if there was ever anyone to settle down with...well, the word *settle* has been right there, all along.

Back in the living room, the women are laughing over the details of our Settle Down Society, which has never been discussed by anyone outside our inner circle. I guess Margot has decided that nothing will stop her now. "I'm staying in New York after all," she is announcing as I walk back into the room, and I nearly drop the fresh champagne bottle. "For good!"

"You are?" I ask, in a voice unlike my usual one. "I thought we were—agreed—"

"I was wrong." Margot shrugs and gives me her most pixie-like smile. "I can't go live in the suburbs. I was crazy to ever think so. And honestly, I think all three of us were crazy to say so."

And just like that, I forget my growing interest in putting my city life back together. We had an *agreement,* and look what it led to. Look at my life! Chase, a literal art thief, my poor emptied gallery, the weekly emails from Detective Patel assuring me that they were doing their utmost to find him, the regular communiques from the insurance company assuring me that I needed to find a way to pay my bills without their help because those funds were about to be used up, my broken heart.

Mason Reilly, his deep voice stirring something deep inside me as he reassured me that I was safe with him.

"And," Margot says, "it turns out Lifer was a bust. I sold my shares and I'm getting out."

I sit down heavily, nearly squashing poor Amanda on the loveseat.

"Hah!" Caitlyn shouts, all the louder for the mimosas she's had. "I *knew* you were involved with Lifer! We were just test subjects, weren't we? You were using us!"

"I really believed in the product," Margot says, shaking her head. "I really thought this was the algorithm that would change everything. But the success rate is turning out to be like, in the negatives. Which I didn't even think was possible."

I seriously consider blowing up at that moment. But if I do, I'll have no one left. These are my friends. Whatever Margot did, whatever lies she told about this app, or whatever she actually believed about herself, these are the people that I have to rely on.

Maybe not forever, I tell myself. But for now, I have to forgive them.

I top off my glass and nod to myself, a resolution.

I'm going to stick to the plan, even if Margot and Caitlyn have given it up.

I don't have any better ideas.

Chapter Seventeen

TWO DAYS BEFORE Halloween, and rain is falling on the sidewalks once again. Jack o'lanterns wilt along the brownstone staircases lining the residential blocks of the Upper West Side; grinning construction paper pumpkins watch the rain stream down from behind wavy glass. There's a discarded umbrella, sometimes two, on every corner, the victims of the bursts of wind which can gust unexpectedly through the Manhattan canyons. It's usually better to just wear a hat or a rain jacket than bother with an umbrella; I've learned that through bitter and expensive experience.

I'm heading downtown to my gallery, and I welcome the cold drops splashing on my neck, the puddles forming at the crosswalks. I splash past tourists shivering and dripping, feeling pretty smug in my blue Hunter rain boots, my thick black sweater tights, and my favorite polka-dot raincoat. It's one thing to get around town without getting your feet wet, it's another to look good doing it.

And I've felt pretty good about my looks lately.

Part of it is Sam's constant attention. He has decided, since Margot's botched wedding, to shower me with love and affection all the time. Whenever I'm around him, I am drowning in compliments and intimate touches and unnecessary kisses. It's like he has decided that I am the perfect project. And as a woman who is all too aware of that "I can fix him" mentality we tend to fall for, I know exactly what's going on.

But I tell myself it's fine. If Sam wants to fix me, I could certainly use fixing. Saves me the trouble of doing it myself, right?

So I've let him shower me with attention and compliments and late-season blooms from the flower stalls in Union Square. Boring poems and Shakespearean sonnets dangle from these bouquets, the dime-store version of literary love—kind of sad that's what the bard has been reduced to, but I never liked Elizabethan literature, anyway.

The flowers lend a brilliant glow to the gallery. Because yes, I've started going back to the gallery regularly. Just a few days a week, and only for private viewings. Abel has been doing well with the place on weekends. If I manage to find a place outside of the city, he's going to keep it going here. My annex.

Sam is in Connecticut for some work meeting today, leaving me on my own. I don't have anything scheduled at the gallery, but when I woke up and saw the gray skies hanging above the

Hudson, I knew I had a seasonal project to accomplish, something that comes up every year.

Today isn't just a rainy day, but a chance for me to look over the gallery and get a feeling for how it will look from November until March, during the short gray days of winter.

The city skyline changes every year, more towers and skyscrapers going up in the place of the tenements and apartment houses of just four or six stories which used to dominate Chelsea, and that means that sunlight patterns and reflections from windows change every year, too.

Today, I'll get a good feeling for the winter light, and make sure everything is going to show up the way I'd like through the dark months. Art can pop off the walls even better when the weather outside is frightful, as long as the set-up is correct for every piece. And the depressingly long New York City winter is uniquely situated to open up wallets, as people seek the pleasure of buying new things along with the stimulation of new colors and patterns on their walls.

I always enjoy this annual event, which tests my artistic eye and my skills as a gallery proprietor. My sense of purpose puts a smile on my face and a spring in my step as I head downtown. I splash cheerfully through a puddle, admiring my waterproof boots, as some tourists scurry around the periphery in their sneakers. Ah yes, there's that old proprietary feeling I used to have for the city, before the shut-downs and lock-downs and the terror in the air. *I know how to live here, this place you can barely visit,* I think, settling into good old-fashioned Manhattan superiority. It feels like a stylish jacket bought for a song at a trunk sale hardly anyone got the address for.

Yes, it's going to be a nice day. I'll order in lunch, listen to WNYC for company, and have a fine old time rearranging pieces and light and temporary walls.

I'm actually humming as I let myself into the gallery and flip on the lights.

Then I stop short, my heart hammering in my ears.

"How did you get in here?" I choke, barely recognizing my own voice.

Chase turns and runs from the front room, his footsteps echoing through the gallery.

I don't chase after him.

You imagined that, I tell myself. *He's not really here.*

The gallery is silent, holding its breath.

Nothing is wrong with the place. Nothing, except for the painting hanging in front of me.

The painting that should not be here.

I walk around the lemur painting again and again, unable to understand how it's here, in front of me. The last time Detective Patel mentioned the missing paintings from the gallery break-in, she was using words like Bosnia and Bucharest. They had gone progressively east before disappearing from radar. I hadn't heard anything about the lost artwork in weeks.

But now the lemur is here, and those big dark circles I've always assumed were his eyes are following me as I pace back and forth across the front room. Someone came into the gallery, took down the work hanging on the front wall, and hung the lemur here.

Not someone. Chase.

Did I imagine him? But if I did, who brought back the lemur?

And now where is he? My head snaps up, and I feel my heart begin to thud sluggishly, too slowly, weighed down with fear. I was so taken aback by the lemur painting, it only just occurs to me that the door had been locked, the gate had been down. The locks were changed months ago. So, the person who hung this painting here had broken in through the back. Which might mean—

I suck in my breath and run through the gallery, slapping my feet hard against the wooden floors, anxious to make as much noise as possible. I want to sound like a riot, like a brigade, like a cavalry charge. I want whoever is here to go scampering out the back door and run away. I don't want to see him.

I don't want to see Chase.

But he's not here.

I turn and turn through the halls, the gallery I've built into this cavernous space with temporary walls and taste. I'm alone. No Chase.

I peer through the back door—locked, I check—and look out at the small pad of concrete behind the building. It's spare and plain back there; I've dressed it up with twinkle lights and Persian carpets for a few cocktail parties but right now, my back terrace is just a gray square of nothing surrounded by high cinder-block walls. The puddles on the concrete ripple as raindrops fall, and the lights of the tall buildings surrounding this one reflect upwards in little quivers of yellow and white.

Alone. I'm alone.

I look more closely at the door until I find it, the mark made by a screwdriver prying at the lock's housing.

He broke in.

Chase broke in. It's impossible for my mind to grasp that it was really him, so I just roll the question over and over.

Why?

I'm standing there, staring at the door, when my phone rings.

I bring it to my ear, afraid of what I'll hear. "Hello?"

"Tracey."

It's him. My heart turns over at the sound of his voice. "Chase. Where are you?"

"Gone. Did you call the cops?"

The cops! That would have made a lot of sense, right? I almost laugh. "Yeah, I called the cops," I lie. "Obviously. Why did you come back?"

"I owed you something. I—" Chase's voice catches. "I felt bad. You deserved so much better than what you got."

"Better than what? Than being wooed and lied to by an art thief?" I want him to say it, admit it. "Don't gloss over what you did to me."

You made me think you loved me. Is there a greater sin?

He answers quickly, like I gave him his line. "Yes. You deserved better than an art thief. And all the lies. But they weren't—they weren't *all* lies—"

My fingers are gripping the phone so hard, I'm afraid it might break. Just shatter in my hands, the way my heart is trying to shatter in my chest. *"What* weren't lies, Chase?"

He sighs, his breath rough against the receiver. "I loved you, Tracey. I really did. When we were planning to buy that house, I *saw* us there. I knew we would go upstate and move into that house and have it all—the picket fence, the two point five kids, the Golden Retriever—"

"No," I whisper, squeezing my eyes shut.

Liar. He's a liar.

"Yes! I could have had everything. *You* could have had everything you wanted if I hadn't... So, I just—I wanted to tell you I'm sorry. That things aren't always as simple as they seem. There are partners involved...I had debts...the only thing I managed to hold back was the Pocchiano lemur. So I brought him back, to say I'm sorry. Hopefully it will pay your bills. I don't want you to lose everything because of me."

He says everything meaning my gallery, my apartment. He doesn't know he took everything in the form of my future. I have insurance for the material things. I'm not stupid. It's trust and confidence and hope that he stole from me. Even today, when I was feeling so confident and hopeful, he managed to steal it away.

I see it all now, so clearly. Chase ruined everything. And for once, my stern voice agrees. *He ruined everything.* I'm not in love with him anymore. Not heartbroken anymore.

I'm over him.

I walk over to the wall near the kitchen door, lift the tab, and press the silent panic button. Too late? Maybe, but it's worth a try.

"Chase," I say, letting my voice wobble dangerously, "just talk to me, baby."

Chapter Eighteen

"YOU DID THE right thing, keeping him on the phone as long as you did." Detective Patel is typing furiously, her laptop balanced on her knees. "Really good job."

"Will you be able to find him? Can you, I don't know, triangulate the signal or something?"

She gives me an amused glance. "Something like that. There are ways to locate the nearest cell tower. More than that? I can't really say."

I don't know if she means she can't say like she doesn't know, or she can't say like she can't tell me, so I leave it at that. I kept Chase on the line until the police got to the gallery. When he heard banging in the background, he swore and hung up.

I sip from a mug of tea and look around the gallery. There are uniformed officers and a few plains-clothes all over the place, doing their CSI things. I've never been big on the TV procedural dramas, despite what Reilly said to me the day we met, over my stolen purse. I wonder why Chase didn't bother to bring back my purse, too. I really liked that bag. Not that the detective here would have let me keep it. Like the lemur, which is being wrapped up with great care by an art specialist from the NYPD, I'd have lost it to the evidence locker.

"You might get another call from Chase," Patel says finally, looking up from her work. She gives me a level gaze. "You're going to want to contact us immediately. One of my guys is going to give you another phone. Just text us your location and we'll do the rest."

"Why do you think he'll call again? That call felt pretty final. Like he wanted a firm goodbye."

"Once they come back, they keep coming back." Patel shakes her head, a pitying smile on her face. "They can't stop themselves."

"So you're just walking around with a burner phone from the NYPD, waiting for this guy to call you back?" Sam leans over the table, his tie nearly falling into his soup, eyes wide with boyish fascination. "Can I see it?"

I slap him away, laughing. "No, you goof, it's just a *phone*. Not even a very nice one. It's just so I can reach them while I'm still talking to Chase and keep him on the line."

"Does it send out a special signal that can track his location?" Sam seems delighted that my ex-boyfriend is an international art thief who is back on the scene.

"Maybe." I stab a lettuce leaf which appears to have made it into my salad plate by accident. We're eating dinner at the diner on Broadway he took me to after Margot's wedding, the one with the high dividers between the booths. I have made the mistake of ordering a chef salad. Sam's matzoh ball soup looks much more appealing. And possibly healthier. "I really couldn't say how the cops are handling this. I'm just doing what I'm told."

"Do you think he'll call you again?"

"I really don't," I admit. "But Detective Patel thinks so. She says they keep coming back." I hadn't asked her if she meant to the scene of the crime, or to the people they'd wronged. But I had no plans to go back to the gallery unchaperoned, either.

"That could put you in danger," Sam announces. He puts down his spoon with a clatter. A waitress looks our way. "I'm going to have to take some time off work to protect you."

"Oh no, please don't." The idea of being followed around by Sam all day is about as unappealing as being abducted by a despondent Chase. "I'm going to carry on living my life the exact same way. And I won't go to the gallery without meeting someone else there."

"So, you won't go anywhere but your gallery and the French bakery? That's life as normal for you, right?"

"Basically, yeah," I laugh. "See? You have nothing to worry about."

Sam accepts this and goes back to his soup, and a few minutes later he orders us both fat slices of cheesecake from the cake stand on the counter. At least now I can congratulate myself on ordering the salad.

I was almost honest with Sam. About my normal life, that is. I really *don't* go many places besides the gallery and the French bakery in my neighborhood.

But that's only if you don't count my walks to nowhere every night. And he doesn't know about those.

No one does. They're my secret.

When I wake up at two a.m. and notice the cold rain has stopped tapping on the glass, I don't even think about going back to sleep. When I'm awake at night, I'm awake for the duration. My mind's not busy or anything; I just stare at the ceiling, or the backs of my eyelids. I figure this insomnia is a phase; it'll pass eventually. And so instead of wasting my night wishing I were asleep when it's clearly not going to happen, I put on my shoes and coat and I go for a walk.

The neighborhood is almost silent. There are just a few night owls on the pavement, and the occasional cab or delivery van driving up the avenues. I take precautions, of course—I don't wear earbuds, I have a slim little bottle of mace in a leather carrying case in my pocket—but I've lived in this neighborhood for almost a decade, and it's about as safe as anyplace else in America. Safer than most, even.

Just to be sure, though, I stick to the avenues where traffic never really dies down, walking past darkened dry cleaners and all-night drugstores, and listening to tires swish through puddles.

At the triangle where Amsterdam Avenue and Broadway meet, a little park with benches facing inward is a welcoming area for pedestrians to take a rest. I walk along the sidewalks as a late-night train thunders beneath my feet; here the pavement is a thin skin over the old IRT lines, and every local bumping its way to the Battery shakes the ground. There's a screeching of brakes, and a hot gust of wind puffs up through the grates in the sidewalk.

"This station is Seventy-second Street," a familiar female voice recites, as if the train is on the street in front of me instead of beneath my feet. "This is a Manhattan-bound One train. The next stop is Columbus Circle." She's half-mechanical, half-real. A perfect bot for the city we have today.

I'm in a robot frame of mind, so I'm not really surprised when my phone begins to buzz in my pocket. I stand over the subway grate, looking down through the grid-work of pipes to the glaring lights of the station below my feet, and answer my phone with a dreamy, "Hi there."

Chase is on the other end, and I find it's easy to picture him, standing in some darkened hotel room, maybe out by JFK Airport, thinking of me before he heads back to eastern Europe, disappearing into the decaying infrastructure of medieval cities.

"I need to see you," he says, his voice husky.

"Of course," I say, like it makes perfect sense. At three o'clock in the morning, what foolish thing doesn't? I feel in my pocket for the other phone, but it's not there. It's in my bag, sitting on my kitchen counter, ten long blocks away. Detective Patel would be so disappointed in me. "Tomorrow?" I suggest hopefully.

"Now," he says, madman that he is. "Come now. Can you?"

"Where are you?" The train has pulled away, but there will be another one in twenty minutes. Or I can run. I can run across the city and find him. Suddenly, with the conviction of insomnia and three a.m., I know it's not over—we still have a chance. It won't be what I thought, but they have picket fences in Europe, right? Golden Retrievers, even? We can start over, new names, new lives. I'm afraid to get on an airplane, afraid of all that canned air, but I push that thought away. We can figure this out. Chase loves me. Chase always loved me. I loved him. I still can. I am drunk on insomnia and second chances.

"Good. I'm at the gallery," he says.

Of course he is.

"Give me thirty," I say. "Late night trains, you know how it is."

Chase sighs. "Take a cab."

Chapter Nineteen

IT'S LATE FOR hailing a cab, and I am considering ordering an Uber when a yellow cab actually pauses in its flight down Broadway, the driver glancing out the window at me with an inquiring look.

Yes, I think. *Meant to be.*

I run through a puddle to stop him, my hand up, waving my phone like a torch. "Wait, wait!"

When I'm settled in the backseat, the driver grins at me in the mirror. He's wearing a turban and he has a close-cropped black beard, dark friendly eyes. "Where to, madam?" he asks, with a courtly air.

I glance down at myself. I'm wearing my polka-dot raincoat and blue boots, the same as I was this morning when I was waltzing through the rain to my gallery, no idea about the way my life would change today. Underneath, though, I just have on leggings and a heavy black jumper. Not exactly romantic assignation wear. Also I'm pretty sure my curls are touching the ceiling of this car, ten times their usual size with the humidity.

Still, I'm not willing to go home and change. I can't take that time. Chase will want me just as I am.

So I give him the gallery address. "As quick as you can, please," I add, feeling appropriately romantic.

My phone buzzes again and again as the cab races through the black streets. I read each text with a zing of fresh excitement, electricity pulsing through my nerves. He's flirting with me, taking me back to the days when we were first chatting, when we hadn't yet met. He's teasing me. I type little teases back and giggle at his replies. The cab driver is watching me benevolently in the mirror; he must think he's taking me to the booty call to end all booty calls.

Dear sir, I want to tell him, *you are not wrong.*

We get to the gallery's cross-street gratifyingly quickly, and I'm thanking the gods of traffic for empty early morning streets as I give the cabby everything in my wallet. The fare, plus an enormous tip. A tip I hope tells him, *Thank you for giving me my life back.* I get out at the corner, so that I can walk down to the gallery, take things at my own pace instead of hopping out at the curb to an unknown reception. I don't know where Chase will be—inside? Could he have broken in again? He'd have to have magic at his disposal to break in this time—and yet I don't want to look around for him like a silly girl, peering into dark corners while he's waiting for me just a few feet away.

I want to walk into this reunion with my head high and my eyes shining, like a movie star about to stroll into her happy ending. I toss my head a little, shake back my curls.

"Miss Tracey?"

I stop, heart in mouth, before I realize it's Ahmed on the corner, standing in the front door of his deli. "You're up early," I say. "Or late?"

"Early," Ahmed smiles. "I start at three a.m., every day. You're never here that...*late.*" His grin is teasing. "Is everything okay?"

"It's fine, Ahmed," I assure him. "I just wanted to get a very early start on something. It's time-sensitive."

"Oh, of course. Do you have time for a cup of coffee? Let me get you one."

I'm bursting with impatience. But I can feel some outward powers at play here. I've never turned down Ahmed's offers for coffee, even when I'm literally holding another coffee in my other hand. Ahmed's one and only love language is doling out free coffee. Indeed, I'm not even sure how he sells the stuff.

So I wait outside his door, my boots in a puddle of water that reflects back the yellow light gleaming from the deli. It's an old-fashioned deli for this fashionable street, with garish signs in the windows advertising specials on meatball subs and all-beef hot dogs and gallons of milk, and I study the artwork, wondering who on earth contracted that one smiling girl to do ads for gyros back in the 1980s that now grace the walls of every establishment featuring a spit of meat in the city.

"Just one moment while it finishes brewing!" Ahmed calls.

"It's fine!" I sing back, because it is fine. In a few minutes, everything will be fine. I glance back down the street. Half a block away, Chase is waiting for me. I squint at the dark sidewalks, the shadows under the storefront awnings, wondering if I can see him.

It's a good thing I'm squinting, because when the entire street lights up with yellow and orange, I'm not half-blinded by the glow.

"He wasn't trying to kill you."

I look up. I've been sitting behind Ahmed's counter for the past hour, wrapped up in the heavy sweater he keeps there for cold days when the deli door never stops opening and closing and the steam heat can't keep up. The deli has a side door onto Seventh Avenue, and he's managed to use that door as an excuse to keep open even after the police have closed off the rest of the cross-street. He's been handing out coffee with abandon to the residents of the apartments on the block, and two silent cousins have been pressed into service at the grill, slicing bagels and frying eggs as fast as they can. There are a lot of crying, displaced people in this space right now, and I would be on the verge of a panic attack, but my brain can't even process the crush.

And anyway, I'm the only one who has been allowed special, VIP access to the small space behind the counter.

Until now, when Detective Patel has arrived on the scene, her face tired and her usually smooth hair in a cobbled-together bun. She's kneeling next to me now, a hand on mine. "I know how you must feel right now, but this wasn't Chase attempting to take your life."

"How do you know?" She can't know, that's the answer. No one can know what happened. Only the very basic fact: there was an explosion. Blinding light, a roar of sound. I shrank to the sidewalk, on my knees in the puddle. Through my fingers, half-covering my face, I saw the smoke rising from the hole where my gallery windows had been. Then Ahmed dragged me inside, shouting words I couldn't understand. He pushed me behind the counter and told me to stay there, where it was safe, until he told me otherwise.

I listened to him, because at that point I'd lost the ability to think for myself.

And now, sitting behind this counter, mulling over the events of the last two hours, I am pretty sure I lost that ability much, much sooner than this morning. Only a person who had given up all sense would have rushed to Chelsea this morning to see the ex-boyfriend who had robbed her blind and abandoned her.

Who tried to kill her. Who blew up her gallery in hopes of blowing *her* up.

Chase, I think, a single desperate word.

How could I be so stupid?

"I know because..." Patel pauses, a line creasing her forehead. "We already had him in custody."

"You *what?*"

"We intercepted his call to you. We knew he was there. We'd already arrested him about ten minutes before the explosion. Which, by the way, isn't looking that bad. The gallery is damaged, of course, but the building doesn't appear to have been affected and they're already letting people back into their homes. He says he doesn't know anything about it and obviously he's being checked for residue, that kind of thing, but we think he's clean. The fire department will know more about the cause of the explosion shortly, but, you know Manhattan…"

Detective Patel shakes her head, and I know what she means. Gas leaks in these old buildings are not uncommon.

Well.

Amazing news. Fantastic news. My ex-lover didn't try to kill me; the neighborhood isn't on the verge of collapse. I might even still have a gallery once a restoration company gets a crack at clean-up. I nod slowly, taking it all in.

"Just one thing," I say at last, feeling my cheeks flame. "You heard the call?"

Detective Patel gives me a sympathetic look. "It wasn't me. I was asleep until about an hour ago. Someone else from the precinct heard the call."

Oh, no.

"Please tell me it wasn't Detective Reilly," I plead.

For the first time ever, I see a little glint in Patel's eyes. Just a spark of mischief, and she suddenly reminds me of Margot, making plots which play with other people's lives. "I'm sure Detective Reilly withheld any personal judgment on what he heard on your call. He's a professional."

I close my eyes. I can handle a lot in one day, depending on your definition of the word 'handle'. But I'm not sure I can take the idea of Mason listening to me give in so easily to my felon ex-boyfriend. "This is so embarrassing," I murmur. "Can you tell him—" I don't know what to say.

"You can explain yourself to him," Patel suggests. "He's just outside, the last I saw him."

"Oh my god, are you kidding? No way."

"Maybe not right now," she says, straightening up. "But you're going to have to tell him eventually. On the record."

Chapter Twenty

Patel's wrong in that. I don't have to tell Mason anything. Because in the midst of all the boring work that goes into preparing a trial, he finds his way off the case again. Apparently, picking up a call during a random late shift is not enough to keep him working on it. Or maybe he just doesn't want anything to do with me and talks his way out of it.

It's Detective Patel's impassive face I eventually spill my guts to, admitting that I'd come back to see Chase like a lovesick dummy. And trust me, that's embarrassing enough.

"I can't believe I did any of it," I say, watching her voice recorder take it all down. "I can't believe that was me. I don't even really remember doing it."

Detective Patel nods slowly, and I think she might understand.

She might have done something crazy once or twice, herself.

Two weeks after the explosion, and a week after the fire marshal's official conclusion that it was all caused by a faulty wire sparking a pilot light in the boiler—a crazy coincidence which could have killed me, Chase, and any number of NYPD officers, Mason included—I find myself wandering Midtown near Rockefeller Center.

The holiday crowds are a little lighter than normal; it's a cold and windy day, with a leaden gray sky and the threat of rain hanging in the air. It's the kind of day where you can either indulge yourself in all those holiday traditions, enjoying the way the Christmas lights glow against the low skies, or you can stay in your apartment and lick the wounds of the past year as the darkness presses against your windows.

I'd love to do the latter, but some errand takes me into Midtown and then I feel stuck there, unable to hail a cab when no one wants to walk, unable to make myself go to the crowded subway platform. My only choice is to walk the thirty-plus blocks home, and I'm shivering a little against the wind when I suddenly pass the courtyard of lit angels blowing their trumpets. I pause and look at them, letting the traffic on the sidewalk eddy around me, and then I decide to do it. Walk through the holiday wonderland of Rockefeller Center. See if I feel anything.

It's been a while since I've had an emotion. And while that's undoubtedly for the best, I kind of miss them, too.

The tourists who are ready to brave the weather bump against me, and for once it doesn't scare me, doesn't make me want to run to Fifth Avenue and throw myself into the street in hopes some cabbie will take pity on me and let me into his car. I decide to just throw myself in with them, and let their patterns carry me through the plaza. In the center, the skating rink beckons. I remember Mason asking me if I ice-skated, and I find myself leaning against the rail, looking down at the hardy souls who have decided to brave the weather for this most cherished of all New York City traditions.

Of course he's not down there, but I feel like he should be. I'm skimming the faces of each person on the ice—they all seem like out-of-towners, to be honest—when there's a tap on my shoulder.

"Miss Adams."

I spin around, gasping.

He's there, so improbable I think I must be hallucinating. So close, just a foot away, and as broad and tall and indomitable as ever.

I look up at him and it's like I'm seeing this man for the first time, all over again.

I think how crazy I was to believe I could be in love with Chase, or that I could have tried to settle for poor Sam, when Mason Reilly is in New York City, and somehow never that far away from me.

I open my mouth, hoping that some kind of amazing Nora Ephron line will fall out and land between us, but nothing is there, and then I see he's not alone. There's a woman in a fuzzy hat standing just behind him, and she's holding the hands of two kids—not Sebastian and Briar, but two smaller girls. The woman is beautiful, and she stands close to Mason in a way that suggests intimacy.

Okay, I think. That makes sense. Roxy's youngish, party-going vibe didn't seem like a good match with him, but this mom of two cute kiddos makes more sense.

"Everything okay, Miss Adams?" Mason asks gravely.

"I thought we agreed on first names," I blurt, squeezing my hands into fists.

The woman lifts her eyebrows in surprise.

But the only thing that matters to me is the moment Mason's polite smile becomes something real. "You're right," he says. "We did. I just thought things might have changed. It's been a while."

It's been a lifetime, I think. I recovered, I was hurt again, I realized I was an idiot, and then you showed up again. "Yeah, I think the last time we saw each other was at Margot's wedding?" A day that is the least of my cringeworthy memories over the past few months.

"Ah, the wedding that wasn't." He turns his head slightly, to address the woman behind him. "Tracey here is an art dealer. That wedding I told you about? The one I went to with the publicist? That was her best friend's wedding."

"The runaway bride!" The woman has a southern accent, which surprises me. "That was such a great story! Where is she? Did everything work out?"

"Margot? She's fine. Everything always comes up Margot. She's one of those kind of people." I shrug; what can you do with the people who are the beloved of the gods? "She's completely thrown herself back into her work, actually. She teaches art and volunteers in a lot of programs for low-income schools."

"Oh, wow! Mason, that sounds right up your alley. You should talk to her."

I look quizzically at Mason, but his face is closed. "Thanks, Steph, but I'm sure Margot gets bugged for help constantly." He gives me a look which pleads *change the subject.*

So I do. It's pretty easy. "Mason, you haven't introduced me to your friend."

Steph laughs. "Manners, Mason!" She leans forward and gives me a mittened hand. "Steph Reilly. I'm Mason's little sister. Came up from South Carolina with these two monkeys." And she indicates the children. "Vera and Nikki. Twins, if you can believe it."

Little sister. I gulp.

"Mo-ooom," one of the children moans. "Please stop saying that to people."

"Well, back home everyone likes to know you're twins! It's unusual!"

"It can be a little more common here," I tell the girl, feeling mischievous. Kids can do that to me. "We see a lot of twins in New York City. More than other places."

"Why?" one of the girls asks, eyes narrowed at me in suspicion.

"It's in the water," Mason says.

We share a smile as the kids blink at each other, confused.

"Mo-ooom," the suspicious girl whines, over our jokes already. "You *said* we could go ice-skating! Uncle Mason said!"

"That's true." Steph looks at Mason. "Were we doing that here, big brother?"

"Central Park," Mason says, his eyes still boring into mine. "Rockefeller Center is a little too small and crowded for the twins."

"Well, I'm going to take them back into that cafe for a hot chocolate." Steph nods at the nearby Dean & Deluca. "You catch up with your friend. You two want anything?"

"Oh, no thank you," I say, just as Mason says, "Two mocha lattes."

"You got it!" Steph winks at me and drags the moping children through the crowd.

Leaving Mason and I alone for the first time in months.

Mason sighs and leans against the railing next to me. I'm hyper-aware of how close he is. "Those two are wearing me out," he confides.

It's so familiar, the way he speaks to me. As if we've been talking every day for months. "That's two sets of kids now," I say. "You've got Sebastian, Briar, Nikki, and...oh, shoot...."

"Vera," he supplies. "Named for another aunt, actually. Yeah, we're a tight family. I was raised in a big crowd of cousins, and even though a few of us have gotten scattered around the country, we try to keep close, see each other a lot. Since Uncle Mason is in the big exciting city, I tend to get a lot of holiday visits. Everyone wants to see, well, *this.*" He nods at the whirl of lights around us.

"And what do *you* want to see at the holidays?"

Mason shrugs. "Oh, you know. This. Where else would a person go for Christmas?"

"There's such a thing as a country Christmas," I suggest, although I haven't ever experienced anything like the movies suggest.

"A cabin in the woods, snow beating on the windows? I suppose I have to build a fire with my own bare hands and chase off bears with a shotgun, too?" Mason's laugh ripples over the crowd. "Every good Christmas song is a song about New York. Listen to them. Even in 'I'll Be Home For Christmas', she chooses to stay away rather than trek home. It's nostalgia versus reality. The real thing—New York—is always better."

"What about 'Jingle Bells'?" I challenge. "You're going to tell me a sleighing song is about the Manhattan streets?"

"Frederick Law Olmsted built sleighing paths into Central Park," Mason tells me. "Next?"

"Well, what about—" I think hard. "Wow, I can't think of any other Christmas songs. Where did they all go?"

He turns around, leans back on his elbows, and gazes up at the soaring towers around us. "Well, then you'll just have to trust me."

I do, I think. I wish I'd know that before. I settle back onto the railing next to him. "So, ice-skating in Central Park? Why not here?"

"I'm not taking those ankle-biters down there to get trampled by show-offs on skates." Mason shakes his head. "Rockefeller Center isn't for kids."

"There's a kid down there right now!" I point.

"Shouldn't be there. This is a place for adults. This is where stories happen—big, important stories, not fairy tales."

"Fairy tales can be important," I suggest. "They can happen in New York, too."

The words hang between us, unspoken: *Anything can happen in New York.*

And I thought Sam talked in cliches.

After a pause, he says, "I thought you were moving."

"I was. I am. Eventually. It's harder than it looks, when your whole life is here."

"Think you'll miss this?"

I shrug, discounting the golden angels blowing their trumpets, the curtains of glittering lights, the scent of roasted cinnamon nuts on the air, like they're all nothing, like they don't have a tug on my heart-strings. I can lie to myself with the best of them. "I guess I could come back and visit," I say.

"It's not the same," Mason argues. "Visiting isn't like living here, breathing here."

"It's the breathing part that gives me hives," I joke. "I need air that hasn't been breathed by a million other people first.

Mason turns and his eyes seem to search my face. "Residual pandemic nerves and all that?"

"Yes," I say simply.

"It was a hard time," Mason says. "No shame in that."

Another pause between us, while we both think our separate thoughts about those days.

Then Mason says, "You shouldn't leave the city because of what happened before. This is a different time."

"I can't stay here, though. It's too hard." The words fall from my lips even though I've often thought, in the past few months, that I still love New York City. But why have an impossible dream if you won't commit to it? I said I was leaving. I'm going to leave.

"That's ridiculous." Mason's voice is stern. "Lots of people had a very hard time. But this is what New Yorkers *do*. We pick ourselves up and we keep going."

"Well, I'm not going to. And maybe we shouldn't." I push away from the railing, suddenly trembling, newly aware of the crush of people in the plaza. "I don't want to just pretend nothing happened and that everything's fine. I'm not going to be locked inside alone again. I'm not going to try and live through that all by myself again. I'm *leaving*."

Mason is staring at me, comprehension slowly dawning across his features. "And you're leaving alone," he says.

I'm not going to be psychoanalyzed by him. "Alone," I repeat. "There, you've figured me out. I'm *lonely* and I'm off to be *alone* in the woods. Congrats. Have fun ice-skating. Tell Steph I had to go, okay?"

And I stalk across the plaza, mindless of the crowds, even though I know I should be afraid of them.

I'm more afraid of the person watching me go than anyone else.

I can't shake the fear that Mason knows too much about me. More than any person should. More than any person every could, and still want to be with me.

And he will never leave the city, I can tell that much. So there's no future here. Nothing to look forward to. Just another dead end.

Chapter Twenty-One

AFTER MEETING MASON and feeling a moment of connection that ultimately feels impossible and painful, I decide I am officially off the horse. It's over. And it doesn't matter how many times Margot tries to get me back on. I'm not meeting anyone else. I'm going to just finish this on my own. Spinster-style.

"I'm glad we disbanded the Settle Down Society," I declare at the next wine-soaked gathering of single girlfriends. "Because I'm finished with dating forever."

"Tracey, please," Caitlyn says. "Although that would be amazing, you know you can't just quit. You wanted to have a partner. Now you're planning to move upstate *alone* and what, just be a spinster?"

"Oh, not the right word," Margot says, making a sour face.

"That's exactly the right word," I say. "I am already a spinster. Why not go with my strengths?"

"You had a good thing going with Sam," Margot says patiently. "You could probably work things out with him. It was just a little break-up."

"I don't think it was little to him." Sam wanted to wrap me up in his arms and protect me after the gallery explosion. It took three days for him to realize I shouldn't have been down there at three o'clock in the morning. When he finally asked, I told him the truth. He'd been shocked and hurt to realize I'd gone back to meet Chase.

Well, I couldn't exactly lie about it. After all, the NYPD announced they'd nabbed an art thief at the scene of the Chelsea gallery explosion. That's the thing about very public affairs; the journalists make sure you get caught. It made the cover of the New York Post and the Times stuck it in the New York section.

I top off the girls' glasses and say, "I don't see Sam coming back to me. And what makes you think I can meet a *third* man who wants to date me in a matter of six months? It's not going to happen. It would be greedy of me to even expect it."

But there is a third guy. That's my stern inner voice, the one that bosses me around. And I don't know what she wants from me now. The third guy is just an idea, a silly daydream. Mason Reilly isn't interested in me. And if he was, a little bit? After our showdown at Rockefeller Center, I don't think that's an issue any more. He told me to stay; I said I wouldn't. What else is there to be said?

Maybe there's another version of me, in another timeline, that ends up with Mason. I wish her well. I wish I could be her.

I shake my head and try to focus on Caitlyn, who has been talking for several seconds. "I'm sorry, I missed that. What did you say?"

"I said I think you're making a big mistake. And you need to slow this whole moving-thing way, way down. You need to slow everything down. You can't rush meeting the right person, can't rush marriage—"

I burst out laughing—the hysterical kind of laughter, not the mirthful kind. "But the whole point of the entire summer *was* to rush through this part! The dating and the waiting and the wondering—we were going to push through as quickly as possible and get to the *results*. Remember?"

"I dropped out, remember?" Caitlyn reminds me cooly. "Because it was a bad, drunken idea, and it was fueled in part by Margot's investment in a truly terrible dating app."

I fall silent.

"Sorry about that," Margot says. "I mean it."

Caitlyn rolls her eyes, but affectionately.

"But seriously," Margot says, "I have been upstate, and I don't think you will be happy there alone."

"Margot is right. Remember when we went on that Rhinebeck farmhouse weekend and you couldn't sleep because it was so quiet? How are you going to handle that *alone?*" Caitlyn looks genuinely concerned.

I look between the two of them. Two of my best friends. The people who have known me since we were baby New Yorkers. When they tell me I can't make it on my own, they don't mean it as an insult. They mean it as a kindness. They mean it as a helping hand. They mean to save me from myself.

But I'm in the thick of things. Next weekend I'm taking Abel to a few towns in the Hudson Valley to look at some small town options. I'm determined to find a space that can serve as home and gallery, even if it's a lot smaller than the Victorian house I'd hoped for until the mortgage company denied my loan.

Suddenly my buzzer starts going off and once we're all done screaming and acting like we've never heard it before, I hit the intercom. Abel's cheerful voice fills the room. "I found a space and we need to go see it now."

"Abel? A space? Where?"

"In *Brooklyn!*" he screeches, the speaker nearly flying out of the wall.

"In Brooklyn?" I mutter, and I hit the button to open the front door. He's going to have to explain this one in person.

"I thought you were looking at spaces upstate," Caitlyn says suspiciously.

"We were," I counter. "I think Abel has gone all sleeper cell on me."

"Okay, ladies," Abel begins, once his coat is off, he has been presented with a mug of coffee, and he is certain that we are all paying him our undivided attention. "I know this one has been selling you on the American Gothic dream, all the hay and cows and corn a person could ever want, but what if I told you we can move Adams Gallery into a beautiful brick warehouse in the fair city of....drumroll please...Brooklyn!"

"We knew it was Brooklyn," Caitlyn points out. "We were all in the room when you shouted it."

"Well, it's exciting," Abel says sulkily. "I thought it would get a better reception, frankly."

"Where in Brooklyn?" I ask, trying to follow his line of thinking. Maybe he means Brookline, Massachusetts. He can't mean just moving across the river.

"In the cutest neighborhood! It's like Park Slope but not. It's by that cemetery, you know the one, with the birds."

"With the parrots?"

"The *parrots!*" Abel beams at me. "It's like three blocks from there. It's a super cute, kind of half-grimy and half-family neighborhood. Multilingual. Close to an express train but not *too* close. And like ten blocks out of Park Slope proper so there's lots of food and good car services and things like that. No one will complain they're bunking out to the back of beyond or anything like that. Which they *would,* if we were to move to Hudson-Jimmy-Joe Fish Camp or whatever hick town you were going to drag me to."

"Abel, we can't move to Brooklyn." He's crazy.

"Why not? Lots of people do it. In fact I have heard of some people moving from Manhattan to Brooklyn and then *back* to Manhattan because Brooklyn is getting so expensive, so, you know...win-win."

"I'm not sure what that means, but the plan is to move *out* of the city. Not just move to a part of it with even less reliable transportation that we have here."

Abel looks sullen. "You haven't even *seen* the space. Or the neighbors! There is a nautical themed bar where they sing sea shanties! It's adorable."

"You're serious," I say, "and that is what concerns me."

"I'm *dead* serious." Abel crosses his legs and sips his coffee primly, looking over the mug at me. It's his way of saying that he's done being persecuted for his remarkable vision, and I am the dumb one now.

I look at the ceiling and sigh. "I guess it won't *hurt* to go look at it."

"There's the spirit." He puts down his mug and stands. "Chop-chop. They're expecting us at two o'clock and the car should be here any minute."

"Right *now?*" I look helplessly at Caitlyn and Margot. They're barely concealing their laughter. "Did you know about this?"

"I might have heard something," Margot chuckles.

"I told him about the space," Caitlyn says, unrepentant.

Great. My best friends are all conspiring against me. What is it about this city? Its converts are absolutely impossible to escape. "I guess you guys can lock my place up when you leave?"

"*If* we leave," Caitlyn says. "You might find us here when you get back, catching up on Netflix."

"Oh, yes." Margot is already picking up the remote. "Bye, Tracey!"

"Well? It's a nice space, isn't it?" Abel has demanded this at least six times, spreading his arms and waltzing around the old wooden floors, or stroking the glamorously crumbling brick walls, or gesturing at the light, which is admittedly much better than in my shadowy Chelsea cave.

"It's a nice space," I agree wearily. "Now can we please find somewhere to warm up?" The real estate agent is locking up behind us, already on the phone with his next client. And this neighborhood, which I remember as so charming and beautiful in summer, is terribly exposed to the wind on a blustery November day like this one.

There is a hint of ice in the gale howling off the harbor and up the steep hill that eventually ends with the statue of Minerva atop Battle Hill. As we hustle up the avenue, we pass people bundled so deeply into scarves and puffy coats, it's hard to make out any faces. I burrow deeper into my own goose-down coat and wish for a closer subway station. The express is a good twelve blocks to our south, and I don't think I'll survive the walk.

"I'm not ready to be this cold," I say, my teeth chattering. "This is like the first winter day we've had."

"Coffee shop just ahead, darling—" Abel angles me through a courtyard filled with empty tables and into a cafe taking up the first floor of a corner row-house. There's no sidewalk vestibule to absorb the cold, so we dart through the doors and pull them shut behind us, hoping we didn't let too much wind inside.

But there's no one to bother; the cafe is empty—just a few round tables with mismatched chairs, a stack of newspapers piled atop a bookshelf filled with yellowed old novels, and a curving wooden bar housing a few trays of pastries and the espresso machine.

"Huh," Abel says. "I hope they're not closed."

"Me, too." I can already feel the warmth of the room soaking through my coat. "Because I'm not leaving unless the police make me."

The swinging door behind the bar eventually opens and a young man emerges. He's happy enough to make us a couple of lattes, and the scent of espresso is wafting through the room as we sit down to wait for our drinks. Once his ass is in the chair, Abel jumps right into his stump speech. "That place is perfect, Tracey Adams, and you know it."

I sigh. It would be perfect, *if* I wanted to stay in the city. "This place is perfect for *you*," I hedge. "But this entire partnership was founded on my going upstate. It almost sounds like you want to run a gallery in this space all by yourself instead of keeping my Chelsea gallery warm for me."

"No, that's not it!" Abel looks around, as if he's afraid a group of people will judge him for such perfidy. "I still want to go into business with you. But I think our initial positioning was... well...a mistake."

I lean back and thank the barista as he sets our drinks down. Then I face Abel. "Well? Prove it."

And then wouldn't you know it, that jerk does?

It turns out, Abel has shown up prepared, with a folder filled with charts and analysis. He's looking at demographics. He's looking at travel patterns. He's got historical data. And he spends the next twenty minutes showing me why our initial plans, for a shared gallery in the Hudson Valley which can capitalize on summer traffic and online sales, simply will not work. But somehow, he illustrates, a gallery halfway between Red Hook and Bay Ridge, Brooklyn absolutely will.

When he's done, I can't even speak. I just stare at him in dismay.

"I'm sorry," he offers. "Didn't mean to burst your bubble, but..."

"Well, what am I supposed to do? This wasn't in the plan." I gesture at the low-ceilinged room. "We weren't supposed to be in *Brooklyn*."

"A lot of people *would* consider a move to Brooklyn the same as a move out of the city," he points out. "Maybe you could move here. A sunny two-bedroom, with a view of the park? Wouldn't that be exactly the same as moving upstate? What would you be missing? Cows? Tracey, are you that committed to cows, really?"

"I'd be missing—I don't know, *space*. Fresh air. The ability to avoid other people if I so choose. Isolation."

Abel shakes his head at me. "You don't want to avoid other people, Tracey. You're not looking to isolate. Stop saying that, honey."

"I do want to isolate." I pick up my latte, and am disgruntled to realize the cup is already down to dregs. I wave it at the barista, who eventually decides to make me another one. "I want to be alone," I say. "Constantly."

I am purposely leaving out that isolation was one of the reasons I wanted to leave the city. And Abel knows it. Jeez, having friends is *work*.

"That's the opposite of what you want," he says. "You set up a whole gag with your friends to get married, remember?"

"And it didn't work! It really backfired! Even Margot ran out on her wedding, and she got all the way to the ceremony. But me? Not only did I choose the wrong guy. I nearly got killed. I am bad at this—"

"The getting killed part was not entirely related to your poor dating skills," Abel murmurs.

"Close *enough!*" I stand up, grabbing at my coat. "I'm not going to be lectured by everyone I know on this. Why does everyone think they know better than me?"

Abel puts out a hand and catches at my sleeve. "Because we love you," he says. "Because we have watched you spiral and we have done everything we can to help you, and sometimes it's been a struggle to prop you up, but we have done it, because we care so much about you."

The emotion in his voice takes me by surprise, and I sit down again. The barista slips a latte in front of me. I reflect that two more shots of espresso is exactly what I don't need, and then take a cautious sip anyhow.

"I'm sorry," I say eventually.

"We just want to help."

"It's been really hard." The tears are threatening to spill over now. "I was alone, and then it was all I wanted, and then I didn't, and now I don't even know."

"I get it."

"And I thought if I could share my space with one other person, just one, that would solve everything. Like we could be alone together. Isn't that a marriage, sometimes? In a good way?"

"It can be. And you deserve that, honey. But it isn't that simple to find someone you can be alone with. So maybe your little Settle Down Society, as cute as that name is, wasn't the best way to go about it. And maybe you got hurt along the way, right?"

"And almost blown up," I remind him.

"And almost blown up," Abel agrees. "Sure. But I think now it's time to just let nature take its course, and stick to the people who love you, even if we aren't going to marry you. Or move you upstate."

"Maybe I'll get that commune idea through eventually," I suggest, sniffling.

"Maybe. You can count me out, but maybe." Abel gives me a tentative smile. "You think you're gonna be okay?"

"Maybe," I repeat. "Could be."

Abel gets up to buy me a danish, because he says I'm pouring way too much caffeine into my body and that's going to keep me all worked up, and I pull out my phone and tap at a map of the neighborhood. I measure the blocks to Green-Wood Cemetery and wonder, with a little jolt of surprise, if we're sitting in the same cafe that Mason was talking about the day we met amongst the gravestones and monuments.

The cafe he had been about thirty seconds from inviting me to join him at when he'd seen Monty and wrongly assumed I was on a date.

Things could have gone so differently, I think sadly. The Settle Down Society could have seen *two* weddings to cap its inaugural year. And I would have gone through with mine, too.

"A danish," Abel announces, placing a heavy white plate at my elbow. "The sugar will burn away all the extra moroseness in your soul, and the cheese will give you protein. For energy."

I try to force away these weird thoughts about Mason and marriage. It's the first time I've considered him in that way, and the daydream stays with me, even as Abel brings out the real estate listing and once again begins to try and sell me on opening a gallery in Brooklyn.

Chapter Twenty-Two

THE DANISH IS nothing but crumbs and our drinks are foamy memories by the time we stand up to leave. Outside the window, the shadows stretch across the avenue, and the east-west facing street is orange with that particularly garish autumn sunset New York shows off this time of year. I am tugging on my coat, thinking how oddly open and bare the streets seem with their low-storied row-houses, when the bell on the door jingles for the very first time since our arrival. A woman and two children, heavily wrapped in coats and hats, stumble inside. And as she takes off their scarves, revealing their faces, I'm shocked to realize I recognize them.

"Sebastian and Briar," I gasp, just as the door opens once more and a taller, more familiar woman walks in.

The first woman to enter the cafe is staring at me furiously, aghast this stranger would know her children's names, but the last arrival in the party pushes forward with a smile on her pinched, cold face. "Tracey!" Steph announces, delighted. "What are the chances?"

"I was just here looking at gallery space. It's a total coincidence. I'm Tracey Adams," I say to the children's mother. "A—um—friend of Mason's."

"Oh, that explains it," she replies, looking relieved. "I don't know why I was so surprised. They could have met you at a play-date or something, anyway. So, um, hi, I'm Kimber. It's so nice to meet you, Tracey, and—uh—"

"Abel," he supplies. "Tracey's business partner."

"And friend," I say teasingly.

"And business relocation specialist," Abel says. "What do you think of a gallery in this neighborhood?"

"Wait, you'd be thinking of moving your business out here?" Steph seems thrilled. "Mason said you were moving to Albany or something."

He talks about me? I try to keep myself composed. "I was thinking of moving to the Hudson River valley. It's not really that far away."

"He made it sound like you were moving to the moon, but you know how Mason is. He can't imagine moving outside the five boroughs. He thinks the Taconic is the highway to hell."

Kimber is wrangling children into chairs by the front window. She plops a bag in front of them. Coloring books and stuffed animals pop out. The kids grouse for a moment before picking out crayons and books. "They used all their screen time this morning," she explains. "And they've just been moping around the house ever since. We have a family reunion tomorrow and everyone's amped up."

"That's why I'm staying there," Steph adds. "To help out. We were hoping for better weather..."

"Tomorrow *has* to be nicer than today," Kimber sighs. "For me. I have been so good and all I'm asking is that it be sunny and sorta warm so I can put everyone in the backyard."

"You have a backyard?" Abel's real estate ears prick. "What's *that* like?"

"A lot of trouble," Kimber tells him. "But worth it to just feel like I have a square foot of ground I'm not sharing with everyone else in the city. And of course, when family comes to town, they all want to get together at my house because of the yard. Which saves me traveling all over the city with those two maniacs." She nods fondly at her children.

"That sounds *amazing.* My partner and I live in a big place, but I always say to him, why don't we have anything *outside?* When I want to commune with nature I have to go to the High Line." Abel laughs dismissively. "And you *know* what a tourist fest *that* place is."

"Oh, please, it's like Disney World." Kimber has warmed to Abel. "Like most of Manhattan is these days. Tourists, tourists, tourists. What about *us?* What about New Yorkers? Don't give me some ad slogan like '*New York is back*' and then that just means folks from Peoria can come go to Broadway shows again. But that's typical. They don't care about us over there in the city."

She says *city* in that particularly Brooklyn way, as if Manhattan is the urban center and Brooklyn is a bucolic village set amongst rolling hills.

"That's what I say!" Abel is over-the-moon delighted with his new friend and, apparently, is now a Brooklyn booster. "I think you have it right, living over here. Maybe I've been too clingy with Manhattan."

"Well, you should come see my house. You wouldn't believe what you can get over here. The space, and the windows! Lots of places over here need gutting, but my god, the bones of them —"

I turn to Steph. "This could go on a while. Abel is really into real estate. It's one of those things that happen to people when they move here. He was perfectly normal in art school."

"Words you don't hear together very often!" Steph laughs. "No, I know. Kimber is a monster about real estate. When she moved out here, Mason fought her tooth and nail. But she was right. This neighborhood is great."

Tell me more about Mason, I think. Instead, we chat about a number of inane things while we wait for the barista to whip up some hot cocoas for the kids. It's not until I hear Abel say, "Well, I just have to see it," and Kimber replying, "You should come see it, in all seriousness. I would love to have you over and show you what we've done, what you could do."

"That would be great!"

I whip around and stare at Abel. Did he really just agree to go visit *Mason's sister's house?*

"But we can't today," I blurt. "We have to get back to—to, um —"

"The client meeting!" Abel cries. "Of course!"

Now I'm blinking at him in total confusion. There's no client meeting. There's nothing going on at all. Is he backing out of visiting Kimber's house just to make me happy? That doesn't sound like Abel, to be perfectly honest. He's a sweetheart, don't get me wrong, and he meant everything he said to me earlier about taking care of me and being my people, but he's also selfish as hell. It's part of his charm.

"You know what, come tomorrow," Kimber says. "What's two more people? Both of you come. The whole clan will be there, but it'll be fun."

"That sounds great!" Steph is handing out cocoas to the kids, who grab at them without looking up. "Yes, come tomorrow, please!"

The whole clan?

Does that include Mason?

"We aren't going to that reunion," I say to Abel. My words echo around the subway.

Our F train car is nearly empty; just a few bold souls are traveling between boroughs on this frosty evening. It can feel hard to do anything after four o'clock this time of year, before we get used to the early sunsets. By the time we get upstairs and onto the street back in my own neighborhood, even twilight will be long gone. The dark days of winter are setting in, and I can feel that creeping sense of dread in my bones, of another lonely season spent indoors.

"Oh, we're going." Abel is playing a crossword on his phone. He has to look up every second answer, but it doesn't stop him from crowing every time he gets a word. I think he looks at crosswords more as a scavenger hunt than a vocabulary quiz. "It's going to be great. I'm going to see inside one of these row houses and take enough pictures to show Robbie just what we can do with them. And then he's going to get off his ass and stop whining we can't afford a brownstone and look at one of these cuties instead. You know under all that vinyl siding there are bricks, right? Bricks!"

"I think some of them are lumber."

"Bricks," Abel insists. "I won't even look at the frame houses. But if I can pull off that siding and there's an adorable brick row house under there, that's the coup of the century as far as I'm concerned."

I let him play his game and murmur about third-floor guest suites and garden-level apartment rentals while I consider what is about to happen. I'm going to see Mason tomorrow. And I don't know for sure, but I don't think he's going to be really happy to see me. The girl who keeps showing up and assuring him she's leaving...then shows up again?

No one likes a person like that.

Chapter Twenty-Three

WE KNOCK ON the front door of Kimber's house at one o'clock the next afternoon. She must have worked some powerful magic last night, because she's gotten her weather wish: the day is a dancing, bright thing. The air temperature has climbed some twenty degrees above yesterday's chill and the long, steep slope from the harbor has been blessed with a soft, tickling breeze from southern climes instead of the howling wind that felt like it was coming straight from Canada.

The weather has let me wear a nice three-quarter length knit coat instead of the heavy goose-down that makes me feel like a swaddled baby, and I think I look pretty good, with knee-length black boots, dark jeans, and a clingy tunic beneath. Plus, something I always forget about winter: knit hats look so cute on my curls. Instead of looking panicked and out-of-control, I look mod and put together. How about that?

If only I felt the same on the inside. My stomach is churning at the idea of seeing Mason again.

"Well, you're looking *adorable*," Steph declares as she opens the door. "Absolutely love that hat. Did you make it?"

I laugh. "I wish! My friend Margot. She knits."

"Oh, Margot! The one we were talking about, who does the art programs, right?"

I feel Abel turning his body slightly towards me, the question in his stance obvious. *We were talking, hmmm?* "That's the one," I say breezily, ignoring him. What am I supposed to do, explain I have a weird former relationship with Steph, through the detective who occasionally works on my case and makes my skin tingle whenever we're within a few blocks of one another?

"I still think Mason should talk to her," Steph says. "We'll work on him. I'm here a few more days." She ushers us in. "The party's out back! We got the weather we needed to kick everyone outside."

I can already hear shrieking children and the sound of trampoline springs wheezing. We're walking through a hall paneled with light wood, and to my right I see the predictable layout of the New York City row-house: the front living room with its bow window, the central dining room, the back kitchen overlooking the yard. A staircase rises to our left and disappears into what will be the bedrooms upstairs. There are small vintage art prints and a few travel posters on the walls, a bookshelf heaving with old paperbacks and well-loved hardcovers, overstuffed sofas and chairs that I think I could sink into and sleep for days.

"This is nice," I say. "Very domestic. Abel, is this what you want out of life?"

Abel winks at me. "Something like that," he says. I know he's judging some of the design choices, but Kimber's style isn't completely out of sync with his. I have to wonder if I'll be trucking out here in six months *anyway,* whether we lease this gallery or not. It looks like Abel is moving to Brooklyn.

Beers in hand, we survey the party. The yard is small, but Kimber has wedged a lot into it: a small round trampoline, a tiny raised garden that's probably home to a bed of organic vegetables in the spring, a little rubber pond in one corner with water tumbling over smooth river rocks. Just outside the back door, there is a brick patio with a gleaming grill and a wooden picnic table.

And that's where Mason is sitting, leaning on his elbow as he drinks a beer and talks with a man in a slouched knit cap and a thick lumberjack beard. He's laughing when he looks up and sees me, and I watch his features arrest for one moment, his jaw tensing. I suspect that Kimber and Steph probably conspired last night, swapping notes on what they knew about me and about their brother, and decided not to tell him I was coming.

I am *so* bad at surprises.

He gets up slowly, as if he doesn't really want to, and saunters over to me. Abel has already darted off, Kimber and Steph guiding him around the features of the postage-stamp sized backyard. I steel myself for whatever Mason is going to say, which is probably going to be on some variation of, "What are *you* doing here?"

But he doesn't say anything accusatory. He just looks down at me, that broad chest of his rising and falling, before he says, "Hey."

"Hey," I reply, because it's as good a start as any. And saying *Twenty-four hours ago I was daydreaming about an alternate life where we're married* would probably get me a very well-deserved crazy look.

"You keep showing up," he says simply.

"Well." I spread my hands. "Small town like this, what can you expect?"

Mason looks around the party, as if he expects the noise around us to melt away. He says, "I have to admit, the backyard of my sister's place seemed pretty safe. And yet here you are."

I smile weakly. *Seemed pretty safe.* He's been avoiding me? Hoping he wouldn't see me in a crowd, or down the block? "I'm like a bad penny," I offer.

"You really are." He eyes me appraisingly, and a smile tugs at his mouth. Something inside of me slowly twists into a knot, pressure rising with every turn. "You polish up nicely, though. Makes me want to try my luck."

My heart is thudding in my chest so hard I'm sure I'm breathy when I ask, "Try your luck with what?"

He leans down and gives me the sweetest little peck on the cheek, the sort of familial kiss an uncle would give to a niece. It's an utterly passionless kiss, but my skin is burning anyway. I blink up at him, confused.

"I just wanted to see if you'd let me do that," he explains. "You know, you can tell how a girl feels about you really quickly just by giving her a little smooch on the cheek."

"What variety of girls are we talking about here?" I ask warily.

"Oh, about toddler-sized through nine or ten. And I should mention I'm only talking about my little nieces." He points to the trampoline, where Briar and Sebastian and the twins are squealing. "They're pretty honest at that age. When Briar was six, I picked them up for a day at the museum. Gave her that little hello kiss and she reared back and wiped her cheek with the back of her hand. Told me to keep my lips off her face." Mason laughed at the memory. "She apologized later, after I'd gotten some chicken nuggets into her. But I told her it was a good reaction to most kisses."

"You're a good uncle," I say, begrudgingly charmed by his story. "Do all kids love you naturally? Are you one of those guys that are just a magnet for other people's kids?"

"I am," Mason admits. "I'm very curious to see if I have that effect on my own. When I have children," he adds. "In the future. Someday."

"You want to settle down and have a family. Where? In Brooklyn?" I hope it doesn't sound like an interrogation. Well, he's the detective. He would know.

But Mason doesn't seem to mind the questions. He nods. "Brooklyn would work. Nice, for the kids to live near their cousins, right? We used to all live here—well, not in this part of town. Down in Bay Ridge. When my mother died and we all sold the house, everyone left but Kimber and me. It's nice to see the family back together." He points out his brother, Jeff, who is busy manning the grill. "We'll get you introduced once he's extinguished the fire. Jeff's a volunteer fireman in a small town in Pennsylvania now. He takes flames very seriously."

"A fireman griller," I say gravely, "is an asset to every family."

"Safety first," he agrees, his grin widening. "Now if only we had a guy for security, we'd be set."

"You're not up to the job?"

"I'm not a beat cop," he says, "just a detective. We take it easy, show up well after all the danger's cleared up."

"Did you always want to be a detective?" Look at me, making conversation like a pro. You'd never even know my stomach is fluttering with a thousand butterflies.

"I've been a Hardy Boy since day one," Mason explains. "But don't make me choose which one."

"I wouldn't know which was which," I say regretfully.

"Frank was the good-looking one," Mason says. "If that helps."

"Looks only get you so far. Which one of them stood to inherit the most from the family estate?"

"Now you're thinking," Mason replies, grinning. "Is that empty already? Let me get you another beer."

He heads back to the table and dips a hand into a cooler, drawing out a can of a local beer. "Here you go," he says. "Brooklyn's finest."

"I thought that phrase meant cops," I say, letting his fingers touch mine as I take the beer. They're warm, firm, strong. "Or maybe firemen?"

"It's always meant beer," Mason says. "Cops and firemen just borrow it to feel something."

For a few moments we stand side by side, sipping companionably, appreciating the warmth of the sun. I think about how right it feels next to him, so incredibly, strangely *right*. It doesn't seem like one person should be able to make me feel like this.

It's possible, I think confusedly, that I've never actually been in love with anyone.

The kids squeal and shriek and do their best to distract me from the sensation of falling inextricably in love with Mason. It's also weird, I think, that those shouting monsters are the result of so many love stories. Hopefully, even mine.

"It's hard to believe you can raise a family like this," I say, taking in the yard, the trampoline, the trees overhead. Just a few blocks away, the trees of Green-Wood glow on their steep slope, giving the whole scene a pastoral feel. "I almost feel like I'm in a small town somewhere far away from New York."

"*That's* why I keep saying you don't have to leave," Mason tells me, but he's not looking at me now, and it's hard for me to judge whether there's some personal meaning in those words. "Plus, think of all the things you can do here that most kids just see on television."

"Like what?"

"Like *what*? Like, oh, I don't know, like the skating rink at Rockefeller Center?"

It's not a coincidence that he's brought up one of our random meetings. I know it isn't.

"But I've still never done that," I remind him. "Most New Yorkers never do stuff like that. We just live here, like we would live anywhere else. And then we get together to talk and all we do is congratulate ourselves on how hard we have to work to live here, and it's somehow a betrayal to say that maybe we could just live normal lives, work our jobs and get in a car and go to the grocery store and eat chicken way too often for dinner in any other place in the United States, and it wouldn't have to be this constant, monumental struggle to survive in the city. Did you ever think of that?"

Mason is looking at me now, and I can see the moment he decides to challenge me. His eyes seem to sparkle. "I can prove to you," he says, "that if that's how you feel, it's because you're living in New York City the wrong way. You might have gotten started on the right foot, but it went wrong somewhere and now you're missing the magic."

I smile and ask, "Oh, really? Is there a challenge here?"

"Oh, *really*. You owe me something, you know." Mason's eyes are twinkling with mischief. There are little crow's-feet around each of his eyes that deepen into ravines when he smiles, and they're making me weak at the knees.

But there's just one question here.

"Me? What do I owe you?"

"An ice-skate at Rockefeller Center."

"Oh!" He's joking, right? He has to be joking.

Mason's grin is positively diabolical. "Come on. You and me, skating around like we're in a classic movie. Do you have a muff? It would be best if you had a fluffy fur muff and maybe a matching fur hat. I'm sure I can find a top hat for myself."

"I don't have a—I told you before I can't skate!"

"I'll teach you," Mason assures me, eyes glittering. "Right there in front of God and everyone at Rockefeller Plaza."

Oh no, I think. I'd better learn how to ice-skate before this happens.

Somehow, it seems inevitable that it's going to happen.

That's how Mason makes me feel, I realize.

Like things are inevitable.

Chapter Twenty-Four

THE VERY NEXT day. The *very* next *day.*

I don't know how he got me to agree to it, but somehow we have a mid-morning ice-skating date at Rockefeller Center arranged before I can make my escape back to Manhattan.

I guess he's very persuasive, and I am very ready to be persuaded by him. It's a worrying state of affairs.

As I sit at the little table outside the rink, waiting for Mason, something new occurs to me: how does this guy have off on a weekday? Shouldn't he be at work, investigating dangerous criminals? Or helping Detective Patel? I know that woman is working way more than nine to five.

But when he finally appears, standing head and shoulders above the crowds of tourists working their way around the ice-rink, my silly questions fly out of my head. What does it matter why Mason isn't at work? What matters is that he's *here*. Coming to see me, with that warm smile of his just for me.

I sit still and watch him approach, trying to appear aloof and arch, but inside my innards are jumping around all over the place. I've got schoolgirl nerves over this meet-up. It's the first time we've made plans together. What if this is a romantic-type of date?

What if it *isn't?*

He greets me with another cheek-kiss, like the one he gave me yesterday. That Uncle Mason affectionate peck.

I feel like it puts me firmly in the friend camp. Non-romantic date, it is. My stomach droops with disappointment.

Well, I should have known. Last night I'd waited for him to give me a more emphatic kiss before the party ended. A more *grown-up* kiss. And I really thought there was a chance. He eyeballed me all evening, and once the twinkle lights were lit over the back garden, I was certainly feeling the mood. Once the kids went inside to play Mario Kart and the atmosphere outside shifted into the adult quadrant, with wine and soft conversation, I thought *something* might have happened.

But, no. He just watched me, always just out of the frame, glancing my way from behind cousins and friends. It was confusing, and suggestive. On the occasions when I caught him, he didn't look away. He just smiled.

Yeah, I'm watching you, that smile said. *Are you going to do something about it?*

I didn't. I wanted to, but I didn't.

I decided to see what today would be like.

And so far, today seems really...platonic, to be honest. He's sitting across from me now, coffee in one hand and wallet in the other. He comments on my lack of a fur muff, and I remind him I was promised a top hat which has not made an appearance, and then he glances towards the reservation desk for the ice-skating rink. He says, "I'm going to go over and get us set up, okay?"

"I think you have to make an appointment," I say doubtfully. He's not going to just walk up and try to buy tickets like some kind of out-of-towner, right?

"Obviously, I made an appointment," Mason scoffs. "There is some *other* stuff I have to get set up. Can you hang tight a few more minutes? You're not too cold?"

I can't help but tuck the collar of my black peacoat a little closer to my chin. I should have worn the stupid goose-down coat again—the weather turned cold and brisk overnight, as if we've been granted just that one golden day in the sunshine for Kimber's party, and shouldn't even consider asking for more of the November gods.

But come on, we always want more.

"I'm fine," I assure him, as his eyes flick to my hands at my collar. "Just a brisk November day, nothing we shouldn't expect."

"If you say so," he agrees, eyeing me. "Okay, I'll be right back."

He leaves his coffee cup, but takes his wallet. I notice his detective's badge is tucked up against one side.

I pick up the cup and study his order, printed on the side: Americano, quad espresso, black.

Damn. This guy is hardcore.

Before he comes back, I hear an announcement asking the ice to be cleared. I look over, expecting disappointed faces and maybe something gross on the rink. But everyone is making their way to the exit as if they got their full money's worth, and I don't see anything Caddyshack-style in the ice. How odd.

At least, I think it's odd until I see Mason coming back, his face bright with anticipation.

I put down his coffee cup. "What did you do?"

"I made us an appointment, like I said. You ready?"

"You did more than make us an appointment. Why is the rink empty?"

Mason is tucking his badge more securely into his pocket. "You said you didn't know how to skate."

"Yeah, and?"

"And I didn't want you to worry about anyone bumping you while I teach you. So I called in a favor."

"What *kind* of favor?" I think my eyes might be bugging out a little. Is this why he had his badge at the ready?

"I just asked them to give us a half hour on the ice alone. Not a big deal. You coming?" His hand is out, waiting for me to take it.

I debate a moment before I put my hand in his. His hands are bare, and I feel the cold radiate through my thin leather gloves. "I can't believe you did this," I hedge, looking at the empty rink. There are people standing all around it, and on the plaza above looking down, wondering if they're going to see some kind of show. Boy, are they about to see a show.

* * *

I can't ice-skate.

I mean, I really can't. We've been out here on this empty rink for twenty minutes, and with ten minutes to go in our private skate, I can tell Mason is about ready to give up on me. But he's having fun, and dammit, so am I. Against my wishes, obviously. Because every time I do a little dip and start to sprawl, Bambi-style, across the ice, the crowds above cheer and whistle.

I'm past embarrassment. I've moved on to some new level, where shame no longer exists, like I've gone past the event horizon of the black hole. Now I just let the city whoop and holler while I focus on Mason.

He's focused entirely on me. The force of his attention is powerful, something I can feel even when my back is to him, like when I'm picking myself up off the ice, his hands gently and firmly guiding me back to my wobbly feet.

Mason tugs me against his chest once again as my legs threaten to split in two opposing directions. I hear some sporadic applause and ask, "How are they not bored of me falling yet?"

He grins down at me. "They think we're practicing for a TV show or a movie."

"What kind? A police drama? Where the victim is found after a terrible ice-skating incident?"

"A romantic comedy," Mason assures me. "One starring America's sweethearts. The perfect date-night movie."

"In this movie, do they ever manage to teach the heroine how to skate?" I ask, as he gives me another encouraging push along the ice. I can feel my feet threatening to skid out of control and clutch at his arm. "Does she pick it up?"

"You know," Mason sighs, "I don't think she does."

"Maybe this wasn't meant to be." I slide wildly, feeling like my kneecaps are splitting loose. "I am much better on solid ground. You know this by now. You've seen me. I can walk and everything. In fact, if you give me gum, I can chew it and walk at the same time."

"A marvel." He grunts as he clutches me against his side before I can hit the ground. "I might have to see this talent. I'm not sure I should just take you at your word."

"Oh, you should *always* take me at my word," I assure him. I look up at him from my awkward position, tucked under his left arm. "Like when I told you I couldn't ice-skate? You should have believed me."

"It's incredible," he says. "You really do seem to have a physical incapability to learn this. I'm in awe of you right now."

I grin, and he grins back. For a moment we're still; I've almost found my balance, and if I move so much as a centimeter, I'm going to feel my feet skid out from beneath me. Mason knows it; his grip around my shoulders is like a steel band. We're locked together, and as the seconds tick past, the laughter in his eyes seems to shift into something more intense.

"Kiss her, already!" some wag in the crowd shouts.

I close my eyes, some new pulse of acute embarrassment flooding through me, and when I open them again, Mason's face is just a bare inch from mine. I feel a shiver of delight ripple through me; if he just tips a little closer, we're going to be kissing—

My locked knees give out and my right leg shoots one way while my left goes the other. I topple, taking Mason down with me.

Exactly what would have happened in a rom-com, I think in exasperation.

Chapter Twenty-Five

WE HEAD OFF the ice after that, Mason raising his hand to acknowledge the cheers of the crowd around the plaza. After a moment, I raise my hand and wave to the spectators, too. I feel like I'd usually be mortified by something like this, but instead I feel kind of—energized? A little *proud,* even? Maybe it's just the fine art of not giving a fuck, that most important of New Yorker traits, finally reaching professional level in my veins. Or maybe it's that Mason is just ahead of me, and when he's nearby, things seem less embarrassing and frightening. I might even be willing to ride a subway with this guy.

Not at rush hour, but still. Off-peak hours on a cold day can get pretty hairy.

It means something, to feel this way.

When we're de-ice-skated and have fended off a small crowd of tourists who think we are definitely a famous couple they can't quite place, Mason holds out his hand once more. He's wearing gloves now, but I still feel a spark of heat when our hands touch. "Madam, can I escort you to lunch?" he asks.

"Please tell me you didn't buy out some expensive restaurant for a private lunch," I tease.

"If only. But my budget only ran as high as the Chipotle on Fifty-seventh Street, and somehow I didn't think that would impress you."

"Depends," I say, "on whether the guac is included."

"The guac is *never* included. That was really the sticking point in the negotiations. I walked. I have my pride, what can I say? But really, I do have a nice place for us. And a cab to get us there."

So close together we might as well before hand-in-hand, we head down to Fifth Avenue and cross the asphalt. Just a few parked cars down the avenue, a man hops out of a black Town Car and smiles at us.

Wait—not a man.

"Kimber?" I blink at her. "You look great in a tux, mama."

Mason's sister straightens her bow-tie proudly. "Thanks! Well, fancy meeting you in the middle of Midtown! I guess I'll just have to give you a ride."

I shoot Mason a glance. "You're making your sister drive us around?"

"She loves it. She borrows that car from Cousin Jamie all the time. You met him last night, remember? Quiet, leather jacket, doesn't smile?"

"Oh, yes." I had actually avoided Cousin Jamie, who made only a brief appearance at the party and spent all of it glowering at us from behind a variety of meat sandwiches. He had a definite South Brooklyn feel that was a little scary to this Upper West Sider via the Midwest. Sometimes you meet people in this city that are a tad too authentic. "He has a Town Car?"

"A fleet of them. One of the best car services in the city. Didn't I tell you? We're all very proud of Cousin Jamie." Mason is ushering me into the backseat of the car. I slide across the smooth leather seat, in the universal city language of *Please don't go around on the side with traffic and get killed,* and he smiles and tucks himself in after me. Kimber closes the door with a smirk over Mason's head that's all for me.

"Are you going to tell me where we're going?" I ask, clipping my seat-belt into place.

"Absolutely not. That would spoil all the fun."

"It's *very* fun for my crippling anxiety," I mutter, looking out the window.

Mason's hand is on my shoulder immediately. "But are you really feeling anxious right now?"

I have to relent, because I'd be lying if I pretended I was anxious right now. "No, not at all," I say, kind of wondering at the release. It's like a weight has been lifted from the top of my head, like whatever misery has been pressing me down into the pavement has finally been taken away.

"I'm just being difficult for the sake of it now," I admit.

"I thought so," Mason says, smiling. "But if you get uncomfortable with anything, you tell me, alright? This isn't about upsetting your balance."

"What *is* it about?" I can't help but hope he'll look deep into my eyes and tell me it's about true love, or something cheesy and unlikely like that.

"It's about reminding you how much you love New York," he tells me.

And that is simultaneously disappointing and touching.

Kimber is an excellent driver, unafraid to accelerate to find her way around slow cars but still capable of finding the smoothest lanes with the fewest potholes. I would have given her a huge tip if she'd been my actual Town Car driver. I might have to give her one, anyway. She whizzes us up Madison Avenue with some kind of sixth sense about when to change lanes and how to cruise through several green lights in one go. It can only be magic. Maybe it's family magic, and Jamie has it too, and that's why he got into the car business.

I know better to ask where we're going, but when we cross 125th Street and are officially sailing through Harlem, my curiosity really ratchets skyward. I rarely come up here, and while for some people it might look like the rest of Manhattan, to me the character of the streets has changed already. The Upper West Side, as much as I love her, can be a little stodgy, especially as more people renovate brownstones and put twee little gas lanterns out front and add underground garages for their personal cars. Harlem, although hardly excused from the constant waves of gentrification that rumble through the city, still has a more free spirit, a more lived-in vibe, and definitely far more sky.

Which is clearing up, I notice. The gray morning is giving way to a blue and sunny midday. It might be storming by sunset—weather on the edge of the cold North Atlantic can be pretty capricious—but for now, we've got ourselves a gorgeous late autumn day.

"Here we are," Mason murmurs to Kimber, and she pulls over, double-parking at a particularly lively corner. Mason steps out of the car, then leans over to help me out. I slide across the seat again, and then my hand is in his. I'm feeling that jolt of electricity that seems to be a little stronger each time we touch, and we're stepping between the parked cars and onto the sidewalk.

Kimber puts the car back in gear and pulls out into traffic. I watch her go. "Where is she going? Driving in circles?"

Mason laughs. "Knowing her, yes. A normal person would just go find a parking spot, but she's really into life behind the wheel. I think when the kids are older she's going to start driving for Cousin Jamie."

"Is that safe? Being a female driver?" Mason has tucked my arm into his and we're walking up the sidewalk, passing a beauty salon with its door propped open, hot air and salsa music spilling out.

"I'm surprised at you, Tracey," Mason says. "Women have been allowed to drive for at least a century. We're not supposed to ask if it's safe."

"No, safe for *her,* driving strangers around," I say, swatting his arm with my free hand.

"Hard to say. Cousin Jamie has been saying no, but Kimber is pretty tough. I think she'll get her own way in the end." Mason pauses. "Here we are."

"What on earth?" I stare at the dark door in front of us. We're standing before a regular brick building, four stories tall and four windows across. It could be any building in New York City, quite honestly. What's odd about it is that we're on a commercial block, and there's no storefront at ground level. Just three windows, with plain white shades in each, and this door, off to one side. "Mason, this looks extremely sketchy."

"Tell me something, when did you move to the city?"

"Right when I was out of college."

"And when you first came here, what did you quickly learn was a sure sign of a good place to eat or drink or generally party?"

I give him a grudging look. "Looking sketchy."

He's absolutely right. The best places in the city, especially when you're young and careless, are the sketchy ones. The incredibly cheap dim sum place that looks like a secret basement used for the illegal sale of medicinal herbs. The alley lined with dumpsters that leads to a fantastic bar. Look at my own favorite place to eat in Chelsea, a no-name falafel place underneath ancient scaffolding. Walking into that joint is like walking through a history of Manhattan written in soot and dirt. But the kitchen surfaces must be wiped clean fairly regularly, because the falafel there has never failed me.

So, let's do sketchy.

I let Mason knock on the door, and I don't even jump behind him for safety when we hear footsteps on the other side. The latch turns and the door opens, revealing a woman in a white button-down shirt and a long, floral skirt. She smiles brightly at us, revealing youthful, white teeth. "You must be the Reilly party! Come on in, your table is ready."

I gape at her, then at Mason.

He smiles down at me. "Sketchy, right?"

We step through the doorway and enter a normal, everyday vestibule with a staircase leading towards the upstairs apartments. The young woman gestures to the open door behind her, and we file into what I would normally expect to be a ground floor apartment.

Except that it isn't.

It is an English library, paneled with wood wainscoting, lined with dark bookshelves, and scattered with a few small tables. A double-decker row of candles lights up the huge fireplace against the far wall. On the mantelpiece, a few pewter cups and china statues stand watch over the unlikely room. Hunting prints and Restoration-era portraits fill in the available space on the walls.

I look around in shock, then stare at the woman. She's smiling as if this is her favorite part of her day. "It's amazing, isn't it? The fireplace is from an old house that was being torn down in England. Derbyshire, I think. The portraits, too. And some of the books."

"What on earth is this place?" I ask.

"Cumbria," she answers. "It's a project."

A *project*. Of course it is. "How long is it running for?"

"Just through New Years," she says. "So you're one of the lucky few."

"I heard about it through a friend at work," Mason supplies. "Somehow I knew it was perfect for a post ice-skating lunch."

"And it's unique," I say, as we settle into our round-backed wooden chairs. "Something you'd only find in New York, right?"

"Or in Epcot," Mason jokes. "But yes. Of course, this is an only in New York thing. This is usually a first-floor retail space in an apartment block. But right now it's an English library where we're about to eat a roast dinner."

"Oh my gosh, seriously? With Yorkshire puddings and everything?"

"I'll slip you an extra," the woman says, and she heads off to the kitchen.

"This is crazy," I tell Mason. "But I love it. I thought you said you weren't buying any places out for lunch?"

"I didn't. Someone else might come and sit at the other table. Or not. It's hard to know how many bookings they get, especially on a weekday."

I raise my glass to him. "Well, you've done it. I'm already more impressed with the city than I have been in several years. You've made me a laughingstock on ice—"

"A *comedy star* on ice," he corrects me.

"And now you've brought me to a genuine English library to eat Yorkshire puddings, one of my *favorite* foods—"

"There will be roast beef also, and roasted potatoes I assume, and some kind of vegetable..."

"Is there a dessert?"

"I think they call it pudding, so I'm anxious to see what that turns out to be."

We smile at each other.

"You know," I say, "I think that Abel is going to move to Brooklyn. And I think he's going to make me lease that gallery space in Greenwood Heights, whether I want it or not."

"And how do you feel about that?" Mason's voice is gentle. "About committing to New York City for another year?"

"I don't know," I admit. "At first, I was against it. But—" I stop, because I'm not ready to go that far. I can't exactly just *tell* him that when we're together, I feel safe. That the city doesn't feel so crowded, and the crowds don't feel so malevolent, and the air doesn't seem so thick and poisonous in my lungs. That maybe, just maybe—I could stay?

I don't tell him because it's way too soon to say anything so feeling to him, and also because I don't know if it's altogether true. Can I really stay here? Am I really willing to throw away all the plans I've made, and embrace this place again?

I don't know if that's a lasting feeling, or something which is related to this big-time crush I've got on Mason.

And now you're calling it a crush, my stern voice interjects. *When just a little while ago you were calling it love.*

Moderation, I remind my inner voice. *I thought I was in love with Chase, too.*

But that wasn't real at all. On either side. It was just self-preservation and weird timing. The right gullible, lonely heart at the right time, for Chase. The right handsome face at the right time, for me.

"You know what I think?" Mason asks.

I look at Mason. His face is so beautiful in the candlelight, somehow older and wiser, as if he has become a courtly gentleman here in this transported country library. "Tell me."

"I think you're going to stay," he says. "And I think you're going to see a lot more of me."

Chapter Twenty-Six

FULL OF ENGLISH roast dinner, we stagger out into the yellow afternoon sunlight. The street stretches out in either direction, humans and dogs on the sidewalk and cars roaring past. It all looks like too much for me to contemplate in this stuffed state. I'd like to snap my fingers and teleport to my bed.

"How do the English eat all of that and then go on with their day?" I ask the universe. "I don't even know if I can make it home to take a nap. Mason, please tell me you don't have some huge follow-up surprise now. If you've made plans for us to jump up and down at an indoor trampoline park, this is the moment to cancel."

Mason looks abashed. "I did make plans but they're just for a nice walk."

A walk, I could probably manage. Along with a latte to keep me awake—and warm up whatever hand isn't tucked into Mason's. "Where? In Central Park?"

"No," Mason laughs. "That would make a lot of sense, right? The perfect rom-com walk. But you know Central Park inside and out. So I had to go a little off-book."

"Oh, god. Is it far?"

"It's not, actually."

Kimber pulls up and double-parks so we can hop into the car. Mason and I do our dance again, sliding into the backseat one after another.

She winks at me through the rearview mirror. "Good lunch?"

"The best. Can you just drive on very smooth roads while I sleep it off?"

"I'd love to," she tells me, flicking her gaze to Mason, "but this one is calling the shots today."

"Randalls Island," Mason says. "But stop at the first Starbucks you see."

He gives me a sympathetic glance. "Ordinarily I wouldn't take you to a Starbucks for your only-in-New-York day, but I didn't think to research cafes in the neighborhood. That's my mistake."

Kimber calls back, "Did you forget something? I've been cruising around the 'hood for the past hour. And I've already finished one coffee. I could go for another." She shakes an empty cup at us.

Mason waves his hand. "Drive on, then, good sir."

Kimber takes us down a few cross-streets and onto an avenue —I'm barely hanging on to my eyelids at this point, so I can't say which one—before stopping and double-parking outside a cafe. "Let me get these for you guys," she says. "Mason, it goes on the expense report."

"A latte for me," I say weakly. "Full-fat, two sugars."

Mason gives me an approving look. "Proper dessert coffee," he says. "Kimber, I'd like a—"

"Quad espresso," Kimber finishes. "I know your order, big brother." She shuts the door and skips into the cafe.

I glance out the window. It's a cute place, with a few tables and chairs out front and lace curtains in the windows. The name is stenciled on the windows in a sentimentally curly font. "Cafe Clementine," I read. "I like it. I think. It might be a little cutesy for the neighborhood."

"Gentrification is a tricky thing," Mason says. "On one hand, everyone deserves a nice cafe in their neighborhood. On the other hand, it usually means a raise in rents is following."

Something occurs to me. "Where do you live? I'm guessing in some old, leaky, rent-controlled apartment you lucked into fifteen years ago and now you can never leave because you'd have to pay more than six hundred a month in rent."

He laughs. "Hardly. Although that's the kind of place Detective Patel lives in. She got it off a tip from one of the families she was working a case with."

"No way! I wouldn't have seen that in her."

"It's New York," Mason says with a shrug. "We don't have boundaries when it comes to real estate. Anyway, no, I have a small and relatively unattractive one-bedroom down near Lincoln Center. In one of those big post-war buildings with the narrow windows and the balconies."

"Oh, yikes. I thought only grandmas with lots of Boston ferns lived in those."

"You'd be almost right." Mason grins. "It was convenient at the time—I worked in Times Square for years before I got down to Chelsea—and I've just never been able to deal with the fuss of moving. Plus, it's still convenient. Lincoln Center, Midtown, the Upper West Side—it's all right there. My delivery options are just fine."

"That's one thing about the city," I say thoughtfully. "When we couldn't go out—and then when I was still afraid to go out—there was an awesome variety of food to order in. I was talking to my mom one day in the middle of lockdowns, and she said they'd ordered Denny's for dinner. I actually felt better about being stuck in New York for two whole weeks after that."

"Come on now," Mason says, "there's nothing like a Grand Slam that's been banging around in someone's backseat for half an hour before it gets to you. How could you ever leave home with that kind of dinner on offer?"

I laugh. "Listen, it's not a tiny town, but there aren't many choices there, either. And I think the only locally-run diner there shut down during the pandemic."

The p-word feels lumpy on my tongue, and I realize it's the first time I've let myself say it in a long time. In the thick of it, when things felt like they'd never end, I'd erased it from my vocabulary. Lots of people had done it—online, the jargon became silly replacement words, as if autocorrect had done it for us: people talked about the *panini*, and the *panorama*, and we knew exactly what we were all discussing. We just liked not having to actually say it. We stopped using its title, trying to take away its power.

But now, I don't feel like the word has power over me. Like maybe, at last, I've gotten the best of a three-syllable word.

"Here we are!" Kimber opens Mason's door and hands in the coffees, her face flushed with the warmth from inside the cafe. The paper cups are toasty. "And I got myself a croissant, but I won't eat it until you two are safely out of the car."

"Much appreciated," Mason tells her. "Neither of us will be looking at food for at least the next thirty days."

Kimber raises her eyebrows, looking between us. "Was it bad, or just too much of it?"

"It was the sticky toffee pudding," I explain. "We shouldn't have finished it."

"And yet, I have no regrets," Mason declares.

"Okay, you two," she says. "No throwing up in my car." And she slams the door.

Mason looks at me. "Do you think you can make that promise?"

"I am actually pretty good at not throwing up. It's one of my strengths."

"Thank goodness. Cousin Jamie would kill me if we got anything on the upholstery."

"So would I," Kimber says, snapping her seat-belt.

* * *

Randalls Island is quieter than the city, even with an expressway roaring through the center of it. The slanting afternoon sunlight sifts through the few tenacious leaves left on the trees and paints yellow-and-black patterns on the sidewalks. We walk along the empty paths near the riverbanks, and Mason tells me scary stories about the island's past.

"Insane asylums, infectious disease hospitals: this strip of land in the East River has seen it all, and most of it hasn't been pretty," he says in a ghost-story kind of voice. "But look at her now."

Randalls Island is mostly park-land, with the crumbling brick buildings of its messy past fenced off and forgotten.

There is a little stable along one path, and we pause as the horses walk over to the fence to look at us. I'm charmed by their pricked ears and soft eyes, and rummage in my purse for something to give them.

"I didn't know to bring carrots," Mason says, pulling back a hand as one of the horses attempts an expectant nip.

"Can horses eat Tums?" I ask doubtfully, shaking a travel-size bottle I've extracted from the bottom of my bag. The horses prick their ears at the rattling sound, and one of them leans against the top rail of the fence, his nostrils fluttering with a silent *Yes, we can.*

"I don't know for sure," Mason says dubiously. "But there's a tin of mints. I know for a fact horses can eat mints."

We give the horses a few mints and then suck on some ourselves. As the coolness spills over my tongue, I'm suddenly aware of what a dating ritual this is. When I was in high school, one of my friends slipped me a pack of Trident when I gleefully announced my first date. "Make sure you're always chewing gum," she warned me, "because you never know when a guy will show up and you've got monster garlic breath or something."

Good advice, Christina. You were really looking out for me, then and now.

I know he's going to kiss me, and it reverberates through my skin, the anticipation becoming almost as unbearable as my full stomach was before our walk. So when he finally pauses at a narrow bend in the path, his hand resting on an oak tree leaning over the railings, I'm nearly quivering with nerves, almost ready to just let my knees go out, as if I'm back on the ice in Rockefeller Center.

Will he catch me this time? I'm pretty sure he will. I don't think Mason would ever let me hit the ground.

Still, I manage to make my wobbling legs walk up to him.

He tips up my chin with one finger. "Well?" he asks.

"Well?" I have a fluttering feeling in my stomach. His eyes bore into mine.

"Well, are you ready to give in? Say you love New York? That you never want to leave?"

"What if I did?" I whisper. "Suppose I never left New York. Then what?"

It's a crazy question; my inner voice snorts. I basically just dared him to propose to me.

But Mason doesn't stop smiling. "Then I would do this," he says, and he dips his head, letting his lips find mine.

Then my knees really do buckle, and wouldn't you know? He catches me.

"I didn't expect you to actually pass out," he says a few minutes later.

"Did I not warn you?" I ask. "It's kind of my thing. I have panic attacks and faint."

"I made you panic? Am I that scary?"

"Oh, it wasn't panic," I say. "But the big crazy heart-rate, all that…I guess I am susceptible to it, in general."

"You should have that checked out."

"And go to a doctor? I'd have a panic attack and faint."

Mason laughs and catches my hand in his, swings it. "I could stay out here all evening with you," he says, looking up the wooded path ahead.

"It's sketchy at night," I say. "But isn't that kind of your thing?"

"Yours, too, you rebel. But you're right, I think this is the end of the walk. We'll have to come out for a really long ramble in summer."

In summer, I think. He wants to bring me here seven months from now.

If there's one thing Mason doesn't seem afraid of, it's making long-term plans very quickly.

But then again, why should he be? Our strides match as we turn back in the direction we came. I've been clear from the get-go that I'm looking to settle down, get married. If Mason wants to date me, then it has to be with that destination in mind, too.

"Come to my workshop sometime," Mason says. "That can be our next New York refresher."

"A workshop?" I glance up at him. "How is that related to convincing me to stay?"

"You'll like it," he says. "Trust me."

Chapter Twenty-Seven

MASON'S WOODWORKING SHOP is in Red Hook, a waterside community in Brooklyn that's an odd mix of light industry and luxury apartments. Like a lot of so-called up and coming neighborhoods, I guess. It's a transportation desert, with no subway service and few buses. It's easiest to get there by car, which suits me just fine.

When we step out of the Town Car—it's one of Cousin Jamie's fleet, though not driven by a relative—I'm struck first by the cold wind gusting off the harbor, and second by the quiet streets around us. There is no one else on the block. There is no one on the next block. In either direction. This street is utterly desolate.

Which is a mean thing to say about a wide boulevard which is lined with brick warehouses and commercial buildings, several of which have elaborately colorful signs hanging above their doors. It's not like this neighborhood is a bombed-out nightmare. But the lack of people in a city that is always teeming with life—too much life, most of the time, for my comfort—is certainly alarming at first glance.

I'm standing with my hand on the car door, arrested by the quiet, for longer than I realize. The driver growls something to Mason, and he takes my other hand. "You okay?" he asks gently. "This guy needs to get going."

"Oh, yes." I jolt away from the car as if it's shocked me; I had forgotten I was holding the door. Mason shuts it behind me and taps the roof, and the car pulls away from the curb. Now we're alone. Just us and the seagulls. Oh, and that rat over there. But he's all the way across the street, not bothering anyone. I turn back to Mason. "Is it always this quiet?"

"Not always. We get tourists in the summer, and there are always a few people wandering around because of the Ikea a few blocks away. But it can be pretty calm." Mason looks around, and takes a deep breath. The air is damp and there is woodsmoke on the breeze. "Definitely out there."

The old warehouse before us beckons with arched doorways and a collection of names and signs by the entrance. I notice that his is just a piece of wood with *Reilly* etched into it, but the wood has been lightly stained to bring out its natural colors, and the edges are smooth. I give it a little tap as we walk into the building.

Mason's workshop is a rectangular space, lit by fluorescent bulbs and heavily scented with cedar and pine; I sneeze as soon as we go in. "Need some air?" he asks. "Give me a second."

He crosses to the garage door at the far end and fumbles with a lock for a moment. Then he shoves the door up, and the cold sea air comes rushing in.

I stare at the gray waves lapping against the seawall just outside. "You have a *waterfront* wood shop? How is this for real?"

Mason laughs at my expression. "It's pretty neat, right?"

"Neat! This is a million-dollar view." Well, maybe not million-dollar. The view is facing east, away from Manhattan, so we're looking at the shore of Red Hook angling away to the left, and the warehouses along the water over in Brooklyn proper. Above them the land slopes upward, thickly covered with jumbled row houses and apartment buildings, until it meets a brown thicket of trees along the hilltop. I draw in a breath. "That's Green-Wood Cemetery, isn't it?"

"Yes ma'am."

"Remember when we saw each other there? Over the summer?"

"Every day."

We go through his shop painstakingly. I'm anxious to see his entire creative method, from start to finish, and he's happy to walk me through it. The raw pieces of wood which sit in one corner are slowly coaxed into beautiful new forms. Some are practical, some are more whimsical.

"This is extraordinary," I sigh, picking up a beautiful little figurine of a dolphin cresting a wave. "How on earth did you get all of these details?"

"By hand," Mason says, tracing the froth of the wave with one finger. "It was always going to be a small piece; I got the wood from a cabinet maker and it was half knot—one big chunk that just didn't want to cooperate. I was just carving away at it, sitting over there in the sun, and I saw a dorsal fin rise out of the water. This was the summer the dolphin showed up in the Gowanus Canal, you remember that? And I don't know if this was another dolphin, or just a really big fish, but that's when I knew what this little difficult knot of wood was going to become."

I held it up to the light, looking at the rich, summery colors in the wood. "And all of that's in here now," I say softly. "Like you trapped a little sunshine from that day in this piece." Somewhere deep inside, an old frustration of mine throbs to painful life. I try to push it away; this kind of thing happens sometimes, when I'm confronted with a particularly inspiring piece. It's the memory of the person I'd been once, drawing and sketching and shading, trying so hard to capture the sensations of a big, beautiful world around me. I've always been easily overwhelmed, but not just by crowds. Beauty overwhelms me, too. And my inability to do it justice is why I have chosen to deal with other, more talented people's art.

Instead of my own, the way I'd planned throughout my entire childhood.

Mason is still gazing at the dolphin, but there is a faraway look in his eyes, and I suspect he doesn't see the wooden one he created, but the one he imagined under the waves that day, the dolphin taking a leisurely tour of New York Harbor before heading back out to more wholesome currents. This little statue is a portal for him, taking him back to a beautiful day in the sun. I'm envious of his memory, and grateful he's been able to share it with this carving.

I hand it back to him with a sudden gesture, moving too fast, and the dolphin nearly falls to the floor. I gasp as he rights it, and even though he just smiles and says, "Whoopsy-daisy," I'm embarrassed and find myself back in the open doorway, shivering in the cold wind.

The gray water slaps against the breakwater, and seagulls are floating on the breeze, their wings lazily flapping once or twice every few seconds, as if they see no reason to ever move from this spot. I focus on the birds, on their nonchalance, until I feel Mason's presence behind me. He wraps his arms around me and I can feel his voice rumbling against my back when he says, "Do you want to try and carve something?"

Interest rises in my brain, *yes, yes, yes!*

"I don't, thank you," I say, pushing back on the feeling, on the desire to create that I've learned will only disappoint me. "I'm pretty sure I would cut off a finger."

"I'd guide you. I wouldn't let you lose a finger. I like all of them too much."

"No, it's not for me. Carving is your thing."

He hesitates. "Is everything okay?"

"It's fine!" My voice is too sharp. I take a breath. "It's fine. I'm so appreciative, bringing me all the way down here, showing me your studio..."

"Shop," he corrects. "I'm glad you're—*appreciative.*" There's humor in his voice now. "But I think there's something on your mind."

"There's always something on my mind. That's the annoying thing about me. I never just relax into the moment."

Mason puts his chin on my shoulder. "Oh, I don't know. I can think of a few times I've known you to relax into the moment. We could work on that now, if you want." His lips find my neck, and I can't help but curve into him.

It's true. There are a few things that I can relax into.

By the time we go back inside the shop, the sky is clouding over in that disappointing way winter days tend to do, only giving us half a day of sunshine before pale gray clouds stream in and overtake the blue. The air has a bitter snap to it now, and Mason pulls down the garage door to block the wind. Even with just the fluorescent light overhead, the wood still finds a way to glow. It's impressive, when you consider how bad human skin looks under those artificial bulbs.

I walk along the table where his finished work sits out. There is variety here: a few signs with family names on them, perfect for hanging on a front wall or fence; some small toy cars and airplanes; a few figurines.

"Are all of these spoken for?" I finger a beautiful little toy car. It's an old-fashioned design, deceptively simple, made of geometric shapes that will delight a small child. "Do you work on commission or what?"

"It depends. The cars and toys are usually sold in a shop on Van Brunt. The bigger pieces and the custom ones, they get ordered there, or online. I run a few ads." Mason shrugs. "I just have to sell enough of the big pieces to pay the rent on this place."

I give him an impressed look. "This pays the bills?"

"Well, sure. There's a lot of demand for hand-carved work. Especially if it's made in the city. You know how the artsy types can be here. They want everything to say 'Brooklyn-made' or 'Crafted in New York City,' as if we're better at everything, even carpentry or, I don't know, beekeeping, just because we live in the city doing rural things in an urban way."

"Or wine," I murmur, thinking of Margot and her ill-fated rooftop vineyard. That had been right around here somewhere. "Have you ever thought of replacing your job with this?"

Mason's smile disappears and he rubs a hand along the granite line of his chin, looking pensively at the toys he's coaxed from wood. "Honestly...yes. All the time. But that's just a little over my head. It's amazing enough I can pay for this shop. There's no way I could cover my rent and everything else. It's alright," he adds, shaking his head. "I'm fine with the balance I've got. I have almost twenty years with the force. This will wait for me when I retire someday."

I glance at his hands, wondering if that's true. I've had some artists tell me the same thing over the years, and while yes, there are fortunate artists who only get better at their art as they age, there are others who deal with arthritis and other impediments. Artists who might have spent their most creative years doing work for other people, forgoing their best work as age takes their talents. I'd hate to see that happen to Mason. "You can retire at twenty years, can't you?"

"Yeah, if I want to move out of town and get a security guard job at a grocery store." He's moving the car back and forth on the table now, and I watch the wheels spin perfectly, no hint of hesitation. How does a person create perfect circles out of hard, unyielding wood? "I'm not going to be that guy, though. This is home for me. I'm not moving to some small town in the Poconos. Or the Hudson River valley. So I need to stay longer, get the full pension, keep my investments cooking along."

He isn't looking at me, but I know that line about the Hudson was aimed directly at me. I hadn't brought up moving from the city since he'd started taking me around the city on this fall-back-in-love tour, but I can tell that was a warning shot: if I'm still thinking of leaving, I'd understand good and well that I'd be on my own.

I wish I hadn't brought it up at all. This is always a thorny subject with the artists I work with, this idea of transitioning from hobbyist to full-timer. Some are desperate to do it, and willing to live on ramen to make it happen. Some are already living on ramen, and know there's no earthly way to stretch their dollars any further, but they're still hopeful things could change some day. And some have simply discarded the idea, certain that a safe nine-to-five is the only way to keep the lights on while they sit up late at night, sketching out their demons because they simply cannot stop, because the art is who they are.

I'm not entirely surprised to learn Mason is in the final camp, but I'm a little disappointed, too. He is such a spontaneous, exciting man, filled with so much heart; for a moment, part of me really thought he might have some elaborate escape plan all ready to go, a scheme to get out of the grind and focus on creating these beautiful carvings all day, every day.

But maybe that's not what he wanted, now or ever. Just because I was once willing to sacrifice every hour of every day to my art, doesn't mean everyone has to feel that way. This could be Mason's outlet, a pleasant hobby; it's not an automatic necessity to monetize every talent and risk driving the joy out of it. Some of us are just intense that way; we can't do things for fun.

So I let the conversation fade away. There doesn't seem to be anything else to say on the matter. And when Mason suggests we go up a few blocks to a diner he thinks I'll like, I shrug my coat back on and leave the shop behind me, not even turning to give the glowing wood within a final parting glance.

This is his. Not mine.

The Dolphin and Ship is a cute little diner housed in one of Red Hook's plain brick buildings. Plate glass windows look out on the narrow streets from two sides, and a counter with swiveling stools takes up the other far wall. We're past the lunch rush, but a few people are chatting in booths and at the counter. The place isn't huge, but it's airy, and when the server takes us to a booth in the back, well away from the other diners, I find I can draw breath without a flutter of nerves.

"This is okay?" Mason asks, and I can see his eyes resting on my chest, as if he's measuring how deeply I'm breathing.

"It's perfect," I assure him. "Thank you for asking."

"I have to take care of you," he says with a grin. "You're a special case. Hard as nails on the outside, and soft as pine on the inside."

"Mason Reilly, did you just use a woodworking metaphor to describe me?"

"I *think* it was a woodworking simile."

The server interrupts with an apologetic smile, and promises to bring us waters along with our beers. The menu is filled with comfort food, and I've decided on a grilled cheese sandwich before Mason can even make up his mind. It seems like the perfect meal for a cold outing to this back of beyond little town.

In fact, everything seems perfect. This diner, the pearly light shining through the windows, the mouthwatering aroma of French fries wafting from the kitchen. There's a pie stand on the counter and I can see an icebox pie topped with a towering crown of whipped cream that has me thinking all kinds of big thoughts about dessert. Mason is smiling at me, and I'm about to tell him about the pie, when I notice a newspaper on the seat next to me.

"Oh, what's this?" I pick up the New York Post. The headlines are lurid puns, as usual, but that's not what has caught my eye. It's a photo, buried down in the bottom left corner. It's of Chase.

My heart does an anxious little skip, as if I've been running and I'm just about to run out of oxygen. The line beneath his photo is short and effective: *Art Thief On The Run: Ex-Girlfriends Tell All.*

The paper slips from my fingers as if its scalding to the touch. Ex-girlfriends?

How many women did Chase dupe?

Mason snatches the paper up and I watch his eyes skim the page. His jaw hardens; a muscle twitches in his cheek.

"It just startled me," I say weakly. "His face, right there—it's weird to see a familiar face on the front page of the Post, right? Has that ever happened to you?" And then I remember that Mason's a cop, so of course he sees familiar faces in the Post. All the time.

He tosses the paper onto the seat next to him—out of my reach, I can't help but notice—and takes my cold hands in his. "That paper is like a dog with a bone. They never just let old stories die. It's incredible how they manage to sell copies with last year's news on the cover."

Last year's news. Hard to believe that I could make a total shambles of my life in one summer, and now we were freewheeling towards spring and it was all last year's news. Not even worth lining birdcages with. I lean back and am pathetically happy when the waitress brings our beers. Maybe I'll take one sip and this will all disappear. Not Mason, of course. But Chase. God, I wish Chase would disappear.

The pie eventually gets ordered. I suspect dessert is one of the many inevitable things about Mason. This isn't a problem for me.

I am filled with chocolate cream and peanut butter crust when the car appears outside, sliding easily into an empty spot along the curb. "There's our ride," Mason says, pulling out his wallet. He drops cash on the table, a habit of his I find endearing—who carries cash?—and slides out of the booth. He holds his hand out to me, and I take it. We're all the way to the door when I realize I've left my phone on the table.

"I'll be right back," I say, and hustle back to the booth.

Mason goes outside to make sure the car doesn't leave, and that makes it so simple to fold up the Post and slip it into my purse, so easy that I barely register the movements.

"I've been thinking," Mason says, as the car starts and stops in afternoon traffic. "I would like to do more with the woodworking, but not necessarily for profit. I was trying to think of a way to work with kids, actually. My sister said something about your friend Margot, that she teaches art classes or something?"

I feel an immediate guilt. I insisted that Margot and Mason had nothing in common. And now he had to come out and ask me for the introduction himself. What kind of girlfriend was I?

Okay, we hadn't been dating when that conversation had come up, but surely I could have acted on that at any point in the last few months.

Stop being so selfish, I warn myself. If I'm going to make things work with Mason—despite the difference in our life plans, I still feel like trying is, well inevitable—I have to start thinking of other people again.

"Of course," I say. "I can put you in touch with Margot. She can be a little flighty. You might have noticed that when she ran away from her own wedding—"

"That was a little bit concerning." Mason is grinning at me. "But I am sure she had her reasons."

"So she says." I wonder if I haven't quite forgiven Margot for jumping out of the Settle Down Society, leaving our promises in the mud. I wonder why I'm not angry at Caitlyn for doing the same thing. Somehow, the two circumstances feel different. "I'll talk to her," I say finally. "Something might come up that would be good for you."

Chapter Twenty-Eight

WHEN MARGOT AGREES to bring Mason in on a class she's teaching to high school students in the Bronx, I can hardly believe it. Everything happens so fast with this one; she's like a salmon, shimmying her way up the waterfall while the rest of us are getting beat down at the bottom. "It's a spring theme," she explains, "so we're going to be doing lots of gardening type stuff. I was thinking Mason could show everyone how to make containers, for gardens outside of the school?"

"That's not very, I don't know, artsy," I say doubtfully. "And doesn't Maeve usually do the gardening?"

"Maeve's going to be sitting the spring stuff out," Margot says, widening her eyes dramatically. "But you didn't hear that from me. She wants to tell everyone at once. I just squeezed the truth out of her when she told me she wasn't doing the school programs after all."

For a moment, I forget Mason. "Are you saying Maeve is *expecting?*" I gasp.

Margot smiles. "I'm saying nothing."

The news that one of our closest friends is finally having a child with her husband of five years is like an electric shock. *The first of us,* I think, trying not to feel too jealous. Maeve and Dane live in a pretty two-bedroom already, so I'm guessing the home office will become a nursery. They're ready for the challenges of raising a baby in the city. I feel like I have so far to go before I could be that person.

Could I ever be that person?

The white picket fence and the three bedroom split-plan is starting to seem more like a misty apparition than a definite must in my future.

When I meet Mason to pick up dinner at another of his favorite New York City places, the Halal Guys cart on Seventh Avenue, he reacts to Margot's suggestion with what I'm realizing is characteristic amiability.

"Practical, that's one of the great things about woodworking," he announces as we shuffle forward in the queue for gyros. "You start small, learning about how wood works, what to feel for, how it joins up. And gain an appreciation for what wood can do. It's going to hold soil, grow food. That's pretty exciting, don't you think? I think the kids will love it."

With that kind of enthusiasm, my personal doubts don't stand a chance.

"White sauce and hot sauce?" the Halal Guy asks, squeeze bottles poised above my gyro.

"Yes," I say. "Please."

We settle onto a bench near the bird refuge on the south end of Central Park, having tucked the greasy paper bag of gyros into a backpack to help them stay warm while we walked up the avenue.

"There's nothing like a gyro," Mason says appreciatively, folding back the foil on his pita. "A *city* gyro."

There's nothing I can say to counter that, because he's right. There's simply nothing like a New York City gyro in the world.

So Mason finds the supplies he'll need to build planters and help little hands with the work from his shop, and with a Town Car borrowed from his cousin, I help him schlep the wood and tools across town to the school where Margot's program is taking place. It's a drab, three-story building built in the sixties, an era utterly devoid of imagination in public buildings, and the place depresses me with its mere presence. But there's a broad, sunny courtyard that's locked up for safety, and inside, Margot has already taped out the areas where they'll put their garden boxes. The cracked concrete can only be improved by wooden planters and green growing things.

"What's Margot going to be doing?" I ask, as we stuff Mason's tools into the steel box Margot has arranged for him. "I mean, I thought this was an art class. Not a garden."

"She's doing the mural behind the container gardens. There are always going to be some kids who just won't participate in painting a mural. That's where I come in. The ones who think they're not artistic? I'm going to show them what else their hands can do."

Mason's voice is excited; his face is animated and he's clearly thrilled about the opportunity. I'm happy for him. It seems like Mason might actually have found his calling—helping people become artistic.

If it's a little ironic, considering that I gave up my own artistic ambitions, I try not to dwell on that.

We go out to dinner the night after his first class, and I can immediately tell he's full of beans. The early spring evening is just warm enough to dine outside, with a sweater on standby and a nearby heater blazing, and he's picked a cafe in between our apartments, an Upper West Side stalwart with a long wine list and a short menu. The sidewalks are still busy, the dusk falling on the strip of sky over Columbus, and a slim crescent of moon is sliding down towards the jagged teeth of Midtown.

"It's absolutely gorgeous this evening," I sigh, watching the city bustle around me under the peace of that blue and gold sky. "I love the first sidewalk dinner of the year."

"You see?" Mason asks, his tone almost forceful, startling me. "Everything's going to be fine. You're going to settle right back into city life before you know it."

I make myself laugh a little, although I know where this is going, and I don't want to talk about it. "It's a nice evening," I say. "Let's leave it at that."

"But you're doing so well," Mason says, unwilling to leave it alone. "Tell me you're not still gung-ho on leaving the city, Tracey."

His meaning goes unspoken, but it hovers over us, somewhere between the skyscrapers and that vanishing moon. *Leaving the city means leaving us.*

"I really don't want to talk about that tonight." I smile at him, feeling the anxiety straining my lips. "Please, Mason."

"I'm just saying a few more pushes and you'll be over all your phobias, that's all. And then you won't have to give up everything you've got here." Mason's eyes seek out mine. "I promise if you put your mind to it, you'll be feeling better before you know it."

I flick my gaze away. "Before I know it? I've been struggling with my crowd anxiety for years now. I think we're beyond *before you know it.* This isn't a fake issue I made up, you know."

"Oh, no, no, no, that's not what I was saying." Mason puts down the wine list and leans across the table, putting his hand over mine. "But you know, I think you just needed a little immersion therapy, and someone to push you into it. I think that's what you've always needed—someone to push you into things. You overthink, Tracey." He glances back at the wine list, that incredible male ability to drop a bomb and move on in full display. "I'm leaning towards this Grenache, do you want to do a full bottle?"

I pull back my hand, tension entering my shoulders. "You think I made it all up. I *overthink* things and that's all this is?"

"Of course I don't. I just *said* I don't think you—"

"You think it's all in my head."

He leans forward, his eyes so understanding and kind that I want to smack him. "Well, of course it's in your head. But not in the way you're saying. I *know* you've been dealing with a real issue. All I'm saying is, you needed a little help pushing through it. That's nothing to be ashamed of—"

"I'm not ashamed!" Well, I am now, because that came out *way* too loud and people are looking at me. "I'm not ashamed," I hiss in a more reasonable, fighting-in-public tone. "Things got really bad in the city. You know they did. You were here. I just— I have a right to take longer than some perfect, wonderful people did in getting over all that."

Now he looks confused. "Perfect, wonderful people?"

"People like you," I fire back, "who apparently were able to bounce right back into normal life!"

"Well, now that's hardly fair. You might not recall, but my job requires me to show up every day, so I didn't stay inside my home like you did. I was out there on the street. I guess I was one of those people you were so afraid of." Mason crumples his napkin up and then flattens it again, plucking at the linen.

"Maybe that was better," I say. "Your life went on. Mine *stopped.* I had to close everything up. Find a new way to pay my bills. Completely change my business model. And I had to be alone through all of it. I was *alone,* all the time, for *months!*" There goes my voice again, but it can't be helped. I slap my hand on the table.

A server appears in the doorway, ready to put a stop to my shenanigans. I'm on notice. I've never been kicked out of a restaurant before.

I lower my voice a half-measure. "Maybe you got to keep on living your life, as surreal as it was. But everyone made me feel like I was a selfish, awful being for even wanting to leave my apartment and I was so—*damned*—lonely!"

The tears come, hot and fast, before I can even get out the last word. They're streaming down my face, and now people on the sidewalk are stopping, staring, asking loudly what that man has done.

I squeeze my eyes shut, like it will help me disappear. *If I close my eyes no one can see me.*

Mason is gripping at my hands, and I hear him urgently explaining to a server that I've had a panic attack and I need a glass of water.

Well, it's *not* a panic attack; it's a rage attack—and I'm angry at him for not recognizing this. But then again, I guess he wouldn't tell the server that he's just downplayed my anxieties and trauma and now he's made me cry.

"He's not worth it, honey," a husky voice says in passing, and someone else guffaws.

That's when I realize I need to pull it together. I'm giving too many people too many stories to run with. I'm going to end up in someone's novel, or their essay about leaving New York, or some grad school poem if I'm not careful. *The girl crying at the Cafe Columbus is all of us.*

Well, I'm not.

I'm my own problem, not a generational problem or a geographical problem or a metaphor to be put on display. I'm just a woman who had her heart broken, first by living through history and then by living through a bad breakup, and in a weird, unpleasant way I know that Mason has hit on a kernel of truth.

I love New York City, and I don't want to give her up, even when she makes me crazy.

But I also don't want to feel that level of crazy ever again.

Nothing has been accomplished tonight. The realization almost makes me laugh.

I sniffle and start to dry myself up. Thank goodness for linen napkins. The server has put a glass of water in front of me and I take a sip to show how recovered I am.

"Are you okay?" Mason's face swims before me. He's concerned, he's trying to make sure I'm alright.

He doesn't fully understand, but you know, I should be used to that by now. Most people don't.

"I'm okay," I say.

"Let's order that bottle of wine," Mason suggests, "and then I'll listen while you tell me why I was wrong."

I have to chuckle at that. "No, let's not dwell on it. As long as you *know* you're wrong, I'll accept that. Tell me about your art class, instead. I want to hear all about it."

Mason walks me home, our fingers loosely intertwined as we walk past the brownstones and apartment houses. I feel a new sensation between us tonight, a recognition that the game has shifted into a new dimension. We can fight now. As a couple, I mean—we certainly had our disagreements before we were together. But this is different.

Something about tonight, realizing we have the ability to argue and shout and cry, then bury it all with a bottle of wine and a nice dinner and a retreat to the bedroom, feels comforting to me. This was the next step I never had with Chase; we never went past the silly romantic first stage of dating. And I thought I was going marry him. Why couldn't I see it was all a big game to him?

And like it said in that horrible article in the Post, the one that's still crumpled into the bottom of my purse, Chase was good at romancing women. Knowing I was just one of a string of heartbreaks he'd left across Europe was not exactly comforting. But at the same time, it seemed to close a door for me that had been resisting my efforts before.

It hadn't been real. Any of it. Not for a second. That means something.

Just like this fight with Mason means something. He doesn't have to understand every little thing about me—I get that. All we have to accept is that together, we still have our own selves, our own mysteries, and sometimes, we will still confound one another.

Before he leaves for work the next morning, I make a promise —I'll come and see the garden project, take some pictures of he and Margot for the school journal. And maybe, Mason suggests lightly, maybe also for his personal website. "Just in case it gets bigger than this," he says as casually as possible.

But I can see through his easygoing air. He's already wondering if this is what can get him out of the force, and into a different kind of life. For his sake, I hope it's true.

For my sake, I wonder if I can fit into it.

Chapter Twenty-Nine

"YOU'RE READY TO go?" Mason is in the doorway of my gallery, dressed uncharacteristically casually for a Friday afternoon. He took the day off from work, excited for the official unveiling of the container garden and mural. It's happening just after the school-day ends, with the kids who worked on the project showing off their handiwork to some representatives from the school board, some local journalists, a few podcasters from WNYC's studios who cover the education and community beats, and of course, Margot and Mason, the volunteers who made it all happen.

All spring, Mason has been working shortened hours at the precinct as his excitement over the container garden rose. Some of these kids were real carpenters at heart, he would enthuse to me over dinner that night. "I can see them starting to understand what they can make with their hands, and it's just beautiful," he said last night. "This whole thing…it has changed me, Tracey. I don't even know how to explain it."

I'd smiled at him, genuinely happy for him. But I've already started wondering what he'll do over the coming summer. Margot usually takes on some mural work and does a few more community projects, but her need for a carpenter will be pretty limited.

"I'm ready to go," I say now, giving a little twirl to add body to my skirt. On this warm day at the beginning of May, I'm embracing polka dots and nostalgia, flared skirts and gathered waists, and the idea that anything can happen, even good things.

I haven't been back to the ugly little public school since the weekend when we delivered his tools, and it feels very different now. The heaviness of weathering an entire school year is evident in the playground debris of rubber balls and scattered granola bar wrappers, the cut-out paper flowers and hearts in the schoolroom windows, the droop of a maintenance worker's shoulders as he drags a few trash cans across the concrete yard. There are eyes in all those classrooms, four stories of windows shutting in packed rooms of children. The idea of all those people pressed together, unruly and un-sanitized, plucks at the parts of my brain I've been working so hard to shut down.

I take a step away from Mason, feeling like I can't be too close to any other person. Even him.

A glimmering of knowledge slips through my brain: *this is how it begins.*

I've felt like this before. Not in a long time, but—I know what's coming.

A dozen coping exercises, gifted by therapists over the years, flutter through my consciousness and disappear. *No time for that now,* my survival brain says. *Time to go.*

Mason notices the distance, the way my fingers slip from his, and his eyebrows come together.

"You're here," Margot sings out, walking up the block with a tote bag swinging in one hand. She's wearing a floral wrap dress that makes her look like a perambulating garden, huge roses blooming all over her slight frame. Her hair is platinum blonde and clipped back from her face. She looks like she's twenty-five again. I have to wonder if she's seeing someone she hasn't told us about yet. For a moment the anxiety eases, and I suck in a shuddering breath of air.

Mason touches my hand and I pluck it away. Not yet.

Margot and I hug at the chain-link gate, and then I take a full step backwards to get away from her, which she notes with a lifted brow before she gets down to business, explaining the people Mason will want to talk to, the hands he'll want to shake, the photographers he'll smile for.

"This is a big deal," she says excitedly. "A couple of guys in this district are looking to make the leap into government and they all want to take credit for this school's improvement over the past year, so I'm going to let them duke it out with the publicity machine and just milk it for all it's worth. We could see a bunch of new donations to the art foundation after this."

"That would be amazing," Mason says, getting into the spirit of things. He has a boyish enthusiasm on his face, and I almost feel like I'm seeing my big, handsome, detective boyfriend for the very first time.

That's what art can do, I think, looking at the work they've done. The corner of the school-yard devoted to the mural and container garden is brilliant with color, like Margot herself—swirls of rainbows and birds splash across the formerly dull bricks, while the wooden containers burst with greenery and blooms. There are even butterflies—real ones—floating idly above the blossoms. I'd love to walk through that garden, I think, and then a bell rings and like a sitcom from the nineties, children burst from the building.

It's just a recess period, but the chaos is overwhelming. I take another step back, until I'm teetering on the curb, feeling my heartbeat fluttering in my throat. I don't know what has set my anxiety off so badly—it's just one of those days, I guess—but the sheer volume of screaming, leaping, jostling children is giving me those first trembling indicators of an incoming panic attack.

The knowledge that there are even more children inside the building presses down on me like a cement block on my chest. What must it be like, to be in those halls between classes, with so many people pressing against one another? What must it be like in the classrooms, breathing on each other, sharing each other's air, for hours on end? I feel a tremble jostle my muscles just thinking about it, a knot rising in my throat, a cough somewhere in my lungs, waiting to be let out.

This is worse, I think suddenly. *I am worse.*

I've spent an entire spring reveling in the city, but now, people—everywhere—too many people—

I step down the curb, and as Mason reaches for me, I slip behind him. I can't go in there.

"Tracey?" he says, turning. His chest is too close to my chin. I step back again, into the street, between two parked cars. A truck blows past, and Mason's eyes widen with alarm. He reaches for me. I watch his hand come towards me but there's a film forming between us, a blur to my vision, and I take one more step backwards.

"Tracey, honey, stay out of the street."

"It's okay," Margot says, her voice low as if I'm a feral creature, cornered in the subway. "Tracey? Blink your eyes, honey."

The children scream and bellow and hurtle around the school-yard. *So. Many.*

It's not safe here. I can't be here. And if Mason and Margot don't feel the same, well, then, I'm going to have to leave them.

I turn on my heel and run, right up the row of parked cars along the street, grateful I wore flats today so that I can escape myself.

Chapter Thirty

MY EYES OPEN to a bright room, and for a moment I don't know where I am. I take a quick, deep breath, and then it comes back to me. I'm in Cold Stream, and this is my house.

It's not a very big house, but it still feels too big to me. A living room, a den, a kitchen, a dining room, two bedrooms. Why so much space, for one person? I wish I had less, a close and cozy four-hundred square feet would do me just fine. But this was the smallest house I could find at the time. Maybe I could have waited, but I was in a rush. From the moment I left Mason and Margot at that schoolyard, I was in a rush. Life was a blur, the big panic I'd been waiting for finally descending.

This is what I was trying to avoid, I'd thought as I pressed ignore on their calls, as I let their texts go unread, as I threw my books into boxes and put in a furious call to my real estate agent, telling her it was go-time. Go, go *go.*

Now, six weeks after my personal panic attack that broke my life in two, I have slowed down, but now there is nothing to slow down for. I struggle to fill the hours. There are so many of them. I walk slowly into the kitchen, I slowly make a pot of coffee, I slowly play with the old radio antenna, trying to convince it to bring in WNYC. It feels wrong to listen to the Capital Region radio station. I don't understand the news about places like Albany and Troy. I can't understand the traffic reports—where are these places, why are people in such a rush to get to them?

I only understand the day is beginning properly when I hear a familiar voice say, "It's seventy-seven degrees in Manhattan, good morning, you're listening to Morning Edition."

I'm an inconvertible, bone-deep New Yorker. But I had to leave to find this truth out.

I figured it out too late, though, so I'm trying to assimilate to this new world I wanted so badly, even if it doesn't suit me at all.

The coffeemaker beeps at me and I settle down on the sofa with a steaming cup. The radio's voice follows me into the living room, and I flip through some nonsense on my phone, waiting until I've woken up properly to dig into the stuff I have to do today, the stuff I don't want to see.

My thumb pauses its scrolling to read a social media post from Margot. *Another splendiferous day of creating with the best kids in New York!* A picture of her smiling from the schoolyard —a different one from the one I ran away from in early June, leaving behind my life like a crazed person.

This is an elementary school in lower Manhattan, one of those old brick ones that looks so respectable and beautiful. She's holding up a paintbrush, and some grinning elementary school kids are holding up paint cans. Another mural for Margot. I wonder where Mason is, and if his plans to change his life have panned out for him. Or if he's still solving cases in deepest darkest Chelsea and wondering when he'll be able to retire.

And with who.

A stab of pain follows that thought, and I try to push it away. It's my daily rule, my constant companion: *Don't think about Mason. Don't think about any of it. The only way out from this is forward.*

Then there's a sharp knock at the door, and I get up, brow furrowed. I can't remember anything I might have ordered online, but that's not always a real indicator of anything...I sometimes wake up in the middle of the night and stress-buy. Two weeks ago, after a particularly bad night, I opened the front door to find a cutting-edge juicer, so shiny and silver that it makes my entire kitchen look like a shabby, dark cave.

I didn't have anything in the house to juice, and I haven't yet bought anything that looks like it might make good juice. I'm actually not even a fruit person and the idea of drinking vegetables makes me squirm. So the presence of the juicer in my house is more of a discomfort than a pleasure, and yet there it sits, a reminder that sometimes I simply can't control my own impulses. And that my unhappiness is entirely my own doing. I didn't have to leave, and I don't have to buy things in the middle of the night.

And yet I had no way of stopping myself from doing either of those things, so what difference does self-awareness make when you're dealing with a total lack of control?

But I really have to stop myself from doing this. Money is tight. In the end, it was the elephant on my wall that got me out of Manhattan—that Pocchiano I'd been hanging onto for some stupid reason, one of the only pieces left in New York once Chase had absconded with the others. He was easy to sell. I called up a few dealers who had been salivating over it for months without feeling any pressing need to buy, I escalated tensions and ran an impromptu bidding war, and I walked away with enough in cash to buy this cottage above the fashionable part of the Hudson River valley.

There wasn't anything after that. I've been living on the proceeds ever since.

The Chelsea gallery is shuttered while I wait for the lease to run out. My apartment lease was easy to break; I was paying half the market rate, if that, since I'd lived there for so long. Giving up a rent-stabilized apartment is the final nail in any New York coffin. I can't even afford to go back.

And now, at the third rap of knuckles on my door, I get up to see who is out there with my nerves twitching beneath my skin —what if it's a delivery of something *really* expensive, that I can't return? Another mistake in a cardboard box?

But there isn't a box on my porch. There's a woman, in her later middle age, with a pinched, nervous face and a familiar look around her eyes and nose.

"Tracey Adams?" she asks me.

"Yes?" I tug my robe a little tighter, conscious of what a disheveled mess I am. I don't wake up pretty. Mason never noticed, or never minded. Chase teased me about it.

"I'm sorry to bother you so early," she says.

It's nine thirty. I should probably be dressed, wearing a bra, by now.

"But, I'm Chase Hugh's mother," the woman says, "and I thought we had some things to talk about."

For a long, awful moment I feel the same way I did in the schoolyard that day—like the world is plunging towards me and there's no one who can save me, no one who can stand up for me. I've wondered, since that day, why I didn't believe Mason could protect me. He'd made it clear, over and over again, that he would be perfectly willing to act as my knight in shining armor, if only it meant he could squire me around New York City without having to worry that I'd disappear. And then, in the moment when it truly counted, I didn't believe it. I just left.

I haven't spoken more than a few sentences to him since, either. I made it a very clean break. It was horrible, and it didn't heal, but at least I tried. I tried to make it easier than the break between Chase and me, for sure.

"I don't think we have anything to talk about," I tell this woman. His *mother.* How could Chase have a mother?

Somehow who raised this psychopath? "I broke up with Chase over a year ago. I've put it in the past."

Broke up with Chase. What a hilarious way to put it.

"It was *only* a year ago," she protests. "This is July."

I raise my brows. "July? Really?" How could it be summer already? That meant I left New York almost two months ago. A lifetime, in city terms. "But close enough. I helped the police, I testified, I did everything I was supposed to do. Chase isn't my problem anymore." I start to push the door closed.

She holds up a hand. "I'm sorry to ask you this—but can you honestly say you're just *over* everything that happened? Because I've talked to some of the other women, and they're not."

Those women from the New York Post. We should have formed a support group and healed each other, but on the other hand, which one of us would have been that open? Which of us would have gotten over the embarrassment of being duped by the same man long enough to call the other women in the article? That's not the New Yorker way. We put our feelings in the basement and we lock the door, because there's no time to deal with them, anyway.

On the other hand, that's probably how I ended up in Cold Stream, miserable and alone.

But I don't give in. "What good will talking about that with you do me? You're his mother, you probably came here to defend him—"

"Nothing of the sort," she says, her eyes flashing. "He broke my heart. I just figure he broke yours, too."

Chapter Thirty-One

SHE WAITS IN the living room, sipping coffee, while I put on clothes and make myself presentable. When I come back out, I marvel at how calm she is, sitting on my second-hand sofa like a queen. There's no sign in her demeanor that she's visiting the ex-fiancé of her criminal son. Although I guess I was a fake fiancé. Ours was probably an engagement of convenience—the convenience being access to my gallery. But still, how do you visit a wronged woman and admit that yes, you've sired a monster? A beautiful, smooth-talking monster?

The woman has guts, I'll give her that.

I throw myself down in the easy chair, the one with a view out into the neighbor's overgrown backyard—hardly the inspiring view of the Hudson I had back in my old apartment—and wave my hand. "Well, let's get this started."

"I'm Sarah," she says.

"And I'm Tracey."

"What made you leave New York, Tracey?"

I blink at her for a moment. It's an odd question.

"I was always going to leave New York," I say finally. "That was how this happened, how it all started—Chase and I were both using a dating app specifically for people who wanted to get married. I wanted to settle down with a nice guy in the suburbs. Keep running my gallery in tourist season and online. So I got on the app and there he was. Why does it matter?"

She shrugs. "It's a big change. I decided to look you up, and I was surprised when I saw your address. So close to where I live, out of the blue. I didn't know if Chase was responsible. And if there was something I could do to...help."

She said it like leaving New York was a terminal illness. Well, Mason seemed to feel the same way. And judging by my radio-listening habits, so do I.

But she certainly can't help me.

"Chase slowed down my move out of the city. We were buying a house—did you know that? South of here, more convenient to the city for summer tourists. We had a mortgage application in and everything."

"I didn't know that." She pauses, casting her eyes down for a moment. But when she looks back up, they're more sure than ever. "I'm sorry."

"It wasn't you that did it," I say. "Honestly, though, I don't see how this is going to help me."

"I'll just say my piece and get out of your hair, okay?" Sarah watches me for a moment, waiting for permission.

I nod.

"Here's the thing. I just want to tell you...you're not alone. And everyone else I've talked to has told me the same thing: Chase has affected their ability to trust. I have to tell you, he did the same thing to me. I find it really hard to believe anyone, ever, means what they're saying. He lied to me for years, and he did it with a smile on his face. The sweetest smile—" and for a moment she falters, her fingers going to her face, pressing against her brows. Then she swallows hard and gathers herself. "I know that Chase can make a person feel like they're the only person in the world. And I know how much it hurts to find out that wasn't true."

I'm taken aback. It was awful for me, yes, but for his own *mother?* I never realized how brutal it could be to discover your sweet, charming son was a liar and a thief the whole time. "Did he steal from you?" I ask, my voice rasping.

"Only my future," she says, shrugging. "The future I had planned out with grandchildren and visits to Disney World, maybe a summer house at a lake, a sweet daughter-in-law to talk with as I got older. I harass my daughter Amy to get married all the time now, to hurry up and get me some grandbabies." She forces a smile. "I lost the life I wanted. Now, I just want you to know that you're still young enough to get yours. I don't want you to feel alone. I just—I wanted to tell you that there are other people out there that Chase hurt, and we're all going to try as hard as we can to get through this. And you can talk to them if you want." She begins to fish in her purse.

"I don't want a list of his ex-girlfriends, if that's what you're offering."

"No." She subsides, looks at the floor again. "Of course not. Some of them did want to talk to each other, but I think it was different for you. They were—he didn't push things as far with them."

"I know," I say. "I read the paper." The Post, that I'd finally thrown out when I was packing up my apartment, had talked to five of Chase's ex-girlfriends. *Five.* He'd tricked all of them out of something: money, inheritances, artwork. But I was the only one he'd proposed to. For a while, I'd wondered if that made me special. I wondered if it made our love real. But of course, I knew it hadn't been anything of the sort. I'd just had the Pocchiano collection. And some other work worth stealing. He'd figured out how to get to me on the dating app that was meant for engagements.

There was nothing else. Nothing deeper. Just fraud.

"I can't trust anyone," I hear myself saying. "I trusted him, and it ended in the most insane way possible. I believed him and I loved him, and now I have nothing."

She glances around. "You have this house," she ventures.

"I don't want this house." As soon as I say it, I know it's true. "I had clawed my way back. I had a boyfriend who loved me. He was helping me. I was getting over all this mania about leaving New York—" I ignore her quizzical look, there are things she doesn't need to know— "and then I fell apart and threw it all away and now I have this *house,* this stupid house in the middle of nowhere, because I didn't believe in Mason! And that's because of Chase," I realize, plowing ahead, "that's all Chase. I would have been fine if I'd never met him, if I'd just met Mason with none of this nonsense in the middle. But Chase ruined it. I'm never going to fix this. Mason is gone, my apartment is gone, my gallery is gone—"

My own art is gone, the last and best part of me, abandoned years ago, like a child I didn't want and refused to raise, and now everything I've filled up my empty world with is gone, too.

There is nothing left.

I put my head down on the armrest of the chair and sob. It's all *gone.* And no stress-shopping is going to change that. I lost everything. Again and again and again.

I feel her hand on my back, the soft pats of a mother. The whispered reassurances. And she stays until I've cried it all out, holding me as if I'm her own child.

"You have to call him," Sarah says later—much later. I'll bet she never planned on staying this long. "Mason. You have to talk to him."

We've switched from coffee to tea—more soothing to the stomach as well as the soul, she says—and the sun has climbed towards noon. A soft breeze is blowing through the open windows. Every so often, a car rattles past on the road. Down the street, a lawnmower is growling away. They are suburban sounds, more annoying than city sounds, which are a symphony of never-ending bangs and rattles. I sleep poorly here, easily startled by loud cars or backfires. It reminds me of the silence of the city during the lockdown days, and I can't understand how I ever thought I yearned for that empty quiet.

"I can't call him," I snort. "I left him without warning six weeks ago. When he finally got through to me, I told him I was leaving the city and we were better off not talking. What on earth would he think if I called him now? He's probably got another girlfriend." A little throb of jealousy pulses through me, followed by a jolt of fear that stabs directly into my heart. "He's probably with Margot."

"Absolutely not," Sarah insists. I've told her all about Margot, and Caitlyn, and the Settle Down Society. In the past two hours my entire adult life has come pouring out, and she has absorbed it all beautifully—like the mother-in-law she might have been. "Margot is your best friend. There's no way she'd even see Mason in that light."

"That's not how love works," I insist, but Sarah shakes her head at me.

"You can't just assign love between two people. You and Mason are in love. That's not going to change. Not because of a few weeks apart. Not because you had a breakdown and ran away. It's going to take longer than that to kill what's between you. And if I had to guess, even then, it would never really be dead."

"How do you know that?"

"Because I've heard your story," she says. "And because I see the way you look when you talk about him. He's your soulmate, Tracey. You're going to have to call him."

"I'll have to build up to it, write down a script or something."

"No." She holds out my phone. "Right now. Go on the front porch and call your man."

I nod, suddenly unable to fight her. I'm going to do it. I take the phone and go outside, shutting the front door behind me. I pull up his number—of course it's still in my phone, how could I ever delete it? And I wait.

"Hello? Is that Tracey?"

It's Margot. I look down at the phone screen in a panic—maybe I called the wrong number, their names are right next to each other's, after all—but no. It's Mason's number. And Margot's voice.

"Tracey? Hey, listen, I can explain—"

The three worst words in the English language. I end the call, jamming my finger down on the red button until it slips from my hand and clatters onto the porch floor.

"Tracey?" Sarah's voice is at the window. "Is everything okay?"

I shake my head. "Margot answered," I say, my words dropping like lead weights. "He's with her."

Sarah opens the door immediately. Her face has changed; she's finally given up that veneer of unflappable certainty. Instead, its ravaged with sadness. She opens her arms. "Oh, my poor girl," she says. "Come here."

I fall into her hug, and I don't realize until she's gone that six weeks ago, I couldn't possibly have hugged a stranger.

Chapter Thirty-Two

I'VE HAD MY heart broken once before—and I don't mean just by Chase, either. Back in the summer before art school, when my boyfriend Niles broke up with me, and boy was that a doozy. Talk about a ghosting—he went from a hundred to zero overnight, as if the distance between our two colleges was between the moon and Mars. The kind of breakup that takes months to get over. The kind of breakup that you're still thinking about a few years later. I mean, the fact that I'm thinking about it right now, close to fifteen years after the fact, tells you how deeply scarred it left me.

The only way I got through Niles' abandonment was through my art. I painted, I sketched, I even tried my hand at pottery (not great). I spent a summer filling up my childhood bedroom with my own art, and even today I know much of it is still there, waiting for me when I come home for Christmas or Thanksgiving.

And so, all these years later, it's what I decide to try again. Art, my first true love, and the one I abandoned because I know I'm no Picasso, I'm no Pocchiano, and why bother playing at what others have already mastered, right?

So silly of me. Mason's woodworking shop, his quiet pleasure in a hobby he'd been gaining skill at over the years, stirred up something in me. And now, I think, I am going to pursue that feeling again.

I haven't really sketched anything in a decade, but I spend a little bit of my dwindling funds on a sketchpad and some of my favorite pencils, a package of kneadable erasers and a sharpener. The cheapest kind of pencil sharpener, it turns out, are the metal school ones that you install on a wall, so I add a pencil sharpener to my kitchen wall. It's the first thing I've done in this house that makes me happy, the first thing I've added which seems to have an aesthetic all its own.

I take the sketchpad all over the place, to the nearby park, to the old cemetery with its graves dating back to before the Revolutionary War, to tourist-ready towns with sparkling white churches and cannons on their village greens. I get addicted quickly; I find myself sketching birds from pictures on my phone late into the night, with the television talking to itself on the other side of the room. I don't waste a lot of time guessing what I'd like to draw. I already know what I want to recreate— my days with Mason. My shot at true happiness. I gave him up, and Margot took him, and I have to live with that. But there won't be another Mason.

So, I try to find the moments that he talked about, when the artwork seems to leap from the scene, and all I have to do is find a way to capture it. That means always being ready to go, a sketchbook and pencil on hand. I develop a blister on the top knuckle of my ring finger from constantly wielding a pencil. I bandage it up and wince through the pain until it heals and a callous develops.

One day, Sarah drops by with a flyer. "The town fair is looking for artists! You should sign up."

"Oh, it's far too late for that," I say, without looking at the dates. She's barking up the wrong tree if she thinks I'm going to exhibit my work.

"No, they still have spots open, see?" She points to the flyer. "Sell your sketches! It's a start."

"My sketches are way too rough."

"People love that. Come on, you used to sell absolute nonsense. People bought it. Tell me they wouldn't love these." She picks up one of my full sketch pads, flips through it, and holds up a sketch of a robin. "This is gorgeous, Tracey. Trust me on that."

It's barely a picture to me, but as the day goes on, I keep looking at that bird, and eventually I start to see her point. There aren't many lines on the page, but the ones that are there all express the essence of the moment: a robin alighting on a branch, the delicate moment when his weight rests on the thin sliver of wood, his wings folding against his sides as he trusts the perch he's found for himself. It really is no different from guessing if the Pocchiano subject is a lemur or a raccoon or an elephant.

So I do it. I pull together my favorite sketches and mount them. I send in my entry. And on a sultry sunny day in late July, I make my debut as an artist.

I don't know anyone at the fair.

It's crazy, right? I've lived here for months and I haven't met anyone, really. Neither butcher nor baker nor candlestick maker, and I knew *all* of those people in my old neighborhood. Well, two out of three.

I really thought that when I moved to the country, I'd have a favorite bakery, and I'd hoped for a *second*-favorite bakery, too, plus a local market where I could chat with the grocer about vegetables and life. I had these things on the Upper West Side, but surely they were better in the country.

Instead, everyone in this town shops at a brightly-lit Hannaford for everything—bread, veggies, batteries. No one speaks about vegetables or life.

It's not the village life I once imagined for myself. I already had my village life. I just didn't know it at the time.

So I stand in my small white tent, which also contains two folding tables presenting my mounted sketches, and I watch a town of strangers pass me by. Occasionally a young mother pushing a stroller will pause outside, and make interested noises at my bird sketches, and once a woman draped in shawls and crystals, sweating in the July heat, comes in and buys two of my tree studies. I hope she'll talk to me about what she sees in the artwork, where she'll hang it, how she envisions it enriching her life. These are the kind of conversations which were part of the art experience in my gallery. But she just gives me a closed-off sort of smile as I run her credit card, and then she slips the sketches into her canvas bag and leaves without a word.

It's the weirdest transaction I've ever been part of.

All the silence in my tent gives me plenty of time to think. And wow, do I *not* need more time to think! Talk about an abundance of unwanted time!

When Sarah stops by around one o'clock with a couple of salads in a plastic bag, I'm almost pathetically grateful for her voice. Anything to replace the one chattering nonstop in my head, telling me about all my mistakes.

"You sold the trees," she observes, passing me a plastic-domed salad container. "That's pretty good. I liked those trees."

"I did too. I'm not sure the woman who bought them did, though."

"Huh?" Sarah pops open her salad.

"She didn't say anything to me about them. Would barely look me in the eye."

"People up here can be closed off," Sarah says airily. "It's the New England way. Anyway, it's a good start."

"Sure. A good start." I have been standing here for four hours and I have sold two sketches. "I'm kind of afraid that's the end of it, though. There's just not a ton of interest in buying pencil art, which I understand. It's not a big market."

"Well, if that's all you sell, at least you know you created something," Sarah says.

"I guess it is nice that someone gave me money for something I drew."

"And it's only the beginning," Sarah assures me. She is wearing the caring expression a mother gives a disappointed child.

It's not the first time I've suspected I'm replacing Chase for her. If I'm helping her heal after her disaster of a son, I guess I've done something with my time in Cold Stream.

We settle down to our salads. They're from the Hannaford, and the lettuce is mostly tasteless. I'm thinking about the salads I used to get from this little deli close to my old apartment, the way they had the most perfect olives, and bitter greens mixed with sweet, and this house-made dressing that just sparkled on the tongue. Every bite was invigorating.

Invigorating. The word sits squarely in the center of my consciousness, defining everything I've lost. That's what I've been missing for so long. The only thing in my present life that comes close to the way certain elements of the city could make feel is my drawing.

Before I began to fill my days with drawing, though, I still had so many other things that enlivened and enriched my life. That salad. My favorite French bakery. Conversation with Abel. Wine nights with Margot and Caitlyn.

Anything, anything at all, with Mason.

I close my eyes against the weight of the memory of him.

And when I open them, there he is.

I drop my salad.

Or what's left of it—thank goodness I am mostly finished the awful thing, and there is just some iceberg lettuce and pools of dressing remaining in the bottom of the tub. It falls at my feet and I let it sit there, draining into the trodden grass, because I'm already standing up to greet Mason. Behind me, I sense Sarah retreating behind a table, trying to stay out of the way of a potential sale.

"What are you doing here?" I blurt, and then I wince, because it's not what I wanted to say at all.

"I'm here with Kimber," Mason says, staring at me with astonishment. "We rented a house near here for the month—the kids needed somewhere besides Prospect Park to run off steam, you know how it is..." He trails off, like he senses he's talking nonsense. Like neither of us need to waste any time on such minor explanations. They aren't the words which need to be said.

There isn't enough air in my lungs for the words which need to be said.

"Sure," I say. "Makes sense."

Mason takes a short breath, as if he's finding the humid air hard to breathe, too.

We are just staring at each other now. There's no telling what he's thinking. His gaze shifts, falls on the drawings. "I see you're back into the business," he says, picking up one of the wrapped sketches. It's a robin resting by a stream, an image I captured in this very park about a month ago. One of my favorites, so much so that I sprang to have prints made so I could keep the original. "I like this. A local artist, I guess?"

"It's hers," Sarah says proudly. "All of this work is by Tracey."

Mason looks at her as if he's seeing her for the first time. Then he blinks. "I know you. You're Chase's mother."

She tilts her head. "Do I know—oh! You're Detective Reilly!"

"Ex-detective," he corrects her. "Or almost. I filed my retirement paperwork about a week ago. In a few months, I'll be a free man."

I gasp.

Sarah gives him a pleasant smile. "Congratulations. You look too young to retire, if you don't mind my saying so."

"I started right out of college," Mason says. "I was too young then, if we're being honest. Now, I feel like I'm just getting started with life."

He looks back at me. "I hope you feel the same."

Sensation floods every corner of my body, tingling in my toes and my fingers and the tip of my nose. I start to open my mouth, still not sure how to say any of it.

And to my horror, Mason puts down the sketch and turns away.

Behind me, Sarah is making an odd noise, as if seeing Mason has brought back feelings she wasn't prepared to deal with. I want to run after Mason, but something holds me back. Sarah has given me so much over the past few months. I can't just abandon her. So I turn and give her a hug, and she lays her head on my shoulder and sighs a long, shuddering sigh.

"Sometimes I think I should just leave and start over again somewhere far, far away," she whispers. "I'm tired of these ghosts haunting me."

I wonder if I'm a ghost. Maybe I'm a friendly ghost to Sarah, because I'm a project, a substitute child.

But children grow up and go away. She can't be planning on watching over me forever. So I stand back and hold her at arm's length. "You've talked to me about Florida," I say. "Why don't you sell your house here and move down there? Get something near the water, enjoy a warm winter for a change? What's keeping you here, after all?"

She gives me a watery smile, and I know that "You" is on the tip of her tongue, so I give her a quick squeeze on the shoulders before I step away. "Can you watch my tent?" I call over my shoulder. "Just this one time. I need to talk to Mason."

"Of course," Sarah says, and she waits in the tent as I dive into the crowd on the village green.

It takes me nearly twenty minutes to find him, and by then I'm absolutely panting with fear that he's gone forever. The heat is soaking through my blouse and reddening my skin, the flush before a burn, but that doesn't matter if I can just find him—stop him—*explain.*

And then what?

Hope. It's not the emotion I'm best at, but it's going to get a workout today.

The crowds thin near the icy little brook that cuts through one corner of the park, and as I run across the downy grass growing near its banks, I finally spot him. He's alone, watching the water as it chuckles cheerfully over the stones. I slow as I realize he's standing just where I sketched the picture of the robin. What are the chances?

He hears my footsteps, or else some sixth sense tells him to turn around.

"Mason," I say, my heart in my throat.

"Tracey," he replies. "What are you doing here?"

"What are *you* doing here?"

Mason tilts his head at me. "Margot saw from someone that you had artwork here today. She texted me. She said you were near where we were staying."

"How is Margot?" I ask. "She didn't come with you?" The words cling to my throat like burrs.

He shakes his head, brows coming together. "Why would Margot come with me upstate?"

The confusion is real, painted across his face, and my heart does a strange sideways motion that surely can't be healthy. I'll get that checked out later. For now, he's not with Margot. I must have misunderstood, that day she answered the phone. Jumped to conclusions. They were probably just working on some school project and I was in no state to be reasonable, or rational—

"Are you okay? Do you need some water?"

I take a deep breath and force myself to start over. "I live here," I say. "I bought a little house."

"Do you like it? Is it what you wanted?"

"I hate it," I say. "I can't sleep at night. It's too quiet. When there's one single noise, one car that goes by, it wakes me up."

Mason smiles slowly, a smile that starts at his eyes and works its way down to his mouth, and something inside me seems to spark back to life. Something I didn't even know had gone out. "What else do you hate about it?" he asks, folding his arms over his chest, the firm but fair detective who will get his answer before he moves on.

"I hate the local grocery store," I tell him fiercely. "I don't know anyone who works there and the baked goods are like cardboard. The croissants are *chewy,* for god's sake. Who wants a chewy croissant? You could eat them in bed, that's how *not* flakey they are."

"That's deeply disturbing." Mason has taken a few steps closer. He looms above me, and I remember the night we met, at the bar in the Lower East Side, the way I had to tip my head back to look him in the eye. "Tell me more. Do you hate the neighbors?"

"I do hate my neighbors," I tell him. "They mow the grass at eight o'clock on Sunday mornings. Except for the one who doesn't mow his grass, ever, and the place looks abandoned. It's bad for my property value, and I hate that I know that."

"And the driving everywhere, you must hate that." He's just a foot away from me. So close, I can nearly touch him. I have to pick up my chin to see into his eyes, but the spark of laughter in them keeps me going.

"I hate the driving," I say. "I hate that there are no sidewalks. I hate having to schlep around in a car every time I want a gallon of milk. I hate gallons of milk! I want to buy a nice little glass bottle of that grass-fed milk from Clover Farms, you know, the ones they sell at the cheese shop on Sixty-ninth Street…"

"I love that cheese shop," Mason says. He's looking down at me. Except for the sunlight and the water dancing over the rocks in the background, this feels like the night I met him. Like we've stepped back in time a year, to the summer I was determined to settle down, and he appeared in my life at exactly the right moment—if only I'd been willing to see it. And kept appearing, throughout that summer and all the seasons after.

I see it now, you gods of love, you old universe of fate and destiny. I *see* him now.

"Tell me what you love," I say, breathless.

The creases beside his eyes deepen. "I love the croissants from the French place by your old apartment. I love the grocery on Columbus where I used to stop on the way over. Please tell me you didn't give up that apartment? Tell me you sublet it."

"I gave it up," I sigh.

"Because you're never coming back to the city?" Mason whispers, the huskiness betraying that it's exactly what he's afraid to hear. And I think, *this isn't over.*

And I think, *he came for me.*

And I think, *yes.*

"No," I murmur. "Because I'm an idiot who *thought* she would never come back to the city."

His hands are on my shoulders now, his thumbs are resting gently on my neck, nearly touching my ears. I'm almost choking with the need to pull closer, and yet I wait, my eyes wary on his.

He could still pull out of this—he could still jump back and say, "Too bad, you should have kept it," and go back to Kimber and Briar and Sebastian, and Margot for heaven's sake, and leave me here to rot with my own stupidity and lack of trust—

"Where is your head right now?" Mason asks gently. "You're a million miles away."

Chase broke my ability to trust. Not Mason.

And Mason is the only way back. Right now, with one step into the void, I can put everything behind me.

"I don't want my old apartment," I tell him. "It was lonesome, and I was tired of being sad there. I want a new apartment." Swallow, breathe, swallow. "I want to find an apartment with you."

The smile that spreads across Mason's face is like fireworks.

Chapter Thirty-Three

I SPEND THE rest of the season shuttling between my house and the summer rental, where Kimber makes iced tea for us while Sebastian and Briar play like wild creatures in the backyard or squabble over Rock Band in the living room. Mason comes up for long weekends, and after all, he points out, there's no point in rushing back to Manhattan in the middle of summer.

And he's right about that. The things I miss about my city do not include the summer smells of garbage or that persistent odor of urine around the entrances to Central Park. Look, the city's not perfect, okay? That's probably why so many terrible decisions to leave are centered sometime around midsummer.

But in late August, after a delightful few weeks spent chasing the kids around the woods, seeking out hidden places to sketch, and sneaking away for a little alone time (never easy with children of Briar and Sebastian's wit and voraciousness), it is time to go back and prove what we're made of.

Together, and apart.

First off, a place to live. It's high time Mason gave up that place near Lincoln Center, even if it is convenient to live near shows and food and everything else. And he knows it.

"We can find convenience that has a little charm, can't we?" I ask hopefully, and that sparks off a month-long search that eats the rest of the summer before we even realize what's happening.

In the end, it's Abel who finds us our perfect neighborhood. And because Abel has embraced Brooklyn fully, it's not even in Manhattan. He drags us to Greenwood Heights, the neighborhood alongside Green-Wood Cemetery where Kimber lives, and shows off a small brick-fronted commercial building that he claims will change my life. It turns out this is his gallery now, since I closed up Chelsea, but it could be our gallery.

"You have to come out here and work with me," he insists. "This place has space upstairs; we'll make it a gallery for your sketch work and you can put a desk under the front window to work at. Then you'll be right upstairs when I need you!"

I look beseechingly at Mason, but he's nodding thoughtfully. "Think about it. Fewer people on this side of the river, so not as crowded—that's good for you. Everything we need is a short walk away, just like on the West Side. And my shop is still just down in Red Hook. Wouldn't it make more sense to live here?"

"*And* I'm buying a house here," Abel cries, as if he is unable to hold back the news any longer. "Just two blocks away! Wait until you see it. A *mess*. The vinyl siding is *hideous*. But there's brick underneath. Brick, hidden away! It's going to take forever to renovate but it's going to be absolutely heavenly."

"It sounds like you're going to need some time off from the gallery," I suggest. "So I guess you really *need* me back in that partnership, huh?"

"Oh, if you must be that way." Abel huffs, but he's laughing. "Yes, I *need* you. Are you happy now?"

"I am, yes."

Mason squeezes my hand.

I look around at the gallery Abel has built out here, a beautiful little home for the art we have loved since the day we met. The quiet street out front isn't packed like a Manhattan block would be, but it isn't deserted either; there are families walking, and young people still in love with their first few years in the city, and yellow leaves on the sidewalk where the tree out front is slowly shedding her summer clothes. A few blocks away, Green-Wood Cemetery looms, topped by Battle Hill with her proud Minerva looking over the water, gazing towards Lady Liberty. And that's where we walk after we've signed the lease on our apartment, a tidy top-floor one-bedroom with a view of Manhattan from the bedroom window. The living room window here won't show off the Hudson River, but the trees of the cemetery. It will be as if we are living in the country.

But with the constant hum of the city to remind us of where we are, of where we belong.

Our coffees struggle to warm our hands as we gaze out over the city and the harbor. In a lot of ways, it's like the day we met up here: an orange blaze of color that is a Staten Island Ferry plowing across the water, a rich blue sky scattered with high, white cirrus clouds. The only difference is the chill in the wind, and the yellow leaves settling around our feet and at the base of Minerva's plinth.

"I think I can see your shop," I realize, pointing to the brick warehouse along the Red Hook waterfront. "Is that it?"

"That's it," Mason says, drawing me close. "I guess this little vacation has to end, huh? You're going back to work with Abel, and I'm going to work in my shop. And with Margot. She has a whole program lined up for the winter."

"We're going to be so busy," I marvel. "The opposite of summer."

"I'm ready for this chapter," Mason declares. "I was struggling, the past few years. So tired of my work. So tired of the reputation I was gaining, just for my line of work. You know, I really did become a cop to help people."

"And you did help people," I tell him. "Look what you did for me."

"You? I got off your case as fast as I could. I knew I was too close to the main witness."

I laugh and stand on my toes, giving him a kiss on the cheek. "You drove me home that night, remember? And you remembered where I lived, even though I'd only mentioned it once. You were there for me, even though it was totally official business."

Mason's smile is positively diabolical. "Trust me, that was not official business."

"Oh, Mason," I laugh. "You caught me at my lowest moment. If that wasn't official business, I don't know what you possibly saw in me that could have told you to drive me home."

"It's simple," he says, tugging me to him. "You're the one. I knew it the night I met you, you crazy thing. And then again the night you sat with your boyfriend and wrote a police report for a purse he'd arranged to have stolen. I saw a woman who had been so roughed up by this city that she'd lost her survival instinct. And I wanted to be the one who helped her get it back."

"You did," I whisper. "And then some."

And we stand there until a flock of green parrots alights in the trees nearby, cackling and screeching with such abandon that we have to leave Minerva to their mischief and totter back down the hillside, leaving behind the trees and graves of Green-Wood. The subway station would be warm with the memory of summer still clasped inside its concrete and tile, and I'd snuggle close to him on the way to Manhattan, breathing through my distrust of crowds, already missing this quiet corner of our urban jungle.

But we'd be back, I know, my hand warm in Mason's grip. As soon as we're all packed, we'll be back.

To settle down and stay, together.

Get the next book in the series!

READY FOR MORE swoony romantic comedy?

Join my VIP squad and be the first to find out what's coming next for The Settle Down Society. I'll throw in a discount code for your next read, too!

Just visit nataliekreinert.shop/pages/vip to sign up!

I'll see you there, readers!

Acknowledgments

THANK YOU FOR reading *The Settle Down Summer!* I wrote the first draft of this story in the summer of 2021, struggling with a deepening pandemic and a sense of desperation to get out of my once-spacious apartment. Over the rewrites, I tried to remove references to the pandemic, because people in the know continued to insist no one wanted to read about it. But in the end, the leftover sense of vulnerability and loneliness Tracey felt had to come from *somewhere,* and it's something I'm sure many readers will identify with.

None of us were alone, it just felt that way.

I'm also a goodbye-to-all-that New Yorker, although I never wrote the essay. I left the city after swearing I'd live there forever, but I have this little thing called the horse bug and I just couldn't ignore it any longer! So now I write from the comfort of my little farm, with my horses just outside and several nice prints of the city skyline on the wall—including one from a music festival I went to called, fittingly, "There's No Leaving New York."

The next book in this series is about Margot's journey to find love, and it's also set in the city—this time it will be in Brooklyn, where I lived happily for five years. *The Business of Fairy Tales* is about books, art, and falling in love. I'm excited to get back to it!

To find out when it's coming, along with all my future rom-com releases, please join my VIP squad at https://nataliekreinert.shop/pages/vip

I'm deeply appreciative to all my readers who make my life as an author possible. To those of you who have jumped genres with me from equestrian to theme parks to city romances, thank you for your faith in me! As long as I'm having fun, I think you will, too.

Thanks so much to my reviewers and beta readers, who jump on every opportunity to read one of my books and share reviews around the Internet. Reviews make this business work, so I couldn't do it without you!

Thanks to New York City, a beautiful mess I will always love, for being my muse in this series (so far).

And thanks of course to my subscribers on Patreon and Ream —your monthly support means the world to me.

Find your name here, lovely friends: Kim Keller, Heather Voltz, C Sperry, Rhonda Lane, Lindsay Moore, Brinn Dimler, Tricia Jordan, Sarah Seavey, Cheryl Bavister, Zoe Bills, Liz Greene, Diana Aitch, Orpu, Rachael Rosenthal, Kathi Lacasse, Mary Vargas, Kaylee Amons, Cyndy Searfoss, Heather Walker, Claus Giloi, Jennifer, Di Hannel, Sarina Laurin, Silvana Ricapito, Katie Lewis, Emma Gooden, Karen Carrubba, Thoma

Jolette Parker, Christine Komis, Peggy Dvorsky, Kathlynn Angie-Buss, Nicole, Harry Burgh, Mel Policicchio, Nicola Beisel, Leslie Yazurlo, Sherron Meinert, Jean Miller, Maureen VanDerStad, Libby Henderson, Nancy Neid, JoAnn Flejszar, Gretchen Fieser, Tayla Travella, Empathy, Dörte Voigt, Laura, Elana Rabinow, Cathy Luo, Mel Sperti, Heidi Schmid, April Lutz, Becca B., Sally Testa, Adrienne Brant, Megan McDonald, Natalie Clark, Jennifer Williams, Kellie Halteman, Raina Kujawa, Pamela Allen-LeBlanc, Karen Wolfsheimer, Nicole Russo, Shelby Graft, Erika Thomas, Jocelyn Bissett, Eris, Ashley Swink, Miranda Mues, Renee Knowles, Annika Kostrabulis, Susan Lambiris, Shauna, Lisa Leonard Heck, Dianna, Megan Devine, Michelle Beck, and Lynne Gevirtz.

Thank you all so very much!

About the Author

I LIVE ON a small farm in Florida, and when I'm not writing, I'm usually gardening or playing with my horses. I've spent most of my life as an equestrian, including several years as a member of the NYC Parks Department's mounted unit along with a few more non-horsey years in the city.

Visit my website at nataliekreinert.com to keep up with the latest news and read occasional blog posts and book reviews. For previews, installments of upcoming fiction, and exclusive stories, visit my subscription and serial site at Ream: ReamStories.com/nataliekreinert

For more, find me on social media:

Reader Group: facebook.com/groups/nataliesreaders

Instagram: instagram.com/nataliekreinert

Join my email list for exclusive offers and news at nataliekreinert.shop/pages/vip

Email: natalie@nataliekreinert.com